ENIGMA

TAMISAN BOOK 2

SUSAN McKENZIE

Cover art © Lauren Dawes of Sly Fox Cover Designs

Ream Stories:
https://reamstories.com/susanmckenzie
Amazon author page:
https://www.amazon.com/author/susancarter
Visit Sue's website:
http://susanmckenzieauthor.com
Follow Sue on Facebook:
https://www.facebook.com/SueMcKenzieAuthor

YOUR FREE BOOK IS WAITING

The novelette

THE ALIEN

is free for a limited time. You just need to tell me where
to send it

When Lilliana crash-lands her spaceship on a Primitive
planet, she'll have to rely on help from an attractive
local to survive.

**Use the QR Code to follow the link, then enter your name
and email address to get your free book delivered to your
inbox**

Or type this link into your browser: https://www.subscri
bepage.com/thealien

WHAT READERS LIKE YOU ARE SAYING...

"This book pretty much picks up where book 1 left off and wowzers what a crazy story! Page 1 through the end is a page turner I couldn't put down! I loved this story! Action, Adventure, and pure craziness on every page of the book! Zhenna is once again in quite the mess."
  — **Stephanie (Goodreads review)**

"Enigma is a fast-paced and well-written read. It is action-packed with vivid imagery that allowed me to get lost in the story. It also has drama and romance that kept me entertained. I was pleased with the ups and downs of the story that had me invested in the outcome. Overall, worth the read."
  — **AC_1098610 (Amazon review)**

"Susan McKenzie created another great story that kept me reading all night long with great characters where I wanted to hug the good ones and on the other side wanted to punch the bad ones. If you're into sci-fi I can really recommend it and you should really read book 1 first."
  — **Amazon Customer (Amazon review)**

To my beautiful mother, Terry McKenzie.

You gave us everything a person could possibly give and I miss you so, so much.

You're forever in our hearts...

CHAPTER 1
Why did I think I could do this?

Stepping out into the sunlight was like stepping into one of my nightmares. The jungle with its vines intertwining around the trunks and branches of trees, the flowers and fungi dotted amongst the green, the smell of earth and damp wood, the humidity crowding in on me. The memories it evoked were choking me.

I took a few deep breaths and tried to push my fears aside.

We'd touched down in a clearing in the jungle made by fallen trees and as I stood at the door of the shuttle battling my demons, I was struck by the sheer beauty of the trees and flowers that were growing beyond the immediate area and by the height of the tallest trees. They had to be at least sixty metres tall.

Despite the magnificence of my surroundings, my breathing became shallow. I had to fight to keep control of my emotions.

Moss grew on rocks and tree roots, vines hung from branches, and flowers of many different colours bloomed in amongst the greens and browns.

The sense of deja vu made both my hearts hammer wildly in my chest. The last time I did this — landing in the jungle — it had ended in tragedy.

The humidity pressed in on me, but, unlike the first time, it didn't bother me. My skin drank in the moisture without causing the least bit of discomfort.

The other members of my team stepped down onto the ground but I hesitated. I forced myself to slow my breathing and calm my thoughts. I could do this if I concentrated on the present.

I forced myself to move and took the three steps to the soft earth and stood behind everyone in the clearing — if you could call it a clearing. It looked like a war zone. Trees strewn about the floor of the jungle, some of them caught by the branches of surrounding trees, which stopped them from reaching the ground. I gasped when I saw blood on one of the nearby tree trunks.

"Looks like a couple of dinos had a wrestling match," Darion said with a chuckle.

That got a few laughs from some of the other men on our search team, but it had the opposite effect on me. It made me think of the two dinosaurs that fought right in front of me while I hid in a crevice between two rocks only a few weeks ago. One had resembled an Allosaurus from Earth's distant past and the other looked like a giant crocodile.

My hearts picked up speed again just thinking about it. I could almost hear the horrific sounds of them fighting.

Darion turned to me. "Are you alright, Tamisan? You look a little pale."

His voice brought me back to the present. "Uh... Yeah. I'm fine."

I took a deep breath to try to relieve the tightness in my chest. I didn't want any of them to know how much being back in the jungle again was affecting me. I needed to be strong. I'd spent a lot of time convincing Darion and our boss, Dr Aimery, that I was up to the task. I wanted to help in any way I could. After all, the man we were searching for was part of my original shuttle crew when I'd first arrived on the planet about six or seven weeks ago.

I closed my eyes for a few seconds and collected myself again. *I can do this.*

Boots crunched in the leaf litter and I opened my eyes to Darion's open arms. I melted into them, needing to feel his arms around me. It grounded me. My heartbeats levelled out and my breathing slowed.

After a while, I reluctantly pulled away from him and gave him a warm smile. I used telepathy to send him a thank you.

He returned the smile and I melted a little. *"Anytime, my love. Shall we get moving?"*

I nodded and we turned our attention back to our mission.

Commander Totino Kozienko gave our team final instructions before heading out. I could see his bulging muscles on his bare arms and half a bare chest, but he didn't look very 'commanding' dressed in a loincloth made of spotted hide. In fact, we all looked strange in skins. But blending in with the natives was key.

He turned to us. "You two, stay in the middle of the group." When we both nodded, he turned back to the group. "Alright. Move out."

As we moved further away from the ship, the fresh musty smell of earth and the refreshing scent of the nearby river filled my senses. Fragrances from the nearest flowers soon followed. It was such a nice change from the air conditioning in the underground base. I breathed in deeply and was hit with a wave of memories from the last time I was in the jungle.

So many things had happened to me after I escaped from the crazy scientist who thought he could play God and transfer my consciousness into the body of one of the natives of this planet, a young woman named Sifayah.

Sifayah was from a race of people known as the Waikari, who possessed psychic abilities. They could speak to each other using telepathy, which came in handy because they lived half their lives underwater. Certain members of the Waikari tribe also had the power of telekinesis. Sifayah was one of the strongest in the tribe with this Gift and had been trained well.

My consciousness had been transferred into her mind and I'd only had her left-over memories to guide me in how to use her Talent. I was still amazed at the things I could do now.

There were also physical differences. I still looked human, but I now had webbed hands and feet, and two hearts.

I'd gained a lot: power and gills and abilities. But I'd lost so much at the same time. My life. My friends. My identity. I didn't really know who I was for a long time.

Things were better now, though. I had a new life and new friends, and my life had purpose again. I could use my abilities to help the Voyager Division study the people on this planet, and help find Janssen too.

I needed to stop thinking about it all and focus, though I was finding it difficult to do.

What was I thinking? I was so naïve to think I could just come back here and carry on like nothing was wrong, like nothing bad had happened to me out here.

Memories of being chased through the jungle and attacked by a man who thought he owned me came rushing up into my mind. My hearts were pounding again.

I can't do this. Why did I think I could do this?

CHAPTER 2
Is this gonna be an issue?

I had to calm down. I couldn't let anyone know how the memories were eating at me.

Darion turned back and realized I'd stopped walking. "Hey. It's okay." He turned back and put an arm around me, steering me over to the nearest fallen tree. "Sit down. Take some slow, deep breaths. You'll be okay."

I did as he said, leaning against his side once he'd settled next to me. I closed my eyes and centred my thoughts.

It's okay. I'm okay. Turak isn't here. He can't hurt me.

I pushed thoughts of what Turak almost did to me aside and concentrated on my breathing while Darion whispered that I'd be alright and rubbed my back. Once my heartbeats slowed, my thoughts turned back to our mission. We had no time for this. We needed to find Janssen.

Darion looked down at me. "Feeling better now?"

"Kind of."

He leaned down and softly pressed his lips to mine, making my body come alive and leaving me wanting more. "How about now?"

I nodded, feeling a little flushed, with a helping of guilt. We were holding up the team. I needed to be strong right now.

"Then why the frown?"

"I... I just don't want to be like this. I don't want to be weak. I want to help find Janssen and be a productive member of the team and not a burden."

"You are not weak. This is the first time that you've been back out here. We knew it would be difficult."

I nodded again. "You're right."

I took a calming breath. *I can do this.*

"Yes, you can!" He'd picked up my thoughts easily as I wasn't shielding my mind from him. It was reassuring to hear him say it and to hear his voice in my mind.

I smiled at him. I just needed to think rationally.

I sighed. "Okay. I'm good. Let's get on with this."

Darion looked into my eyes and smiled.

"Andiyar," Commander Kozienko barked. "Is this gonna be an issue?"

"No, Sir," Darion assured him. "It is her first time back in the jungle, but she's okay now."

The commander grunted in reply. "Alright, let's get moving."

We stood up and started off into the jungle again, moving along the river's edge. I looked back and saw the shuttle disappear as its cloaking device was activated. The pilot would stay with the ship until we returned, unseen by any natives or animals that might happen to pass by. As long as they didn't bump into it...

We had a couple of trackers in the group — Commander Kozienko, who used the old-fashioned method of tracking footprints and looking for clues, and Corporal Lazuli Idrial, who used his psychic ability to 'find' people and objects. His rating was only a T6, but he was good at his job. He'd been sick recently, which had slowed down our search for Janssen, and we were hopeful that this mission would be successful now that he was back on the team.

We were also hoping that if Janssen was still alive, he would still be wearing his boots. That would separate his footprints from any others. The natives were usually barefoot or wore boots made of animal hide.

The natives were unaware that there were people in their midst from the other side of the universe studying them from an underground base. We were wearing clothing that looked like it was made from animal hide to try to blend in. Well, except for mine. Mine were genuine jungle cat. They were given to me by one of the natives to replace my damaged wetsuit. It had been cut through from top to bottom by a being who was half-man, half-beast. I shuddered at the memory.

As we meandered along next to the river, I tried to push any negative thoughts aside and enjoy the scenery. Plants were tangled around each other while the larger trees stretched high up into the canopy and blocked out most of the sun's rays. It was slow-going as we had to duck under low-hanging branches and vines and climb over roots, rocks, and fallen trees. Just about everything was covered in a bright green moss and the leaf mulch was thick on the ground.

I tried to ignore the creepy crawlies we passed, but it was difficult. Spiders and beetles and large ants and some seriously weird-looking hairy caterpillars with spikes and a colour pattern on their backs that looked like a big eye.

The humidity was extreme. I watched Kozienko pull out a handkerchief and mop his forehead and noticed that Nykolar was panting and I sympathised with them. Nykolar was the only other person besides Darion and I that wasn't a soldier and he clearly wasn't as fit as the rest of us. He worked with electronics in Security. I wondered what he was doing out here. I thought it was odd that he would volunteer to be on the search team.

After about five minutes, my breathing and heart rates were back to normal. The sights and sounds of the jungle stopped making me jumpy and I started to feel more confident. I could do this.

I was able to think about the job at hand. It wasn't going to be easy to find Janssen; the jungle was so huge and so dense that it was probably like the proverbial needle in a haystack. But we were hopeful. I'd survived, even though I'd been poisoned by a plant that made me hallucinate and had been captured and sold by slave traders. I was hoping that Janssen, being a tall well-muscled male — who had some experience with hiking and camping according to his files — would be able to do a better job than I had. A *lot* of people could've done a better job than me. I was born and raised in a city back on Earth and was totally clueless. Which was why I'd been doing some self-defence classes since I'd recovered from being attacked by Dr Starrick, the scientist who had captured my crew and I in the jungle and experimented on us.

The thought that he'd only grabbed us because he needed some test subjects to play with still sickened me and I was glad he was dead.

Movement caught my eye. One of the men was trying to squeeze past a small tree covered in flowers and fruit and my stomach dropped to my feet. "No! Don't!"

He turned to me with a questioning look.

"Keep away from the flowers!" I yelled. "They're dangerous!"

He rolled his eyes and continued on.

I was running towards him before I realized it. "No! Stop! It will—"

Chapter 3

Incoming!

It was too late. The plant had a self-defence mechanism. The bulb on the base of the flower popped and the pollen went straight into his face. I quickly pulled him away from the tree.

"Water!" I cried out to no one in particular. "We need to wash his face!"

I was already pulling out my water bottle and as he slowly sunk to the ground, coughing and wheezing, I rolled him onto his side and poured water on his face. I had to get the pollen off. The others helped me and poured some of their water on him as well.

Memories of the horrific hallucinations I'd experienced from this plant raced through my mind. My hands shook as I tried to move faster. It was already too late. The pollen had started to affect him. He was disoriented and looked at us with a dazed expression. This guy was in for a rough time.

Darion knelt down next to me, looking me over. "Are you okay? You didn't get any on you?"

"No. I'm fine. Don't worry."

His eyes were intense. "Are you sure?"

"Yes. I'd tell you if I did. There's no way I want to go through that again."

I couldn't blame him for worrying. He saw what I'd gone through last time. And helped me use my telekinetic ability to expel the poison from my body.

I gave him a reassuring smile and looked up at the commander. "He needs to go back to Jannali, right now." Station Jannali was the underground base we were working from. "The hallucinations will hit him hard and fast."

Some of the men just looked at each other. Darion stepped forward. "I'll take him and be back in a few minutes."

Everyone looked to Kozienko. "Do it," he said.

As Darion approached the guy, he started to scream and lash out with his arms and legs. "No! Keep away from me!"

Darion moved back. "We need to take you to Jannali," he told him.

"No! How could you— What— No, no, no, no, no!" He batted his arms at an invisible foe and screamed again.

Darion turned to us and said, "I'll be back," and before anyone could say anything more, they both disappeared.

The rest of the group looked dumbfounded.

Kozienko finally spoke. "You all need to listen up," he barked. "You were briefed on this. There is a good reason that Tamisan is on this mission with us. She's been in the jungle before and has experienced this shit first-hand. Some of you have been out here too, but others haven't. Anyone else who refuses to listen to her warnings from now on, gets teleported back to base immediately and will have to answer to me! Is that clear?"

"Yes, Sir!" was the hasty reply.

He looked at each person in the group. "Good! Now we wait for Andiyar to get back. Be alert."

I couldn't help wondering how I was supposed to give these men guidance if they wouldn't listen to me. I had to hope that they'd listen now that the commander had spoken to them.

Once Darion reappeared, we travelled through the jungle along a wide animal track. I shuddered to think of what might be able to easily walk through here, but pushed it aside. We were armed and alert. We understood what could come trudging along on its way to the river for a drink.

When I was in the jungle by myself, I narrowly escaped being the next meal of a smallish Allosaurus look-alike. I say smallish, but it was at least two metres tall.

I looked up as it seemed to be getting darker down here on the floor of the jungle. It was hard to see through the canopy but it looked like it might rain.

At the sound of crashing footfalls through the underbrush, I turned and jumped back a couple of steps as a large dinosaur that resembled an Anatosaurus stumbled out onto the track and veered away from our group. Relief flooded through me once my mind registered that it wasn't a predator.

Everyone raised their weapons and I shouted, "Don't shoot!" They didn't lower them, but they didn't shoot either. "It's not dangerous! It is a herbivore. A rhodon."

Everyone visibly relaxed and watched the rhodon as it tried to decide what to do. I was so glad they'd listened to me as I didn't want to see it hurt.

We stood still and watched it pass. It had four solid legs similar to an elephant's, and a long tail protruding from its large body. Its neck was thicker and shorter than the tail, with an oval-shaped head. It finally chose to avoid us and trudged off into the foliage.

Once it was gone, I added, "I told you about them in the briefing. The natives have domesticated them and use them like horses, although that one looked wild."

They all lowered their weapons and we started moving again as the sounds of its footsteps died away. It took a while for my heartbeats to return to normal. Having two hearts was good for swimming long distances, and I assumed that to be one of the reasons why the Waikari had more than one, but having both pounding against my ribcage the first time I woke up in this body had made me think there was something wrong with me.

As we walked, I looked at the trees that seemed to go on forever. I hoped that Kozienko knew the way back to the shuttle, because I hadn't been paying attention while trying to wrestle with my fears. All I knew was that we were still near the river.

In a pinch, I could teleport back to where we'd landed. I could easily picture the fallen trees in my mind.

There was an order from the commander to halt and we gathered around where he crouched in the middle of what looked like a smaller animal path heading off through the bushes.

When we reached him, he pointed at the ground. "There," he said, as if we could all see what he was seeing.

I looked closely, but couldn't see anything unusual.

He looked at us, then clenched his jaw in frustration. "Can't you see it? Look. A boot-shaped print."

He pointed at an area to the right and I leaned closer. There was an indentation in the soft black soil, but whether it was boot-shaped was up for debate in my mind. But then again, what would I know?

Just as I was straightening up again, someone screamed, "Incoming!" and all hell broke loose.

CHAPTER 4
You Shouldn't Be Here

I turned to see a huge mass of spotted fur and claws and teeth. A jungle cat. It held one of the men down on the ground with its huge front paws and had sunk its teeth into his shoulder. His screams of agony ripped through me and I stood frozen in the chaos that ensued.

Shouts mixed with the zaps from laser pistols and Kozienko shouted out orders over the top of it all. The men changed positions and focused on bringing the monster down.

The cat roared in pain and took a swipe at another soldier with one of those deadly claws, knocking him sideways. He landed with a thud against a nearby tree root with a sickening crack, then slumped down onto the ground.

My mind replayed the last time I'd seen one of these nightmares that resembled a sabre-toothed tiger up close. I'd narrowly missed being its next meal and the native I was with, Anjou, had killed it with a spear through the chest.

Finally coming to my senses, I threw out my hands and pushed with my mind just as the cat was about to take another chunk out of whoever it was on the ground. It flew backwards and landed on its back, but quickly flipped over and stepped forward.

The lasers focused on its head and chest and it finally crumpled to the ground, thrashed around and gave a last attempt at a roar before going still.

I was surprised it took so long to go down, considering one spear through the chest had killed the other cat. No wait. Anjou had leapt on it once it was down and had cut its throat. And I had turned away to throw up, so I didn't really see how long it had taken to kill it.

The men were now an organized team. Some checked to make sure the cat was dead and others tended to the injured men.

My brain was still trying to process what had happened. Their voices seemed far away. Someone said that it was Lazuli and Private Rowton that had been hurt. I gasped in horror as I saw that Lazuli was the one lying at my feet in a pool of blood.

No, no, no, no, no!

Lazuli was a good friend. He'd only just recovered from a fever.

Blood was everywhere and as I stared at the shredded flesh of his shoulder, I thought he had to be dead. How could anyone survive that?

I couldn't move. Couldn't speak. I couldn't see if he was breathing. Tears sprung to my eyes.

"He's alive!" someone called out. "But he's in bad shape."

I rushed forward and fell to my knees by his side, not knowing what I could do to help. I wished I was a Healer. We'd applied to the company for one because of how dangerous the jungle could be, but that wouldn't help Lazuli. He needed someone right now.

Tears streamed down my cheeks and my stomach roiled, threatening to spill over at any second. I swallowed hard and realized that I was kneeling in blood.

Kozienko carefully put Lazuli in the coma position and pressed a couple of gauze pads from the first-aid kit on his wound, holding them firmly while another man put a cushion under his head. Lazuli must have passed out from the pain.

I looked around. Darion and Braydac were attending to Rowton.

"What's the damage over there, Andiyar?" Kozienko asked.

"Rowton has a broken arm and some deep lacerations to his chest," Darion reported.

"Can you port them both at once?" Kozienko asked.

"Yes, Sir."

"Good. Lazuli is bad. If you don't take him *now*, he's a dead man."

Darion stood up from where he'd been leaning over Rowton. "I've let them know we're coming..."

I got to my feet and immediately felt light-headed. Darion's voice faded away. The blood was everywhere. I had to get away from it.

If I hadn't leaped out of the way in time so that Anjou could kill that other jungle cat, I would have been ripped open like Lazuli. And probably worse.

My knees were buckling and darkness clouded my vision. I couldn't get enough air into my lungs.

Darion had teleported the injured men to Jannali. I needed to be away from the blood on the ground.

Out of nowhere, Nykolar appeared by my side. "You don't look so good."

Well, I don't feel so good either.

"Let me help you. Let's go to the river and wash the blood off and you can have a drink."

I looked down at myself. I'd somehow gotten blood on my hands and the blood on my knees was running slowly down my legs and into my fur boots. My loincloth thing had soaked up a lot of it too as I'd knelt next to Lazuli.

Oh no. The lightheadedness increased.

"It's okay." He put an arm around my shoulders and it helped to keep me upright. "Come. I'll help you."

He steered me away from the mess and the people who were all talking at once. We would need to stay here until Darion returned from the base.

We ducked around a few large tree trunks and made it to the riverbank. "Just a little further. We'll get you sorted out in no time."

I looked back and couldn't see the others.

"Don't worry. I took you down this way so you couldn't see what's going on up there. It will help you to feel better if you can't see it."

That made sense. I took a deep breath and let it out slowly. "Thank you."

I looked into the depths of the water as I knelt down to wash myself, checking for any lurking predators. I could see a lot of submerged rocks and a sunken branch under the fast-flowing water, but no crocodile look-alikes or anything else that might want to eat me. I let relief flow through me and I started to wash my hands and arms.

I hoped Lazuli would be okay. He didn't look okay. He was probably dying or maybe even dead already. My chest tightened at the thought. I needed to think about something else.

I couldn't help wondering how we were going to locate Janssen with our Finder gone.

Then guilt crashed down on me for only thinking of him as our Finder. He could be dead and I was worried about our mission? *Gah!*

I was too hot. I thought about just diving into the water, but decided against it. I splashed water on my face instead. Then I moved my long hair away from the back of my neck so I could splash water on it. It was such a relief to feel the coolness and the droplets of water running down my back.

"Feeling better?" Nykolar asked.

"Yes," I answered, and I was. The lightheadedness had mostly subsided and my heartbeats had slowed. This was a good idea. "Thank you for helping me."

After a few moments of silence, he spoke again. "You shouldn't be here," he said quietly.

I frowned. I didn't turn around while I washed the blood from my knees, but was hurt to hear him say it. "Why would you say that? I'm capable of carrying on with this mission. I just needed to calm down, like you said."

"I'm not talking about the mission. You shouldn't be alive."

There was a sinking feeling in my chest. Something cold touched the back of my neck and caused a weird stinging sensation that made me jump.

My hand automatically went to the back of my neck. "*Ouch!* What was that?"

Thinking I'd been bitten by something, I spun around, only to see Nykolar holding a stunner. *What the?*

He gave me a creepy smile. "I've disabled your tracking device."

"*What?* Why?" *How did it zap the tracker without zapping me?*

His eyes filled with hate and his voice became flat and hollow. "So no one can find your body and bring it back to base for further study. You're an abomination. Made in a lab. You don't deserve to live. You have no soul."

My stomach pitched. He flicked the switch on the stunner to the highest setting, which was strong enough to kill a person. My first thought was that it needed to be set back to stun. As he squeezed the trigger and pain shot through my body, I could only hope that I'd switched it back in time.

My whole body seized up and I couldn't control my limbs as I fell backwards into the cool water, and as pain exploded across the back of my head, everything went black.

CHAPTER 5
How Did I Get Here?

My eyes drifted open. I was lying on my stomach on something hard and cold and my head was hurting. My cheek resting on something wet. I lifted my head to see what it was and a stabbing pain shot through the back of my head. I yelped and jerked up from the ground, which only caused more excruciating pain. It was so intense that I was forced to lay my head back down. There was pain in my back too. Under my left shoulder blade. *What...?*

My head throbbed and my vision blurred as I lay there waiting for my head to stop spinning.

Sand. I was lying on wet sand. My chest tightened. *What happened? How did I get here?*

No answers came. I couldn't remember how I'd ended up here or how I'd hurt my head.

I flinched as water washed up against my legs. *A beach? How...?*

My breathing started coming in shallow bursts. The more I tried unsuccessfully to remember what had happened to me, the more panicked I became.

Calm down! I told myself. *Breathe! There has to be an explanation.*

I forced myself to take slower, deeper breaths and tried to relax.

I looked from the sand in front of my face to the rocks that were further away from me. I blinked a few times, but everything was still blurry. There was some green here and there that I assumed were plants.

I couldn't see enough of my surroundings to help me recognise where I was. I needed to get up and have a good look around. But I wasn't willing to put myself in that much pain again so soon.

I tried again to remember how I'd ended up like this. Something — anything — but there was still nothing there. Nothing at all. I couldn't even remember my name. That scared me more than anything else.

There was a blank space where my memories should be. It felt like I had a tight band around my chest.

Why can't I remember anything? Surely, I should be able to remember my own name?

My heart pounded and there seemed to be something wrong with it. The rhythm was wrong. Or something.

And the pain radiating from the back of my head was unbearable. I touched it and flinched at the pain and the size of the lump I found. It was wet and my hair was matted and stuck together. I pulled my hand away and it was covered in blood. Nausea swelled in my stomach and I fought the urge to throw up.

Then I spread my fingers wider. They were webbed. Why was I surprised at that?

There wasn't a lump on my back, but it was very painful to touch.

How did this happen to me? Did I fall and hit my head? Maybe that's why I can't remember anything.

I tried to lift my head again to look around and the world spun. I put my face back down on the wet sand and lay there feeling the waves rolling over my legs in a rhythmic motion.

I don't even know where I am. Or how I got here.

Had I washed up on the beach? Was I in a boat and had fallen out? Did I swim to shore? But then, how did I hurt my head?

I had no answers.

I desperately wanted to be able to look around to try to piece together what was going on.

Blackness clouded in at the edges of my vision. I did *not* want to pass out. Not now. I needed to find out what happened.

Who am I?

There was no answer. It was just blank.

I didn't know how long I had lain there in the sand. Time was hard to judge; I think I passed out for a while because the waves were suddenly washing up to my armpits.

The tide was coming in.

On the heels of that realisation was the thought that if I couldn't get up, the tide could eventually come up high enough to wash me into the sea and drown me.

I tried — slower this time — to push myself up. Although it was painful, I managed to turn and sit up and the world tilted. I managed to stay upright and waited for the dizziness and nausea to subside. The ocean stretched out before me and gentle waves kept rolling in and splashing around me.

Turning my head proved to be too painful and nearly made me pass out, so I turned my whole body around to see behind me. There was sand for a few metres, then the ground rose where there were some rocks and grass and small bushes. A few metres past that, the small bushes gave way to a dense tropical jungle. Although I still couldn't remember anything, the jungle scene seemed wrong somehow, like it wasn't where I was supposed to be. That was odd.

Why would it feel wrong to me when I couldn't even remember anything at all?

I looked down and saw that I was wearing a sort of crop top thing made out of spotted hide and some kind of loincloth. I had jet black hair that hung down to my hips. It was tangled and messy and even had some seaweed in it.

Looking down was causing too much pain and when I straightened up my head spun so fast that my stomach pitched and I threw up on the sand. I wiped my mouth with the back of my hand when I'd finished and shifted away from the mess. I ended up lying back down again to avoid passing out.

I lay on my right side with an arm under my head to avoid putting pressure on my wounds. It was uncomfortable and painful, but I had no choice. No position was going to relieve the pain.

I trembled, feeling lost and alone. Tears pricked at my eyes. My mind was desperately scrambling to find answers. How was I going to get help or even find my way home? I didn't even know where home was.

After the pain subsided a little, I slowly got to my feet. I had to do something. Lying on the sand wasn't going to give me any answers. And there was the whole tide-coming-in issue.

I turned in a slow circle. Nothing looked familiar. I had absolutely no idea where I was or which way I should go. I picked a direction and walked slowly, careful not to turn my head or look down.

The beach seemed endless. I didn't know whether I was heading toward help or moving further away from it. My bottom lip trembled and I felt the sting of tears, but I tried to push it aside. I needed to stay strong. I needed to keep going.

After stumbling a few times, I found that it was much easier to walk on the wet, flat sand than it was to walk on the dry stuff. I frowned. Shouldn't I know that kind of thing instinctively?

I stopped and looked into the jungle. What if my home was in there? A distant roar split the silence. I shuddered. *I'll stick to the beach.*

I didn't know what kind of creature had made that noise, and I didn't *want* to know.

I pushed myself onward as I tried in vain to remember something. How did I get such a terrible head injury? What had happened to my back? Did I fall or did someone attack me? Or was it some*thing?* After hearing that roar, I thought anything was possible. But my mind was still empty.

A wave of nausea hit me and the pain in my head increased. I stopped and took in some deep breaths, which only made me feel marginally better, then I kept going.

Time was hard to judge, but I must have walked for almost an hour. I didn't know what else to do. I was just aimlessly walking.

I'd had to stop a few times and wait until my head stopped spinning. I'd even thrown up again on the sand a couple of times.

As I rounded a bend in the beach, I saw that the next section of the shoreline curved around in an arc, culminating in a rocky outcrop. Something stirred in my chest. Did I know this place?

CHAPTER 6

Are You Well, Sifayah?

I increased my pace. I needed to get closer, to see if there was anything familiar. I desperately needed something to latch onto. Something that I could remember. Maybe if I found just one thing, it would trigger other memories. I *had* to get there.

Only, the faster I walked, the more my head throbbed in time with my heartbeat. It felt fuzzy and I started feeling cold, despite the warmth of the day.

My stomach roiled and threatened to bring up its contents again, but I kept going.

The sudden sounds of laughter startled me and my knees went weak, but I kept up the pace.

As I got closer, I thought I saw movement. It looked like someone had dived off the rocks and into the waves. I felt a pang in my chest. This place must be familiar to me.

More laughter.

I tried to call out, but nothing came out. I was overcome with nausea and dizziness and my legs gave out. My knees hit the sand and I pitched forward and vomited. Only, there was nothing left in my stomach and I only brought up bile.

As soon as I'd finished retching, I crawled a safe distance away. I knew I was going to pass out and the last thing I wanted was to wake up in a puddle of my own bile. My vision faded as I slipped sideways into nothingness.

———— ◦ ————

I woke to what sounded like footsteps squelching in wet sand and tried to turn toward the sound, but pain shot through my head. When my eyes finally focused, there were three faces hovering above me. I jerked away from them and the pain made me cry out.

It took a few seconds for me to remember why my head was sore.

Three young teenage boys stood over me, dressed in loin-cloths that were a strange shade of grey.

I couldn't quite follow what they were saying as they were all talking at once. They were speaking a foreign language, but I could understand them perfectly. I still couldn't remember a thing, but apparently, I spoke at least two different languages.

They were asking if I was Sifayah. Was I? My mind didn't give me an answer.

From what I could make out, they were happy to see me and couldn't believe that they'd found me after so long. They asked where I'd been, but I didn't have an answer.

I cringed, mostly from the pain, but also from the intensity of their gazes. They were still leaning over me and I noticed that tears were running down their cheeks. That scared me. Why were they crying? How long had I been gone? Was I hurt more than I'd thought?

"Are you Sifayah?" the boy closest to me asked. He looked older than the other two.

"Um... I... don't know," I stammered.

They exchanged looks and frowned at me. "How do you not know?"

"I don't remember," I told them.

They all spoke at once again and I had to close my eyes against the pain in my head.

I opened them to see one of them pushing the others back. "Give her some air." To me he said, "Are you well, Sifayah? Where are you hurt?"

"My... head..."

"Okay. We can help you. Take you back home. Your family will be pleased. Jarleth has been searching for you."

The name didn't stir anything inside my brain. "Jarleth?"

He frowned. "You do not know Jarleth?"

"No."

"Oh. That's... bad... I mean... sorry. It will be okay. You will probably remember him when you see him, right?"

I frowned. "Um, right. I guess."

His smile returned. "We can take you home. Can you stand?"

"I... don't know."

They helped me to stand and I swayed a little. They led me toward the water, saying it would be easier. Quicker. Adrenalin shot through me. Were they going to *drown* me?

My heart raced as I pulled against them, but they wouldn't let me go.

"Come," the boy said. "It's okay. It will be easier for you than walking. We can just pull you along through the water."

"*What?*"

I fought against them, but I was outnumbered and they were too strong. I struggled and screamed and tried to hurt them so they'd let me go, but it made no difference.

They were puzzled by my reaction and kept telling me everything would be okay when we got home. "It will be quick. We won't hurt you," the boy told me.

My head throbbed and the world spun and I couldn't stand anymore.

They told me it was okay over and over, probably because I wasn't listening. They kept calling me Sifavah, but that name didn't seem right somehow. Just like the jungle.

They pulled me under the waves and terror gripped me. They weren't here to help. They were going to *kill* me. How could I have trusted them so easily? I was going to die.

Chapter 7

Do You Remember Me?

I held my breath. My lungs started to burn, desperately needing air. I struggled harder, but it was no use. Their grip was too strong.

I couldn't hold my breath in any longer. I let all the air out of my lungs but resisted the urge to breathe in.

When I couldn't hold out any longer and felt I'd pass out from lack of oxygen, I resigned myself to my fate and breathed the water in, expecting to cough and splutter, but I didn't. It was a natural fluid motion. My eyes flew open. I breathed more water in and felt a strange sensation on either side of my ribs, like water was passing over them faster than the other water around me. Each time I breathed water in, I felt it. The water I was sucking into my mouth was being expelled from my body.

I had *gills?* Like a fish?

I felt faint and looked at the boys. They were swimming along without any problems, and I could see their gills opening and closing as they breathed underwater. It was so surreal. How could this be possible?

They gave me smiles of encouragement and kept pulling me along through the water, but the cloudiness crowded in on me. Right before the darkness overtook me again, I swore I could hear them talking to me as if we were still above-water.

The first thing I felt was a dull ache at the back of my head. I frowned. Why was my head so sore?

The memory of waking up alone on the beach trickled through my mind. The pain. The long walk. The boys finding me and dragging me into the water. Me *breathing* underwater. Did that really happen? My mind was muddled.

And no matter how hard I tried, anything before that was still blank.

I had to focus on what I *could* remember. They said they were taking me home before I passed out. So the fact that I was lying on my side on something soft like a bed gave me some relief.

I was about to open my eyes when I heard hushed voices. A male and female. I feigned sleep and listened. Maybe I could find out more about what had happened to me.

"But they said that she can't even remember her name." That was the male voice.

The woman, whose voice was cracked with age, answered him in a matter-of-fact tone. "It would be the bump on the head. It happens. It could be a temporary thing, or could be more serious."

"More serious? What do you mean?"

Now she had my attention too.

"Sometimes the memory does not recover. But we shouldn't dwell on that now. We need to wait till she wakes to find out how things are."

"Yes. I understand."

"And we will need to only speak to her with our voices for now. No Mind-touch."

Mind-touch?

"Why?"

Yeah, why?

"She may not remember that we can do so. I am told she panicked when the boys took her into the sea, most likely forgetting that she could breathe in the underwater."

The male shifted his position and my eyes almost flew open when I realized that he was sitting on the bed I was lying on.

"What will I do if she doesn't remember me, Tasha?" he asked, and there was pain in his voice. "I don't think I could stand it... after all this time... She's been gone for so long. Most in the village believed her dead..."

How long was I gone? Where did I go? Why did I leave? Did I run away?

"It is okay, my son. She is here now." There was a pause. "And you can ask her if she remembers you. She is awake."

I sucked in a breath. *How did she know that?*

"It is okay, my daughter," she said to me. "You can open your eyes now. You are safe here."

Daughter? Was she my mother? Was the male my brother?

I slowly opened my eyes. The old woman was sitting on a wooden chair against a rock wall. She was smiling and her face was filled with lines so deep, they looked like they would be painful.

As I took in the rest of the room, I realized that I was in a cave. I turned my head, which caused sharp pain in my head and back, and saw a young man sitting on the edge of the bed looking at me with intense brown eyes that started to fill with tears.

If he was my brother, I didn't recognise him. My heart started to pound erratically and I looked at the woman again.

"Hello, my child," she said gently. "Are you well?"

My breathing was shallow. I didn't remember this place. Nothing was familiar.

"I... um... no." I didn't know what to say to her. I was far from being 'well.' I should know these people; they obviously knew me. How hard did I hit my head? *How* did I hit my head? Was this permanent? What if I never recovered and could never remember them?

"Do not panic. Everything will be fine." She gave me a toothy smile. "I can see that you don't remember us and that's fine. Take things easy. These things happen. We will take care of you. The main thing is to rest."

Rest? How could I rest when my brain was empty?

The male glanced at Tasha, then turned back to me. "Sifayah? Do you remember me?"

I cringed inwardly as I looked up at his handsome face, hoping for some recognition to hit me. "No. I'm sorry."

The hopeful look he'd been giving me seemed to crumble and it made me feel terrible. But there was nothing I could do or say to make things better. I would just have to rest and recover and hope that my memories returned.

"We were close," he told me. "We were... just close." He looked so helpless.

What did he mean? Were we close siblings? Or a couple? I looked to Tasha for answers but she remained silent.

He reached out to touch my arm, but then his hand fell to his lap. Maybe he thought it would be too much for me. "Do you remember anything? Any people?"

"No. Nothing at all."

He sighed heavily and ran a hand through his long black hair that fell to roughly elbow-height. "Okay then. My name is Jarleth and your name is Sifayah." He gestured toward the old woman. "This is Tasha. You have a family here. Your mother is called Tamari. Your father is Silurian and he is the leader of our tribe, the Waikari."

The word Waikari stirred something in my empty cavern of a mind, but it was like something out of reach.

He played with a bracelet made of seashells on his wrist as he continued. "Jadidi and Axiak are your brothers and Shanae, Melina, and Channia are your sisters."

My heart sank. None of those names were familiar. I had a huge family that I couldn't remember.

Tasha cleared her throat. "We see that you don't remember. Do not worry your pretty head, child. It's too soon yet."

I sighed, feeling like a failure. And her mentioning that I was pretty made me wonder what I looked like.

Jarleth leaned forward slightly. "They have missed you and would like to see you — but only when you are ready, of course."

I wasn't ready. I needed time. Having two people in here was bad enough. I felt like I needed air. I took a deep breath as if that would help. It didn't. I felt a little dizzy.

I looked at him again. Surely I should remember someone that I knew well, that I'd been close to? It dawned on me that he hadn't listed himself as part of my family. So, not my brother then.

"How long was I gone? Where was I?"

He frowned. "You went missing two moons and six suns ago. No one knows what happened to you or where you have been all this time."

A chill crept through my bones. No one knew? That was *not* good. Was I lost, wandering around in that jungle I saw? Did someone hurt me? Hit me on the head and leave me on the beach?

Two moons and six suns. My mind was telling me that they were called months and days, not moons and suns. Why, if I was supposed to be from this tribe, did they use different words and speak a totally different language to the one in my head?

The one in my head was my native language — I knew that deep down. So it didn't make any sense to me.

But I couldn't dwell on that now. I needed to try to remember what happened. And apparently, I wasn't the only one who wanted answers.

Tasha pushed herself to her feet and shuffled over to a small table that I hadn't really noticed and brought over a tray of fruit and a crude cup filled with what looked like water.

"Here you go, my daughter. You must be famished."

I was about to ask her if she was my mother, but I remembered that Jarleth had said that my mother's name was Tamari. So maybe it was just a term of endearment that she used with everyone. She called Jarleth her son, but she probably wasn't his mother either. I wondered how she fit into the picture. How did I know her?

I had to push myself up into a sitting position to eat, which almost caused me to pass out again, but I felt really hungry once Tasha had mentioned food. Before that, it hadn't entered my mind.

I took a few big mouthfuls of the water, but I had to stop myself from drinking it all at once. I was so thirsty, but I needed to take it easy or risk throwing it back up.

Tasha sat back down and cleared her throat again. "There is something I need to tell you."

"What is it?"

"It is about our people." She smiled and clasped her hands together in her lap. "We can speak to each other using our minds."

CHAPTER 8

Your Family Would Like to Meet You

"What?"

"It is part of who we are as a people. Like breathing in the underwater."

I just sat there with my mouth hanging open.

She smiled again. "How else could we talk in the underwater?"

That made sense. But it was still overwhelming to think that there was a whole race of people who could speak to each other using telepathy.

Then I remembered what I'd heard before I blacked out. "The boys... They were talking to me when we were underwater."

"Yes. They were using Mind-touch."

"And everyone can do this?"

"Yes. Well, the Waikari and our brothers and sisters of the Shinnari. I am certain that the Jungle People cannot do this."

"Jungle People?"

"Yes. There are other tribes who don't go into the underwater. We keep away from them, and we keep them away from us."

"Why?"

"They do not understand us and can be violent. We simply keep away. That's the best thing for all."

It seemed like a good strategy and I wondered how we kept them away. It wasn't like we could put up a fence... or was it? Maybe these people could build fences.

"Eat up, my child."

I'd forgotten about my food. Feeling silly, I picked up a piece of fruit. It had smooth skin and when I took a bite, the sweetness burst into my mouth. It tasted like a nectarine, but was more of an oval shape.

They let me eat without bombarding me with more things I couldn't remember, then Jarleth took the tray and put it back on the table. I would have enjoyed my meal more if the two people in the room hadn't been staring at me.

So, now what?

Now that my hunger was gone, I noticed that I felt dry all over. My skin felt like it needed some moisturiser. Really badly.

Why is it I can remember what a moisturiser is, but can't remember my own name?

"The mind is a strange thing," Tasha told me as she leaned back in her chair. "In these situations, it recalls some things about everyday life and usually retains things like language, but it can lose memories."

How did she know what I was just thinking?

She looked into my eyes. "I can see what is in your mind, my daughter."

"What? *How?*"

She waved a hand casually. "We can see what others are thinking in the front of their minds if we look, but we don't pry without permission. Some of us have other Gifts and can go further into another's mind. This is how I can help you."

I shifted my position on the bed. "How?"

"I will try to help you remember, when you're ready."

Questions popped into my mind about how she would do that.

Tasha smiled. "I will answer your questions another time. We will leave you to rest. We will return later." She turned to Jarleth. "Come, Jarleth. Give her some space."

He dragged his gaze away from me and turned to her.

She frowned at him. "Come."

I wondered if they were having a telepathic conversation.

They both said their goodbyes and left me in peace.

I sighed and carefully lay back down on my surprisingly-comfortable bed. It was a relief that they were gone, but I couldn't help feeling utterly alone.

It took a while to get into a position that didn't hurt my head or my shoulder blade. I must have been exhausted because once I was settled, I drifted off to sleep.

It was a dreamless sleep, and when I woke up, I felt a little better, but the pain was still there. I felt the lump on the back of my head and it felt like it was covered in some kind of gel. Something to help it heal, I guessed. When I pulled my hand away, the gel on my fingers was clear and had traces of blood in it. I cringed and felt a little ill thinking about how much blood there was the last time I did that.

I looked around the room and was relieved to find it empty. I knew I'd have to face more people I didn't know soon enough, but I wanted to be alone for a while.

Someone had refilled the cup, so I slowly sat up and had another drink.

Just as I finished the last of the water, the rickety wooden door opened slowly and Tasha shuffled in.

She smiled. "Are you well, Sifayah?"

"Yes. I'm feeling better. Thank you."

Something in my mind screamed at me that the name Sifayah was wrong. It was not me.

Her smile grew. "That is good. Your head is still empty?"

I nodded, which caused me a lot of pain. And the thought that she could read my empty mind was unnerving.

As she reached the bedside, she clasped her hands together in front of her. "Your family would like to meet you. Are you feeling up to it?"

I started to shake my head, but besides the fact that it would hurt, I thought I might as well get it over with. "Okay."

Without her having to say a word, a woman with a curvy figure and long black hair walked cautiously into the room. My mouth fell open. She was beautiful.

"This is your mother, Tamari," Tasha told me.

CHAPTER 9
I'm Your Favourite!

Tamari gave me a wobbly smile as the tears started to slide down her cheeks. "Sifayah, my child!"

She crossed the room quickly and wrapped me up in a warm embrace. I tried to return it, but it was awkward. She was a stranger.

I patted her on the back as she sobbed, feeling uncomfortable. What else could I do?

I tried to remember something, *anything*, but came up short. It was frustrating to have nothing there. My mind felt hollow and cold inside and I desperately wanted it to change. To go back to normal — whatever *normal* was.

A tall man walked into the room. He had to duck his head a little to get in through the doorway. His long dark hair was tied up in many braids that hung down past his waist and his shoulders were broad and muscular. *This must be my father.*

His smile was tinged with sadness. "I am your father. It is so good to see you, my daughter. We had thought you lost to us."

I could see he was trying to control his emotions. We must have been a close family. My parents' emotions were starting to rub off on me, even though there was no spark of memory for either of them. No wait. I could *feel* their emotions. Was that normal?

He came over and joined my mother and I in a group hug

When they finally pulled away, I could see they knew I didn't recognise them.

Tasha shuffled forward. "Let's not be sad about this," she said. "It is too soon yet. Maybe when she sees the others, something will spark."

She looked at me. "I will send your siblings in and let's hope something jostles your memory."

Five people came pouring into the room. My three sisters and two brothers. I looked at each of their hopeful faces, trying to find something, but it wasn't until I saw the face of the smallest boy that I got a weird sensation, like I'd seen him somewhere before.

I smiled at him and he charged forward, wrapping his small arms around me and sobbing. "It's you! You're h-here!" he cried.

I cradled him in my arms on the bed with me and looked at Tasha. "There's something. I don't know what... with him..."

Relief sparked in her eyes and my brother lifted his head. "Really? Because of me?"

I looked down at him. "Yes. But I... I'm not even sure what it is... Just something."

He looked to Tasha, as they all seemed to do. "That's good, right?"

She patted him on the head. "Yes. That is good."

He turned his smiling face back to me. *"I knew it! I knew you'd remember me!"*

I sucked in a breath. He hadn't said those words aloud. They were in my head.

His smile faded. "Whoops. Sorry. They said not to use Mind-touch yet. I forgot."

"It's okay," I told him, even though it was strange to have his voice in my mind.

Now his smile returned and he gave me another hug. Meanwhile, I was reintroduced to my siblings. The one in my arms was the youngest, Axiak.

I was the oldest child. Jadidi was the oldest of my siblings, then there were my sisters, Shanae, Melina, and Channia.

I said hello to each of them as they were introduced, but had to disappoint everyone in the room by telling them I didn't remember anyone. I didn't really even remember Axiak. It was just a spark of some familiar feeling.

"Rylar!" The name just came to me when I looked at Axiak. "I remember the name Rylar!"

I looked around the room hoping to see smiles on everyone's faces because I'd remembered something, only to find eyes that welled with tears. I didn't understand. "What's wrong?"

It was Tasha who answered. "Rylar was Axiak's twin brother." I looked into her teary eyes. "He was killed by a Water Dragon." I frowned at the name. "A very large water reptile with very sharp teeth."

My heart sank. "Oh. I'm sorry. I thought... I'm sorry." I didn't know what else to say and tears pricked at my eyes.

Tasha changed the subject quickly and we chatted for a while. I noticed that my older brother, Jadidi, was kind of standoffish. He kept looking away, his lips pursed together in a straight line. Why didn't he seem happy to see me? I pushed that thought aside for now. I would have to find out what was going on later.

When she could see that I felt too overwhelmed, Tasha ushered them all out. She returned with another tray of food and some water.

"Jadidi seemed upset," I said. "It's like he's not happy to see me."

"Ah, yes. It is complicated for him."

"What do you mean?"

"He is conflicted about your return. It means different things to him, and a major change in his life."

"What kind of change?"

"All in good time, child. I do not wish to overburden you with the details."

I shook my head slowly and regretted it instantly as my head throbbed.

"You shall learn of it soon enough. I will let you rest now."

And with that, she left the room and left me to my thoughts.

———— ◆ ————

Later that day, I was able to get out of bed and walk around the village. I was still sore all over and my head was a bit fuzzy, but I didn't want to stay in bed or sit in that room any longer.

Apparently, we lived in caves that dotted the side of a tall cliff encircling a small cove. We lived on land and spent a lot of time in the sea. Jarleth had explained that our skin needed moisture regularly or it became too dry, so that explained my need for moisturiser.

There were people staring at me wherever we went and it unnerved me. Especially when none of their faces were familiar. I needed to find somewhere where I could take in my surroundings without feeling like I was in a sideshow.

They all kept their distance. Maybe they'd been told not to overwhelm me. To give me some space.

Jarleth wouldn't let me out of his sight, and Axiak was holding my hand the whole time. They told me who was who and where the cooking areas were and the village meeting place and the Zheav's cave. Zheav meant leader, so it was actually the cave where my parents lived. I felt anxious until I saw that they weren't in there.

It was hard to get used to the fact that I was the daughter of the leader of the tribe. That was a bit too much. And I was the oldest child too. I wondered what that entailed. Did I have a significant role within the tribe? Was I supposed to attend official gatherings? I had no idea and didn't want to ask Jarleth for fear of what he might tell me.

I wondered how close Jarleth and I had been before I disappeared. He was handsome with those intense brown eyes and jet-black hair and he had a lean, muscular body, but I didn't feel an attraction to him. If we'd been close before, wouldn't part of me remember it? Surely he would be the one that would trigger something in me.

Axiak had sparked something, even though it was only something like deja vu. And Rylar. I still felt guilty for making them all relive that.

A headache was creeping in but I did my best to ignore it. I was trying to piece together the family dynamics and remember our ages.

I turned to Axiak. "You're my youngest sibling, right?"

He nodded enthusiastically. "Yep. I'm your favourite!"

Maybe that was why I'd had some kind of reaction to him. I smiled. "Am I your favourite too?"

"You bet! We used to do all kinds of things together, and I was worried that you wouldn't want to spend time with me anymore after you married Jarleth, but you told me that you'd always love me and always have time for me."

Jarleth's face flushed. We were engaged? It almost felt like a punch to the gut. *It must be so devastating for him that I can't remember him.*

"Why didn't you tell me that we were engaged?"

"Engaged? What's that?"

What? "Uh, we were going to be married." How could he not know what *engaged* meant?

"Oh. Yes. We were betrothed." He ran a hand through his hair, clearly uncomfortable. "Tasha thought it best that we didn't tell you everything all at once."

I didn't know what to say to that. It felt like a betrayal somehow that they hadn't told me something so important, but it did make sense. "Okay, but this is important. This is huge. I mean, we were really going to spend the rest of our lives together?"

"Yes. We have known each other since we were younglings." He ran his hand through his hair again, clearly agitated. "Do you not remember even *one* thing about me — about *us?*"

Tears formed in his eyes. I searched my mind and still came up blank. There was nothing there. I couldn't answer. I just shook my head. Then I wondered if that meant 'no' in their culture — in *my* culture that I had no clue about.

The look on his face told me that that was exactly what it meant.

"I'm sorry. I'm trying. There's just nothing in my head... It's just empty. Haven't you looked into my mind and seen for yourself?"

His eyes snapped to me. "Not without your permission."

"Oh. I didn't realise. Sorry." I was confused. "Tasha—"

"Tasha is looking after your health. She is the only one allowed to look without first asking permission."

"Oh. Sorry."

"Do not be sorry. It's okay."

I sighed. There were so many little things that I didn't know that I *should* know.

I decided to let him see my blank mind, just to ease his worry. "So, you can look if you want to."

He gave me a lopsided smile. "Are you sure?"

"Yes."

I felt a weird sensation as he looked into my eyes. I could *feel* him in my mind. Was that normal?

"Yes," he answered me inside my head.

"But I can't tell when Tasha is in my head."

"That is part of her Gift. She can disguise her presence."

I shuddered. That was *not* a comforting thought.

I could somehow feel Jarleth searching for my memories. He could see that there was nothing. Nothing besides the things that had happened to me since I'd woken up on that beach.

I felt it when he left my mind.

"That was weird."

"I'm sorry if it disturbed you. Are you well?"

"Yes. Fine. It's fine."

Axiak looked at me. *"You're going to be okay, Fayah."*

"Fayah?"

"Yep. I couldn't say Sifayah when I was young, so I called you Fayah, but I'm grown up now."

I suppressed a giggle. I wondered if I was that confident when I was eight. "So, everyone can do this Mind-touch from when they're born?"

Axiak nodded. "Yes. And some can do more."

"Axiak," Jarleth warned.

He looked up at Jarleth. "What? She has to know. It's about her. We need to tell her."

I looked between them. "Tell me what?"

"That you can do more," Jarleth said.

"What do you mean?"

Jarleth looked directly into my eyes. "You are one of the few that can move objects with your mind."

CHAPTER 10
So, it's True

I gasped. "What?"

"It is part of who we are, to have other abilities of the mind besides Mind-touch, but most cannot do what you can do. You had been training with Tasha for a long time to learn to master this power. You cannot feel this power now?"

"No. Nothing." I was feeling like I needed to sit down. "Why do I have this extra ability?"

"No one knows why some have the Gift and some do not. You and Tasha are the strongest here. It is strong in your family. Your father can lift some objects as well, and your mother is Gifted with the ability to find things, but it is not strong enough for her to find people over long distances. She has been sad that she could not find you."

My stomach twisted. *The guilt she must feel...*

"What happens if I don't get this Gift back? How will it change things?"

"I'm not sure if it will change things any more than your disappearance has."

"What do you mean?"

"Well, I may as well tell you now. You were next in line to become Zheav, but your oldest brother, Jadidi, has been preparing for the role in case you never returned." He faltered on those last two words.

I sucked in a slow deep breath. Zheav. I couldn't imagine myself as a leader of anyone, but then again, I didn't know who I was or what I was capable of. I might have been a warrior, trained in battle, ready to fight any army that might dare invade our little village. What would I know?

And that explained the 'complicated' problem Tasha was referring to regarding Jadidi. It made sense, but I felt I should talk to him about it.

A group of young boys walked past at that moment and they turned to look at us. At me.

They greeted us and smiled politely. Some of them looked familiar and I was wondering if I was remembering something from before I disappeared. Hope started to stir within me, but was crushed with the next thing Jarleth said.

"Sifayah, these three are the boys who found you on the beach. Aarish, Calizar, and Kaidan."

So, not a long-lost memory then. I couldn't help the disappointment weighing heavily on me. I was really getting sick of this.

Jarleth introduced the other four boys that were with them, but I forgot all of their names except for Calizar — which was unusual for me. Calizar was the oldest of my three rescuers and the one who'd talked to me on the beach.

Wait. How did I know it was unusual for me?

I forced a smile. "Thank you for bringing me back home."

They all blushed furiously and fidgeted. "Anyone would have done the same," Calizar said.

It was a small village and everyone seemed to know each other well, so he was probably right.

When I thought about the state I was in when they'd found me, I cringed inwardly. "I don't know how long I would've lasted out there with no memories to help me. I didn't even know what to eat. So, thank you."

He smiled. I don't think any of them knew what to say.

Axiak turned to us. "Can I go fishing with the boys?"

My smile faltered and I froze. He was asking me? I didn't know if it was okay for him to go off with older boys.

Jarleth came to my rescue. "Of course you can. Off you go."

Axiak looked to me and I nodded.

"Thanks!" He gave me a big squeeze and joined the boys as they turned to go, waving goodbye as they went.

Fishing? Well, of course they'd eat fish. It would probably be a major part of their diet. I just hoped that they cooked the fish before eating it.

Now where had that come from? Why was I wishing for cooked fish? Surely that was the way we ate it.

And I still couldn't figure out why I didn't naturally speak their language. It didn't make any sense. It was like someone had sprinkled puzzle pieces from a different jigsaw puzzle in with mine. They weren't fitting together.

I didn't ask Jarleth if they cooked their food; I felt stupid enough.

"Do you want to go and see where they fish?" he asked me.

"Yeah. That would be good."

We walked down to the shore and saw the boys diving into the water. I wondered how they were catching the fish until I saw Axiak take a small thin spear from a pile on the sand and race into the waves.

I could see Jarleth looking at me from the corner of my eye and turned to him.

He smiled. "Do you—"

"So, it's true. You're back."

We both turned to find a tall woman with long auburn hair glaring at me.

I guessed that she expected me to know who she was. "Um... hello."

Her scowl deepened. "They say you lost your memory."

Under the weight of her stare, I shifted from one foot to the other. "Uh, yeah."

"I don't believe you."

CHAPTER 11

Dakawa

My anger flared and I glared back. Who was this woman? "I don't care what you believe."

She looked like she wanted to hit me.

Normally, I wouldn't react that way, but her attitude put me on the defensive.

Jarleth stepped forward. "Dakawa! What are you doing?"

She dragged her gaze away from me and glared at him. "She is lying to you, and you're falling for it!"

"No. She does not remember."

"No! Don't you see? She is seeking attention! She knows that you have moved on while she was gone and she is trying to get back into your heart."

I felt like there was not enough air getting into my lungs.

Jarleth's face had turned red. Could it be true? Did he find love in this woman's arms, but didn't want me to know it? Why would he hide that from me? Because I was going to be the Zheav and as my husband, he would be someone important?

He lifted his chin. "Dakawa. You have it wrong. I have not—"

"Don't lie to me! Don't lie to *her!*" She turned back to me. "He is not your love any longer! You need to stop this game and leave him be."

Before I could say another word, she turned on her heel and stomped up the beach.

Jarleth turned to me. "Sifayah. Do not worry about Dakawa. She has a temper. I don't know what's gotten into her. She is usually more reasonable."

Not 'usually nice' or 'usually a pleasant person,' so did that mean that she was a horrible person, but was extra nasty today?

I looked into his eyes. His face was flustered and he seemed embarrassed, but I couldn't really tell why. Did he love her? Were they close? Or was he just embarrassed that she'd caused such a big scene out here in front of me and everyone else on the beach?

I wasn't sure.

"Come. Let's get back to your cave. You look like you need a rest."

I did need to rest — my head was pounding — but was that the reason why he was eager to get back?

I wished I had my memories back. Then maybe I could work out what was going on here. I didn't know these people well enough to judge the situation.

We headed back up to my cave in silence.

The next morning after I'd had something to eat, Jarleth took me to Tasha's cave on the edge of the village.

On the way, I was having trouble concentrating on what he was saying. I couldn't stop thinking about the discovery I'd made the night before that I could see in the dark. I'd lain in bed looking at all the things in my room and wondering why I had this ability, until it hit me. How else would I be able to see where I was going in the depths of the ocean?

Tasha welcomed me and asked Jarleth to leave. She would call him when we were done. He was reluctant, but did as he was asked.

"Why am I here?" I asked. I thought there was no point in beating around the bush.

"Hmm. Why *are* you here?"

Why answer a question with a question? I closed my mouth tightly. I thought if I opened it, I would have said some snarky comment. I was frustrated and wanted answers to the millions of questions spinning in my mind and didn't think I'd get them by being a smart-arse.

"We need to try to unlock that mind of yours. Then you will truly be home."

Yeah. She was right about that. I didn't feel like I was home, or that I belonged here. Maybe she could help, but how?

"How can you 'unlock' my mind?" It sounded ominous.

Tasha smiled gently. "It's okay, my daughter. It's not as scary as it sounds. I will enter your mind and see if I can find a way into your memories." I cringed inwardly. "Do not worry yourself. I will be gentle. I will not hurt you."

I took a deep breath and tried to release the tension in my shoulders. It didn't help as much as I'd hoped.

"Now, sit down and try to relax. Open your mind to me. I will place my fingers on your temples. These things can be done without touching, but it is good to have the touch to help strengthen the connection." She pulled up a chair and sat opposite to the one she had gestured for me to sit on. "Is this something you will allow me to do?"

"Yes. Okay." I sat down and took another deep breath.

I tried to calm my panicked brain; I was willing to do this if it meant regaining my memories, and my mind. I felt incomplete. Wrong. I *needed* this.

"Close your eyes, child."

I closed them and felt her calloused fingers touch my temples. I tried to only focus on the touch of her warm skin. *Breathe in... Breathe out...*

I felt it when she entered my mind this time. She moved slowly, carefully. I let her in and didn't try to stop her. Could I stop her? Surely people who could do things like this naturally would be able to guard against someone invading their minds without permission.

"Yes. That is right." She told me. *"We have all trained to use our natural mental shields to guard against that very thing. If I cannot access your memories of it today, you will need to be retrained."*

I groaned inwardly. I really hoped she could fix things. I didn't want to be trained in something I should already know — something that my youngest brother would already know how to do, even at his young age.

I didn't ask any more questions about it. I tried to relax and let her do whatever she needed to do. It was like there was a big black wall in my brain and she was nosing around trying to find a hidden door. Maybe that was exactly what she was doing. Maybe that's all it took. I really hoped that this would work.

"Relax, child."

I hadn't realized that I'd tensed up. I breathed in slowly and deliberately, then let it out just as slow. I concentrated on my breathing, even though the whole thing was unnerving. It was like trying to ignore someone doing something in the corner of the room while you're trying to concentrate on the program you're writing...

What?

What was that? A computer program? How could I possibly know what a program was when these people didn't even have electricity? It didn't make any sense. Even Tasha had stopped poking and was trying to work out what was going on.

I 'thought' a question at her. *"Why do I know things that I shouldn't know?"*

"That, child, I cannot answer. Maybe once I've unlocked your mind, we will find out where you've really been."

This was creating more questions than it was answering, but I was determined to find answers. *"Okay. Keep looking."*

She gave what could only be described as a 'mental nod' and continued her work.

The waiting was grating on my nerves.

I was about to tell her to give up when I was plunged into total darkness. I opened my eyes, but couldn't see anything. I tried to move, but my body wouldn't obey. I could blink in the darkness, but nothing else. And the darkness didn't change; it didn't matter whether my eyes were open or closed. Panic started to choke me. How did this happen? I was just sitting in the cave with Tasha. Where was I? What was happening to me?

CHAPTER 12

Some Time Alone is What She Needs

"Breathe, child. I am here."

"What's happening?"

"This is a memory."

"But I can't see! I can't move!"

"Yes, but it is only in your memory. You are still in my home. You are safe."

I tried to relax, but nothing worked. My brain couldn't get past the fact that I couldn't move. Tasha's presence didn't help. I started to take shallow breaths and the panic crept up and seized me by the throat.

"Shhh, child. It is okay."

Within a few seconds, I was plunged into bright daylight and I could move again. Objects were floating around in the air and a large pot clanged against the wall. I jumped up out of my seat and looked at the chaos surrounding me.

Before I could ask what was causing it, Tasha spoke. "Calm yourself, Sifayah. You need to stop this. Relax and let them fall."

"What?"

"Let the objects in the room fall to the floor."

"I'm doing this? But how?"

"Jarleth said he told you that you had this Gift."

"Yes, he did, but... how do I make it stop?"

"Calm down and concentrate."

I tried, but it was hard to calm down with so many things flying around in the air, knowing that I was the one doing it. My head started to pound, as if using my mind was giving me a headache.

Tasha kept talking to me and put a reassuring hand on my arm, which helped to anchor me enough to stop the carnage.

Once it had stopped, I immediately started to apologise. I had ruined a lot of things in her home. Guilt wrapped itself around my chest.

"It is okay, my daughter. You had no control. The fault is not yours."

"But, your things..."

"I will survive. They are only things."

"If we do this again, we do it outside somewhere, away from your house."

I couldn't believe the damage I'd done. There were clothes strewn all over the floor, hanging wooden frames had been pulled from the walls and smashed to pieces, and clay bottles and pots were everywhere — most of them shattered with their ingredients mixing together on the floor.

People came rushing into the cave and stopped short, taking in the scene.

Jarleth stepped forward. "Tasha! What happened?"

She gave him a small smile. "Sifayah remembered something very unpleasant, which seems to have awakened her Gift."

He mumbled something incoherent and ran his hand through his hair. "Are you okay?"

I let Tasha answer him as speech evaded me. We were okay, but I couldn't say the same for her belongings. I couldn't stand the fact that I had ruined just about everything Tasha owned. I had to get out of there.

"I'm sorry!" I almost shouted, and ran for the door.

"Sifayah!" Jarleth called out.

I pushed past him and the other people I didn't recognise and kept running.

"Let her go," I heard Tasha say. "Some time alone is what she needs."

I ran out of the village and along a sandy beach. I couldn't stand the curious looks everyone was giving me. How was I going to fix this mess? I'd caused so much damage, and with my eyes shut. What if I have a bad dream and end up wrecking everything in my cave? What if I hurt someone next time I'm upset?

Tears ran down my cheeks. And what was that memory? Not being able to move or see was terrifying. What had happened to me? How did I escape that? There were no answers.

My head pounded to the rhythm of my heart, which still felt strange, like there was something wrong with it.

I sank down onto my knees in the sand to catch my breath. My head felt fuzzy and my stomach roiled. I just needed to sit for a while. I turned to the ocean and watched the waves roll in. It made me think of when I'd woken up on that beach and it sent shivers down my spine, but I forced myself to just see the beauty of the ocean for what it was, and to just enjoy nature.

It was so peaceful here. I didn't want to go back. I needed time to myself. Everyone crowded me and made me feel guilty for not remembering them. I knew it wasn't their fault.

I tried to put myself in their place. It would be horrible to lose someone you love and not have any idea what had happened to them. After a while you would start to think that maybe they were dead, as much as you hated to even think it. Then I guess you would feel guilty for thinking that they could be dead. Maybe you'd feel like that would be giving up. Then you'd try not to give up, even though there's that nagging thought in the back of your mind that maybe you're wasting your time searching and hoping.

I sighed. All the time they'd been searching and worrying, and it was almost like I didn't care. Like I hadn't been worried. I was sure that I'd had a worse time of it than everyone else, especially after what I'd just remembered.

I wished that I could get my memories back. Now. I searched my mind and came up blank. Would I ever remember?

A noise startled me and I turned to see a young woman with long blonde hair walking along the beach.

She paused when she saw me. "Sifayah?" Her breath hitched. "Is it really you?"

I looked more closely, hoping I'd remember something, but there was nothing. "Um, yes. It's me."

She came closer, but was hesitant. "They said you lost your memory. Is... is that true?"

"Yeah."

She shifted her weight from one foot to the other. "So, do you remember me?"

I looked at her for a few moments, hoping that something would click. "No. Sorry."

She closed the distance between us and sat on the sand in front of me. There were tears in her eyes.

There was a flash of recognition in my mind. I remembered seeing her face before, and she was crying. Sobbing uncontrollably. I sucked in a breath and her eyes widened. "What is it?"

"Something. I remember seeing you crying. Really crying. Sobbing. Is that right?"

Her face fell and big fat tears rolled down her cheeks. "Yes. That did happen. My..."

Her breath hitched and she couldn't continue. I'd done it again. Whatever had made her cry was obviously something painful and I'd just dragged it up. "I'm sorry. You don't have to say. It's just that... that's what I remembered."

She took a deep breath. "It's okay. You didn't know. My betrothed was killed by a Longtooth."

CHAPTER 13

You're Not My Sister!

"Oh! I'm so sorry!" I didn't remember what a Longtooth was, but I didn't really have to.

She wiped her cheeks with the backs of her hands. "It's okay. You didn't know."

I looked down at my sand-covered feet. "How did I know you?"

"We were — *are* — best friends."

My gaze snapped up to meet hers. "Really?"

She nodded.

"Maybe that's why I remembered something. There was something with Axiak too. At first it was only a feeling that I knew him somehow. Not an actual memory. But then I remembered Rylar... and then I felt terrible for making everyone remember him and what happened..."

"You couldn't have known."

"I know, but I still felt like I'd dug a knife into an open wound for them. And now I've done the same to you." My gut twisted at the thought.

She opened her mouth, closed it, then looked down at the sand for a while. "Maybe if I stick around, you'll remember more stuff."

"Okay. We could try. Hopefully it will be something happy next time."

She gave me a wobbly smile.

I ran a hand through my hair. "Umm. I was wondering why I haven't seen you in the village since I got back."

"Oh, I've just arrived from visiting my cousins that live among the Shinnari. I came as soon as I heard you'd been found."

"Who are the Shinnari?"

"They are our sister tribe from across the sea. I was seeing their healer as well while I was there to help with my grief..."

"Oh. I'm sorry." There was an awkward silence. "Tell me about us. How did we become friends?"

She seemed to cheer up a bit at that. "Well, it was when we were only younglings. A girl called Dakawa was pushing me around and you came over and set her straight. You threatened to punch her in the face if she didn't stop."

"Dakawa? I met her already."

"Really? Did you remember her?"

"No. She remembers me though. And she told me that Jarleth had moved on. She also said that she didn't believe that I'd lost my memory. That it was all an act to get him back."

"That sounds like something Dakawa would say. She's had a thing for him for a while now. Everyone knows it."

"So, is she telling the truth about Jarleth? Has he moved on?"

"No! Of course not!" She pushed her hair behind her ear. "She is crazy to think he'd want to be with her at all, even if you'd— Well, you know. If we'd known that you were..."

"Dead?"

She nodded and shifted in the sand, the tears welling up again.

"It's okay. I understand. I was gone a while, from what I've been told. It would be hard not knowing."

"Yes. It was." She sniffed.

I picked up a shell and turned it over, admiring the pearly interior. I felt bad, but I didn't know why I'd left the village or where I'd been.

Did I leave on purpose? Did it have something to do with Dakawa? Did I run away or did something bad happen to me? I hoped that my memories would return before I drove myself mad with these questions.

I thought I'd change the subject back to when we were kids. *There I go again. She said 'younglings' and I thought 'kids.'*

"So, we became friends after I threatened Dakawa?"

Her smile returned. "Yes. We were inseparable and did just about everything together. Until it was found that you had... um..."

"My Gift?"

"Yes. I wasn't sure if they'd told you yet. I didn't want to mess things up."

"It's okay," I assured her. "Even if they didn't, I would have found out just before I came down here."

Her eyes went wide. "What happened?"

"Tasha was trying to find my memories and I remembered something really horrible. I made everything in her cave fly around and... broke a lot of her stuff."

"Oh."

"I didn't mean it." I kicked some sand around. "I couldn't control it. I don't know how. I don't remember my training."

"Maybe Tasha can help you remember."

"I'm not sure I want to go through that again."

"Why not?"

"It was terrifying. In the memory, I couldn't move or see."

"Oh. That sounds awful."

"What if the next thing I remember is just as bad, or worse? What if I hurt someone?"

"You can't help it. Maybe get some training before you try again? Maybe go somewhere where there's nothing in the cave to break?"

Maybe the training would work. I took a slow, deep breath. I needed to calm myself down. Change the subject.

"So what happened when my Gift showed itself?"

"Okay. So, once they found out what you could do, you had training with Tasha every day and I couldn't go with you."

"What did you do while I was training?"

Her face flushed. "I spent my days with Jakaren and saw you after training. We were eventually betrothed and... well... you know what happened."

"Oh. I'm sorry."

Her tears returned. "It's okay."

It was clear that it wasn't, but what could I do? I leaned over and gave her a hug and it didn't feel awkward like it did with my own mother.

<hr />

"I remembered something."

We were in Tasha's cave and I was trying not to cringe at the mess.

"Tell me, child."

Samura and I told her what I'd remembered.

"This is good. This is progress. Maybe you should spend some more time with Samura and your youngest brother. Spending time with your betrothed is not bringing your memories to the fore."

I thought it was odd. Wouldn't the closeness of our relationship trigger something? It was strange to me that there was nothing.

Tasha praised my efforts, even though I hadn't done anything, and suggested that I meet with more people in the village to see if something triggered more memories.

It was a logical idea, but I didn't really want to face more people I didn't know staring at me like I was some kind of monkey in a zoo.

Monkey in a zoo? There were no monkeys here, and no zoos. Where did all this other information come from? It was like I'd been taken to another world while I was gone. But even that didn't make sense.

I had to put those questions aside for now to avoid making my headache worse.

Before Tasha shooed us out to go 'meet people,' she checked my head again, and my back. Apparently, the pain I felt was from a huge purple bruise under my shoulder blade. Either someone had hit me hard, or I'd fallen and landed on something. Maybe I hit my back and my head in the same fall. Probably. Maybe. Will I ever remember?

The fact that there was little clothing covering my back made it easier for her to examine my wound and put some kind of ointment on it.

I was wearing clothing made from the skins of a jungle cat when they'd found me, which had puzzled everyone in the village. The Jungle People wore those skins, but not the Waikari.

Our clothing came from a durable seaweed that we cultivated and softened.

I had been given short filmy dresses to wear, which I assumed were mine.

We headed out and walked around the cove, with Samura pointing out some of the places that Jarleth had shown me, as well as others I hadn't had the chance to see. Now I could see more of my home.

Home. That word didn't seem to fit and I couldn't work out why. I'd lived here all my life and never known any other place. The Waikari kept away from the Jungle People. They spent a lot of their time under the sea, swimming and playing and hunting. How could I think of Akilina Cove as anything other than home?

Nothing made sense. The only way I was going to have answers to my questions was to get my memories back. It made me more determined to look around at everything and everybody to try to spark something.

"Maybe my parents' home? Surely there would be memories there?"

Samura smiled. "Let's try it."

As we approached the Zheav's cave, one of my sisters approached us. I couldn't remember her name.

I gave a pathetic little wave. "Um, hi."

She kind of smiled, but she didn't look happy to see me, which I thought was odd. "Hello. Are you going to see Mama and Papa?"

"Um, yes. I'm trying to find things and people to help me remember."

Her eyes narrowed and it looked like she was trying to see into my soul. "There's something not right about you."

I felt my eyes go wide. "Well, yeah, I can't remember anything before I was found on that beach—"

"No. It's something else. I can sense it. It's my Gift. You don't belong here. You're not my sister!" She covered her mouth with her hands and ran off down the path.

CHAPTER 14

It is Your Fate

I didn't know what to think of that. But there was this nagging thought in my head. Something telling me that she was right.

"Don't listen to her. She's upset. Everyone is upset and things are all upside-down now that you're back. It will sort itself out. You will remember everything and then things can get back to normal."

"Yeah, but what is normal?"

Samura blinked. "You will see. You will know soon."

I hoped she was right.

We set off again toward the cave. Once we reached it and were permitted to enter, we walked in to see my father lying down in his bed. I didn't remember him so I didn't know if this was normal behaviour for him, but surely the leader of the tribe wouldn't be lying around in bed in the middle of the day. My immediate thought was that there was something wrong.

"Are you ill?" I blurted out without even thinking.

He gave me a steady look. "Yes. I am not well. It has been a while since I was well enough to hunt."

I felt tears stinging my eyes, which was kind of weird considering I didn't even remember this man. Obviously, my heart felt something for him, even if my mind had forgotten.

"Should I get Tasha? Is there something she can do to fix this?" She was obviously the person they turned to for medical help, as well as matters of the mind.

He shook his head sadly. "No, my daughter. There is nothing. I will not get better. There is only waiting to be done. One day, I will have to give up my position as leader and pass it on to another."

He was looking at me so intently that I wanted to hide. Not me. He couldn't mean for me to take over. I knew nothing about our people or our culture. I was a blank slate. I would have to pass it on to someone else.

"I can't do it."

"I know that you cannot remember, but we were preparing for this before you left. It is your fate."

I cringed. "It can't be my fate if I can't remember anything. I need time to figure this out."

"Yes, Sifayah. It is okay. We will sort things out."

I nodded. I couldn't help feeling overwhelmed. I took a deep breath and tried to push some of those feelings aside. I wanted to get to know my father again and there was that hope in the back of my mind that talking to him might spark a memory.

We sat and talked to him for a while before Samura suggested we go swimming.

After we left the cave, I couldn't help feeling down. Seeing my father like that was upsetting.

Samura turned to me as we walked along the sand toward the beach. "Let's go for that swim now and get away for a bit."

The memory of the boys dragging me into the waves flashed through my mind and I hesitated, but I knew I could breathe under the water and there was nothing to be afraid of. I needed to do this. To face my fear.

My fear turned to curiosity as I looked out toward the vast ocean. "Let's go."

Samura's face brightened and we headed to the waves.

As my feet touched the water, I was surprised to find that it wasn't cold. It was a tropical climate here, so I didn't know why I'd expected it to be too cold.

I kept walking as small waves washed up against my legs and once I was in knee-deep water, a bigger wave crashed into me and I was suddenly wet up to my waist. I could feel my heart pounding, this time with excitement. I couldn't wait to see what was out there.

Samura turned with a look of concern, but my face must have shown how I was feeling because hers morphed into a smile. "Come on," she almost squealed, "let's get wet!"

We started forward but as we entered the deeper water, we were slowed down to a snail's pace.

Samura took my hand. "Sifayah, are you ready?"

I smiled. "Yes."

I watched as her head disappeared under the water and took a deep breath before following her.

Opening my eyes felt strange and I watched Samura's long hair being tossed about in the current caused by the waves. Mine moved to the same rhythm.

"Let's go!" She turned and started to swim away from the shore and I could feel the urge to surface and breathe. It was so strong that I almost did it.

I followed Samura while telling myself that I could breathe under here. I blew the air from my lungs and the bubbles rose around me. I had to keep fighting the desperate urge to get to the surface. Why was this happening? If I was born to breathe underwater, why was the instinct to breathe air so strong?

I forced myself to suck in water and expected to cough and choke, the fear that I would drown almost strangling me.

CHAPTER 15
Only, You Did Not Return

Samura turned back. *"Are you well?"*

Breathing in water was just as smooth and easy as it had been the last time and I couldn't understand why something so natural to a being that was amphibious could cause such a reaction. It was unnerving.

"I'm okay now," I told her. *"I don't know what happened."* It was the truth.

We started off again. It took me a while to get the rhythm of swimming. I was flailing around for a few strokes and as I watched how Samura was moving, it all clicked somehow and I shot forward, using both my legs together to propel me through the water, and my hands by my sides to help manoeuvre my body. Samura gave a laugh that I could somehow hear in my mind and we sped off toward a coral reef and a drop-off.

The coral's colours were amazing and so diverse. Orange and green and white and grey, pink and purple and blue. Some were shaped like little trees and some were large flat growths that grew from short thick stems.

Fish with colours and stripes and spots and odd-shaped fins darted in and around the coral. It was so beautiful. I was glad I'd agreed to come out here.

Movement caught my eye and I turned to see a huge sea turtle gliding through the water. *"Look, Samura! A turtle!"*

"A what?"

"A sea turtle." I pointed to it as I spoke.

"That shellback?"

"What?" Why did we have different names for the same thing?

We frowned at each other. *"The shellback. You don't remember what it's called?"*

"No."

We approached and swam alongside it for a while and I touched its shell. It was rough and hard and it was difficult to convince my brain that it was part of the turtle and not just a shell it had crawled into. I touched one of its flippers and it felt so different. Smooth. It changed direction and darted away from us but we didn't try to follow.

Below us were at least a couple of hundred silver fish that were about as long as my hand. It was incredible to watch them change direction at the same time as if they shared a hive mind.

My attention was drawn to my feet and I gasped. There was a flap of skin sticking out from the outer edge of each foot, which made swimming easier, but I hadn't known they were there. I just shook my head and returned my attention to the swarm of fish.

They parted to reveal a large groper. We swam closer to get a better look. I avoided calling it a groper in case Samura's name for it was different.

It swam slowly with its mouth agape. We watched for a while before Samura said that we should get back. Water Dragons liked to hunt at dusk. I shuddered. I couldn't remember what they looked like, but after what I'd been told about Rylar being killed by one, I didn't want to stick around to see one.

As we turned toward the shore, I got a flash in my mind of me swimming along the bottom of the ocean and pulling a camera off my shoulder and letting it fall to the sand.

I tried to keep pace with Samura and make sense of the memory. A camera was something else that was far too advanced to belong to the Waikari and it frustrated me to know that it was yet another thing that didn't fit in with me living my whole life here in this primitive village.

As soon as we had walked up on the beach and squeezed the excess water out of our hair, it started to rain heavily, and we laughed at the irony as we headed back to the village.

Once I was back in my cave, I tried to relax but I couldn't find a comfortable position that didn't hurt my head or back. I was startled by a knock on my door and Jarleth asked if he could come in. I wasn't sure if I wanted to see him, but asked him to come in anyway.

This was crazy. I should be eager to see him.

"Hello," he said. "Are you well?"

I sat up and the movement hurt my back. "I'm fine. A bit tired from all the walking and swimming. I guess you heard that I remembered something about Samura?"

"Yes. It is good progress." He smiled, but I could sense the hurt.

"I wish I could remember more. We walked all around the cove and nothing seemed to look familiar." I didn't want to tell him about the underwater memory with the camera. How would I even begin to explain a video camera to these people?

I frowned. 'These people' were supposed to be *my* people.

"Do not worry too much. It will come."

"Will it?" I looked up into his dark eyes. *"What if it doesn't?"*

He sat on the chair. "It's only been such a short time and you've remembered things already. We can go back to Tasha and she can try to—"

"No! I don't want to go through that again!"

"Why? What did you remember?"

"I couldn't see and I couldn't move. I don't know where I was or how I got there or even how I escaped from it all."

"You may have been in a dark cave."

"No. I don't think so. We can see in the dark, right?"

"Yes."

"Well, I couldn't see anything when my eyes were open. Not even shapes in the darkness."

"Maybe it was a form of torture? Maybe one of the land tribes found you and tortured you. We keep away from them for good reason. They are our enemies."

"I don't know. I don't know anything." I sat and thought for a while. "What do you know about when I disappeared?"

He looked uncomfortable. It was probably very painful for him to think about, but I had to know. "We had been diving off the rocks at the Dive and you decided to head back for your training—"

"The Dive?"

"Yes. It is a place outside the village where there is a rocky outcrop. We take turns diving off the rocks and into the sea. It is near where you were found."

"Oh." I remembered seeing the boys diving into the sea.

He continued. "We were there with Jadidi and Axiak. You headed back for your training session with Tasha. Only, you did not return. Until the boys found you there yesterday, no one had seen you at all. Your tracks had just stopped in the sand. There were no clues as to what had befallen you. We called, but couldn't reach your mind."

I took a slow breath. It was hard to picture what it would be like for everyone to try so hard to find me, only to come up empty-handed. I wished I could put their minds at ease.

Jarleth shifted anxiously in his seat. "Are you sure you don't remember anything about me?"

CHAPTER 16
You Love Him!

I felt an ache in my chest. It must have been so hard for him. "There's nothing. Yet. Maybe there will be soon."

"What if I held you in my arms? Maybe that could trigger something."

I hesitated because he felt like a stranger to me, but he looked so hopeful, and it might actually work. "Okay."

We stood and I stepped forward into his outstretched arms. It felt kind of awkward at first, but then he pulled me a little bit closer and I felt him relax more. He'd probably been dying to hug me since I'd been found. It must have been torture.

I closed my eyes and breathed in, smelling the scent of salt water and a fresh smell I couldn't identify as I put my head on his shoulder. Maybe it would trigger something. I tried to relax and searched my mind for something, anything.

But there was nothing.

We stayed like that for a long time, then he finally whispered, "Is there anything?"

I shook my head, not daring to say it out loud. I'd just crushed his hopes.

I lifted my head. He looked into my eyes for a long time and then started to lean toward me. He was going to kiss me. I flinched instinctively and he apologised, but then I thought that maybe we should try it. Maybe we needed something more than just a mere hug.

"It's okay. I... I think we should."

"Really? Are you sure?"

Not really. "Yes. Maybe I'll remember something."

He leaned in again and our lips met. He was tentative and gave me short little kisses, then longer ones. It felt kind of nice, but also kind of awkward, like I was kissing some random stranger from off the street.

He stopped. "Anything?"

"No," I whispered.

I stepped back and he dropped his arms. He looked so lost. I couldn't stand it. "Maybe if we got Tasha to try again..."

His face brightened. "Or I could try."

"You?"

"Yes. I can do it. I've had a bit of training."

I was reluctant, but thought it was worth a try.

We sat on the edge of the bed facing each other. I closed my eyes and tried to slow my breathing. Jarleth put his fingers on my temples like Tasha had done. I felt his presence in my mind.

At first, there was nothing, but after a while, there was motion. Something out of reach. I let Jarleth push at the memory and it kind of burst out into my mind.

I was lying in a strange bed and there was a shirtless man with short brown hair sleeping next to me. I watched his chest rise and fall. There was a feeling of peace and contentment while I looked at him. I felt alive and so in love. I loved him with all my heart.

I was suddenly pulled from the memory and was disoriented for a few seconds until I realized I was back in my cave and Jarleth had moved away from me.

"Who was that?" He demanded from near the doorway.

"I-I don't know."

"You love him!" It wasn't a question. He'd felt what I'd felt.

"I..." What could I say? I couldn't deny it. "I don't know who he is. I don't know why I... I don't know anything!"

The anguish was clear on Jarleth's face as he turned and stormed out the door. I called after him, but he didn't stop.

———◦———

Tears slid down my cheeks. I'd hurt Jarleth, but not purposely. I had no control over it. Who was this other man that I'd felt so much love for? And why didn't I love Jarleth? What had happened?

I had nothing. I sat for a long time, replaying the memory over and over in my head.

Darion.

I had no idea where that had come from, but I knew that that was his name. It didn't really help me, but I was glad I had a name for the face I saw in my mind. Who was he? How did I know him?

I became aware that the sun was fading and my stomach was rumbling, so I left my room and went to find some food.

Once I'd reached the cooking area, I saw Axiak and headed over to where he was talking to our mother.

I said hi to my mother and looked down at Axiak. "Hey, squirt."

He frowned up at me. "What's a squirt? Why do you talk funny?"

Huh? Why didn't he know what that was? "It's a term of endearment for someone shorter than you."

"I'm not short!"

"No, but you're shorter than me."

He huffed, but then moved over to where they were serving fish. "Do you want some Big Fin?" He was pointing at some fish on a platter. Cooked fish. Thankfully.

"Um..." I trailed off. Did I even like it — whatever it was?

"It's one of your favourites," he informed me with a grin.

"Oh. In that case, yes." My cheeks warmed. I hated that I knew nothing about myself.

We grabbed some Big Fin and some raw vegetables of some kind with our mother and sat down at a table with some of my family members. My sisters.

Tamari and Axiak talked about what life was like in the cove and I listened intently, trying to remember everything they told me. I needed to learn as much as I could about life here if I was to survive and live a somewhat normal life. I couldn't just expect that my memories would return. Plus, they seemed happy to do all the talking.

As I bit into the Big Fin, I wondered why the dish was one of my favourites. It was okay, but not something I'd rate as a favourite. That didn't make sense. Why would one of my favourite foods suddenly not be one of my favourites?

Axiak turned to me once we'd finished eating. "Why don't you remember me?"

I wasn't expecting the question and was a bit stunned. "I, um, I'm not sure."

"But I'm your favourite," he said, tears welling up in his eyes. He didn't understand.

Well, neither did I.

I gave him a big hug. "I'm sorry. I can't control what my brain does. And I'm trying, I really am."

I looked to my mother, who gave me a watery smile. There was nothing I could do. I just had to hope my brain recovered.

"Maybe if you tell me about something that happened, something that we did together, it might help," I suggested.

He smiled. "Okay."

My sisters leaned in to hear what he had to say.

He thought for a moment. "Ummm. You taught me how to do a backflip off the rocks at the Dive."

"Did I?"

"Yes. And Jadidi too."

"I taught Jadidi?"

"No. I mean, he taught me too."

"Oh. Okay."

"You told me how to turn around and stand right on the edge and how I had to count to three and push really, really hard and go up and back."

I tried to picture the scene in my head. It sounded like fun, but it didn't spark anything. And the thought that he'd have to teach me now made me cringe inside.

I shook my head, wondering what it was going to take to bring my memories back.

Axiak hung his head.

"Hey, don't be sad," I said. "Keep going. What else?"

CHAPTER 17
I Don't Want to Be Zheav

He told me about the time he caught his first fish. And his first crab that nipped him on the finger. The day he fell out of the tree just as I tried to stop him from climbing up there. I'd managed to stop him from hitting the ground using my Gift.

But there was nothing in my mind. No spark. No feeling in my chest.

Once we'd finished our meal, he'd ducked over to another table and came back with some wonderfully juicy pieces of fruit that I couldn't remember the names of.

When I had only two pieces left, I saw him eyeing my plate. "Do you want one?" I asked while trying not to giggle.

"Oh. Yes, please! It's my very favourite!"

I gave him one and popped the other in my mouth and something flashed in my mind. Hope stirred in my chest.

"Hold on. Did I...?"

He leaned forward. "What?"

"No... that can't be right..." I couldn't have shared my dessert with him like in my memory because it was in a cafeteria and there was nothing like that here.

"What can't be right?" My mother was leaning forward too. How could I explain?

"Oh, I thought I'd remembered sharing my fruit with Axiak, but the location was wrong. It wasn't here. It wasn't him."

They looked disappointed, but I couldn't tell them anything more about it.

Where was the cafeteria and what was I doing there?

The word Jannali popped into my head. "What's Jannali? Is it a place? A person?"

Every face showed a frown.

"I never heard that name before," Tamari offered.

I frowned too. "I don't know where it's from then."

I was really getting sick of this.

After dinner, I felt exhausted and decided to head back to my cave alone. I didn't know whether it had been mine before or whether it was just a place they'd stuck me while I recovered. I'd been meaning to ask someone because it didn't feel like home.

My older brother fell into step with me as I walked. "Are you well, sister?"

I smiled. "I'm doing okay. It's not easy, but I'm hoping I'll remember everything soon."

When we reached my cave, I invited him in. He sat on the chair against the wall and I sat on the bed. I told him who I'd had dinner with and we talked awhile.

He seemed unsettled, which bothered me. I'd been wanting to talk to him, so I decided to just come out and say it.

"What's wrong?"

"What do you mean?"

"You're upset about something and it's really bothering you."

He struggled to answer me. "I am having trouble because... I don't know how to tell you. I am feeling these feelings and I know it's wrong and it's making me feel guilty... and I'm sorry."

"What feelings?"

"Well, I was told that you know this already, that I was being prepared for the leadership once we could not find you?"

"Yes. They told me."

"Well, I feel... I don't know... I have worked so hard and..." He put his hand to his heart. "I just have this heavy feeling in my chest... now that you have returned and will be Zheav." He cleared his throat and squared his shoulders. "I know that it is rightfully yours and I will not stand in your way. I love you and respect you, and that is why I feel so—"

"Don't worry, Jadidi. I don't want to be Zheav."

His eyes snapped to mine. "What?"

"I don't want to lead. I can't lead. Not without my memories."

"But they will return."

"Maybe, but I've been thinking and I don't want to lead. Even if I remember everything tomorrow. I know it deep down. I think you should lead. Mother and Axiak told me while we ate about all the things you have been doing while preparing to take over from Father."

There was relief on his face, but he frowned. "Mother? Father?"

"Oh, um, Mama and Papa."

"Oh..." He was still frowning at me.

Why would I be calling my own parents something different? Something that my own brother was frowning at? It seemed that every minute that passed pointed to me not belonging here. All the more reason for him to lead.

Maybe, somehow, I was the impostor my sister had accused me of.

I turned to him. "I will talk to F— I mean Papa. I'll tell him that you should be Zheav."

His eyes widened. "No. You should wait."

"I'll do it tomorrow."

He put a hand on my arm. "No. Wait till your memories return. You'll feel differently then. I'm sure."

I thought about it. I was positive that I wouldn't feel differently, but I agreed to wait a while.

Jadidi gave me a warm hug before he left. I knew deep down that I wouldn't change my mind.

As I lay down on my bed and tried to relax, a voice pierced the silence.

You shouldn't be here.

I sat up and looked around the cave, but realized as I did so that it wasn't a voice I was hearing now. It was a memory.

CHAPTER 18
We Will Fix Things

They had arranged for me to start training with Tasha the next day. I sat on a chair in her cave, taking some slow, deep breaths and trying to relax.

I'd insisted that we go somewhere else, but she had shut me down. I was afraid that things would get out of hand again. The guilt I felt hadn't faded. She didn't have many possessions, so I felt that a couple of crazy sessions with me would wipe out the rest and she'd be left with nothing.

I had to push those worries aside for now. She had asked me to focus my energy on a pebble she had placed on the floor in front of me. She wanted me to move it up just a little bit into the air, and put it back down again. I'd been at it for a while and had nothing to show for it, except the beginnings of a headache.

I sighed. This was never going to work.

"Do not sigh, child. Concentrate."

"But I can't do it."

"You've done this many times before."

"Yes, but—"

"No buts. Do it."

"Easy for you to say," I mumbled under my breath.

"Oh, yes. Very easy. You forget. I trained you before and I can do it again. You used to be able to move fallen trees. And you will again."

Fallen trees? Whoah... How could I have done something like that?

"Quite easily. Your Gift is strong. You will be able to do these things again, with or without your memories."

I'd forgotten that she could see my thoughts. I'd have to be more careful.

"I will need to teach you to strengthen your mental shield. This will help you. Now that you no longer have your training, sometimes your thoughts are broadcast to anyone nearby."

"What?"

"You can accidentally broadcast what you are thinking, especially when you're upset, and sometimes we can just read your mind without trying to because your shield is down. We need to fix that, and quickly."

"Yes." Now I was wondering what people had heard.

"Do not be concerned about that now. We will fix things. Now, pick up this stone."

"Okay."

Tasha had told me that I needed to have more telepathic conversations so I could get used to doing it again.

I took a deep breath and focused. I tried to ignore the headache that was building.

Staring intently at the stone and willing it to move was hard going but I stayed there, concentrating, hardly moving, and just when I was about to give up and walk out of there, it moved.

I think my heart stopped. Did I really do that?

"Yes, child." Tasha said. "Now do it again."

I turned back to the stone and kept trying until I was able to lift it up and put it back down. It was amazing. It was hard to believe that I could do it, yet I knew that this was just part of life. Mundane even. It shouldn't be a big deal at this stage of my life. I needed my memories back or this was going to take forever.

I practiced for another hour and managed to lift a wide variety of things — without breaking a single one.

Tasha smiled. "Would you like to try a Mind-link again?"

"A what?"

"A Mind-link. That's what we call the link we used before when I unlocked that memory."

The guilt slammed me in the chest. "Can we do it somewhere else so I don't wreck your house again? Please?"

She hesitated and I thought she was going to say no, but she finally nodded. "We shall go to the small alcove near the beach on the south side."

So with that, we headed out the door. I couldn't help wondering if the headache was normal.

"It is the bump on the head and the extra concentration needed to relearn your Gift."

"Oh." I needed to learn how to shield my thoughts.

On the way to the alcove, Tasha explained how to build a wall in my mind to shield my thoughts. By the time we got there — moving at her slow pace — I'd been able to successfully shield my thoughts from her. Well, when she poked my brain with the same amount of pressure as the average Waikari. It would take a lot more training to keep her out.

Once we'd arrived, we sat opposite each other on the sand. Tasha told me to relax and put her fingers to my temples once more. "Open your mind to me."

I did as I was told and felt her in there, looking around.

When I'd told her what had happened with Jarleth, she had become angry and told Jarleth not to try it again. I wasn't sure whether it was because he didn't know what he was doing, or if she was worried about what other memories he would see that would be upsetting. Maybe it was both.

Thinking about that distracted me and she told me to focus.

"Jarleth is a good man," she told me, "but he should have left it to me. Now he has upset himself, the silly boy. I know he was just trying to help you. His hearts are in the right place."

My eyes snapped open. "Hearts? As in, plural?"

She frowned. "Yes. We have two. You know this."

"I... I don't remember having two... I only thought I had one. On the left." I put my hand to my chest, as if I was checking to see if my heart was where I said, but then moved it to the right. It was too hard to feel anything with just my hand. That explained why my heartbeat was weird, but didn't explain why I didn't just instinctively know it, like I knew I had two arms and two legs...

"Right," she said. "Let us return to our reason for being out here."

We started again. It was like we were both wandering around in my head together, looking for a way into another part of my brain, and I guess that's what we were doing.

A flash of something burst into my mind and I gasped. I was in a room with a computer in front of me. The words on the screen were written in the language in my head. The language of my thoughts.

I spun lazily on a chair that swivelled around and started talking to a young woman with short brown hair. Oliana.

"Should I do this?" I asked her.

"Yes! You should go for it. I thought we'd already discussed this. I thought that Kaliya and I had already talked you into going."

"Yeah, but it's so far away."

"We talked about that too. We can still call each other. And once I'm done with my studies, I'll apply for a job out there too. I can't believe we're having this conversation again. Just go."

That room and her face faded away and I saw a man standing over me while I was hooked up to a bunch of wires. He was asking me questions, but he looked bored. He went back to his screen and started reading the data being displayed on it.

I wasn't sure how, but being linked with my mind made it possible for Tasha to somehow understand what we were saying, even though we were speaking Basic.

Then I was under the sea with two men in diving suits. For some reason, I was planning how I was going to get away from them.

Next thing I knew, I was at the Dive with Jarleth, Jadidi and Axiak. So far, this was the only thing that fit with this life. We'd been diving off the rocks and I had to get back to start training with Tasha. Something about this sounded familiar. Isn't that what Jarleth told me happened the day I disappeared?

I kissed Jarleth goodbye and waved to my brothers. As I walked along the beach, I sensed danger. I couldn't see where it was coming from. Then I sensed that it was coming from above. I drew my dagger instinctively, but it looked like I wouldn't stand a chance against the giant wingless metal bird above me. In a flash of light, I lost consciousness.

I was thrown back into the present and Tasha quickly removed her fingers. We looked at each other, shocked by what we'd just seen.

After a while, she said, "It seems that there may be more than one person up there in your head."

Chapter 19

He is Mine!

The words kept spinning around in my mind. How could I have more than one person in my head?

Since we'd found those memories, more little things had been popping up in my mind. I was lying on my bed just trying to relax and 'let the memories come,' as Tasha had put it. It seemed to be working, sort of.

She must have told everyone to keep away as I'd been lying here for a couple of hours and no one had come to my door. Which was a good thing. I needed some time alone.

I needed to put some distance between me and the rest of the village. I felt almost like I couldn't breathe here.

And the last person I wanted to see walking through my door was Jarleth. He needed to keep away from me. He didn't deserve this. I kept hurting him every time I saw him. The guilt was crushing me.

I took a deep breath and pushed thoughts of him aside for now. I needed to see how many memories I could coax to the surface. It was like a cork had been pulled, but there was only a small amount getting through.

I'd seen a couple of things related to that other life, including travelling through space, which was something that the Waikai had no concept of. And the fact that I knew what space flight was scared me.

Other memories included Axiak, and there was finally one with Jarleth. We were standing on a large rock at the Dive, staring into one another's eyes, the sea spray hitting us every now and then from the waves crashing up against the rocks. We hadn't needed any words to convey what we were feeling. I could feel a genuine love for him while I was reliving the memory, but afterwards, it faded.

Had I stopped loving him? If so, why? Was it because of Darion? And how did Darion fit into the picture? How did I meet him? Where did I meet him?

From what I could work out, I'd been captured on the beach; the light coming from the ship had to be a transporter beam. Someone had taken me away from the life I'd known, but that's where things didn't make sense. I couldn't have learned about all that technology in the two months I'd been gone.

And then there's the fact that I had memories of a childhood on another planet surrounded by technology.

There were large pieces of the puzzle missing. The holes were too wide and I couldn't even begin to guess what was in the missing parts.

Closing my eyes, I breathed deeply and tried to calm myself. I was getting frustrated and frazzled, which wasn't helping.

A loud bang had me opening my eyes and jumping up out of bed. The door hit the wall as Dakawa barged into my room, her face red.

"What did you do?" she demanded.

"I-I don't know what you're talking about."

"Yes, you do! Jarleth has been really upset since yesterday and he won't tell me why, but I know you've got something to do with it."

"Umm..." What could I say? She was right. But it was none of her business. I wasn't about to discuss it with her.

"Just as I thought. Stop playing games with his hearts. I told you. He is mine!"

"That's not the impression I got from him."

She clenched her fists at her sides. Would she actually hit me? "You... You need to back away. You need to call off the wedding. He doesn't want you anymore! He pledged his love to me while you were gone!"

My hearts sank. I knew in my hearts that for whatever reason, I didn't love him that way anymore, but it hurt to think that he'd pledged his love to someone else while I'd been gone. How important was our betrothal to him?

But that didn't make sense. When I thought about it, there was nothing that told me he'd moved on. He wouldn't be trying so hard to get me to remember him and he wouldn't be heart-broken now if he didn't love me.

"You're wrong."

"No. I know things that you don't. I know that even Samura managed to turn his head."

"What? What are you talking about?"

"The bracelet he wears. Samura gave it to him. Why is he wearing it if he is devoted to you?"

"That doesn't mean anything. You're—"

"Then why does he wear the hair beads I made for him?"

"I—"

"See? A lot has happened since you ran away from your responsibilities."

"I didn't run away! I was captured!"

"I thought you couldn't remember."

"I've remembered some things. Tasha has helped me."

"Or maybe you're just choosing to tell us certain things and pretending to remember."

"No. That's not true. I—"

"No. You don't get to tell me more of your lies. I think you remember everything and you've been with the Jungle People. They've sent you back here as a spy and you're going to tell them everything about us."

CHAPTER 20
That Girl is Not Right

"No! I don't even remember if I met any Jungle People when I was gone! You need—"

"I don't need to do anything! I want you to leave Jarleth alone! You've upset him and you've just made everything worse since you showed up again!"

"You're wrong!" I lost control of my Talent and things flew around the room. Something hit her in the head. A small clay ornament that looked like it was made by Axiak. I'd noticed it when I'd come back to my cave.

She fell back toward the door and landed on her butt. Blood trickled down from her hairline. She touched it gingerly and looked at her bloodied fingers, her eyes going wide.

"You'll regret that!"

She got to her feet and rushed out the door. And the weird thing was, I wasn't thinking about her. I was wondering why I'd thought of my Gift as my Talent.

<hr />

After a couple of days of training in telekinesis, shielding my mind, memory mining, and some more mistakes where I'd smashed things, I was summoned to visit my father.

I'd seen him briefly and spent some time with my mother in between everything else, but I was still nervous.

My mind was busy as I headed to their cave. As I walked along the sandy path toward a corner made of rock, I could hear voices up ahead. I caught a few words of the conversation and stopped in my tracks.

"... out of control. How can we follow her?"

"She has changed since returning to the village. She is like a totally different person in Sifayah's skin."

"She even talks differently. No one in the village talks that way. And some of the words are so foreign."

"Maybe she is one of the Jungle People now."

"Or working for them somehow."

"That girl is not right."

Had Dakawa been spreading that story around the village, or had these people come to the same conclusion on their own?

You shouldn't be here.

Who had said those words to me? And why?

The voice had been male. Was it Jarleth? Jadidi? My father?

I shuddered despite the warmth of the day.

I turned around, tears welling in my eyes. I couldn't face those people. I would have to go the long way around to get to my father, which would take me closer to the beach.

As I walked, I was glad the village was small, otherwise I'd get lost easily, which was weird considering I'd lived here all my life.

I froze when I heard voices ahead through the trees. Not again.

I was about to turn around until I heard Jarleth's voice. I crept forward to try to see who he was talking to. They were sitting on a rock ledge near where it dropped off toward the beach. Their backs were to me, but I recognized Samura's blonde hair.

My stomach dropped. What was going on?

"It's just so hard," he was saying.

"I know," she said. "But we don't really know what happened to her while she was gone."

Oh, great. They were talking about me too. I should have crept away, but I couldn't help myself. I wanted to know what was going on around me.

You shouldn't be here.

I thought that maybe my family was trying to protect me so no one could hurt my feelings, but I needed the truth.

"I saw him in her mind. They were sleeping next to each other. Maybe—" his voice cracked, "— maybe she lost her memory when she first went missing and fell in love with him."

Samura leaned closer to him. "It is possible. We won't know until she remembers more things." She rubbed a hand over his back. "You may have to face the fact that you can no longer marry."

His breath hitched. "I know."

She kept rubbing his back. I wondered if there was something going on between them. First Dakawa, and now my best friend?

CHAPTER 21
The Elders

The things that Dakawa had said went through my mind. He was fidgeting with the bracelet while Samura's hand made circular motions on his bare back.

It was shocking to think that maybe Jarleth hadn't been faithful to me while I was gone.

But then again, I couldn't expect him to stay loyal to me forever. I could have been dead. Surely, I could expect him to be loyal for at least a few months though... or something.

Dakawa might have feelings for Jarleth, but I was sure that he didn't feel the same.

But Samura...

Jarleth turned to her. "Thank you for being there for me through all of this."

She smiled. "No need to thank me. You're one of my best friends. Sifayah is the other. I would do it all again in a heartbeat."

He gave her a wobbly smile in return. "Thank you."

She sighed. "You know, I didn't think we'd ever find her. I'd lost hope. It had been too long." She pushed some hair out of her face. "I'm sorry. I feel so guilty, especially since you did not give up."

He ran a hand through his hair. "It's okay. Most people believed her lost to us."

"Yes, but you didn't and I should have listened when you said you knew deep down that she was alive."

"Do not do that to yourself. You couldn't have known."

She sniffed. "But I should've been able to feel her too."

"You had your own problems."

She wiped away the tears from her cheeks and nodded.

They stood and he gave her a hug. Was this it? Was he going to kiss her too?

I waited without breathing, but they drew apart and I could tell that it was only a friendly hug and nothing more. They said goodbye to each other and went their separate ways and I felt guilty for being suspicious. What was I doing? Why did I let Dakawa put those thoughts in my head?

———◆———

I knew something was wrong before I'd reached the cave. There was something in the air. A mood, maybe.

Silurian was in bed, but he didn't look like a healthy man lying down for an afternoon nap as he had the last time I'd been here. He was pale and had lost weight. A heaviness settled on my chest. He was dying. I knew it.

Yes, he'd said as much the other day, but I didn't think it would be so soon. I'd brushed it all aside. It was too painful to think about. But now I was forced to confront it.

Tears welled in my eyes and my bottom lip quivered. I hardly knew him, but I felt a connection to him.

"Now don't be upset, my daughter."

I couldn't speak. He knew that I knew.

"There is nothing to be done." He told me. "I will pass on and life will go on."

"But..." I didn't really know what to say. "But surely there's something that can be done."

He shook his head. "All things have been tried. The Rot cannot be stopped."

Cancer.

He was talking about cancer. That wasn't the Waikari name for it. It was from my language.

He beckoned me over and took my hands in his. "You have progressed well with your training. You will need to prepare to take my place—"

I pulled my hands away. "No!"

He took my hands again. "It is the way of things."

"But I can't remember—"

"You will remember. You can do this."

"But I no longer want to lead!"

That stopped him.

"I don't know what it is. I am different now. I'm not the same person. I don't like the same things. I don't love Jarleth anymore and I don't know why. And I don't want to lead. Please, you have to understand. I know Jadidi has been preparing for this and I know he'd make a great leader, like you."

I couldn't bring myself to tell him that some of the villagers didn't want me to lead them anyway. I hoped my mental shield hadn't slipped.

Sadness and pain and a touch of pride played out across his face. "Are you sure, my daughter?"

"Yes. Please summon him and tell him that he will be the next Zheav. I know he's been feeling bad because he wants to lead so badly, but knows that now I'm back, it's not his place."

"I will need to think on it."

"Good."

"And Sifayah?"

"Yes?"

"I want you to think on it too."

"But I already have—"

"Think on it. You need to be completely sure. This will be permanent. You cannot make a claim on the leadership later on if you change your mind. You must know it in your hearts that you will not have regrets."

I nodded. "Yes, Papa."

The following morning, after a huge downpour of rain, Samura came to take me to see the Elders of the tribe. I was surprised because I didn't know there were Elders. I'd only heard people mention the Zheav and his wife in regard to the leadership.

I agreed to go and see them, but by the time we'd reached their cave, I was feeling anxious about why I was summoned.

I didn't know what to expect. As we entered the cave, the air seemed to become dense. More humid. Was it the humidity or the tension in the air?

I made sure my mental shield was firmly in place.

The cave was quite large. There were two women and one man sitting on large chairs with high backs and cushioned armrests. A long table separated them from Samura and I and was draped in a delicate-looking embroidered cloth. The Elders had an air of authority that set my nerves on edge.

I didn't know how to greet them. Samura gave a deep, respectful nod and the Elders nodded in return. I gave an awkward nod and they returned it with a look of disdain on their faces.

Was it disdain? Or was I just reading that wrong?

I shifted from one foot to the other. What was I supposed to do now?

"Greetings," the man said. He was quite imposing with broad shoulders and long, dark hair.

"Um, hello."

He frowned, then turned to Samura. "Samura, you may leave us."

She nodded and left without a sound.

I had to say something to break the silence. "Um, you wanted to see me?"

The woman to his left cleared her throat. "Yes. We would like to ask you some questions."

"Okay."

"Why have you not come to see us before now?"

"I didn't know you existed?" I'd said it as a question, even though I hadn't meant to. "I thought there were just my parents in the leadership roles."

That raised some eyebrows. It might not have been the right thing to say, but it was the truth.

"How could you not know?"

"I don't remember anything about you or our customs."

The man gripped his armrests. "Then how can you lead? You must step down as our future leader!"

"You're right. I can't lead." There was a lot of throat-clearing and shuffling of feet, but I continued. "I'm not going to lead. I want Jadidi to lead when our father is... um when he retires."

The woman to his left almost leaped out of her seat. "This is not our way!"

The man put a hand on her arm. "But Jaitar, it is our way. She can renounce the leadership and then name the next in line as her successor."

She pulled her arm free. "Yes, I know that! I meant that it isn't done! It hasn't been done that way for... many, many seasons."

The woman on the other side of the man spoke for the first time. "Sifayah. If you do not remember us, allow me to introduce myself. I am Franzen."

I nodded. "Pleased to meet you." I wasn't sure if that was the correct greeting.

She gestured to her left. "This is Eredor, and Jaitar is to his left."

I repeated my greeting, but Jaitar did not respond.

I looked at Franzen. "Thank you."

She inclined her head.

Jaitar started again. "Sifayah. We need to know where your loyalties lie."

What? "What do you mean?"

"I mean exactly that. You have been missing for many suns and you return to us speaking differently and using foreign words and can't — or won't — tell us where you have been."

My jaw tightened. "I can't tell you. I don't know. I don't remember."

She narrowed her eyes. "Perhaps you only tell us this to avoid your responsibilities and your betrothal to the warrior, Jarleth."

CHAPTER 22

Traitor!

"No! I wouldn't do that! I don't remember him!"

"Hush, child. Do not raise your voice to us!"

"Sorry." I hadn't realized that I'd raised my voice. But she was wrong. I was not pretending just to get out of doing the things I had to do. My mind seemed like it was permanently broken. *What if I never remember?*

This was starting to sound like the things Dakawa had said to me. What was going on here? Was everyone in the village talking about this?

Jaitar flipped her long brown hair over her shoulder and glared at me. "You do not show us the respect we deserve."

"I can't remember the customs that dictate how I should behave in your presence."

She frowned. "Or maybe you say these things in order to be able to disrespect us."

"No!"

Franzen gave Jaitar a look that seemed to say that she should back off. She turned to me. "Sifayah. I believe you that you have no memory of us."

I sighed. "Thank you."

At least *one* of them was willing to listen. Jaitar made a small noise in the back of her throat, but otherwise kept quiet. Eredor's features were blank.

My nerves were jangling now. I knew this interrogation wasn't going well, but didn't know how to make them believe me. Not knowing how much authority these people had wasn't helping. What could they do to me if they didn't believe me? Did they overrule my father? Was he powerless to help me?

Eredor cleared his throat. "Sifayah. We have had a report about you hurting a member of our tribe. What do you have to say to this?"

"Dakawa? It was an accident. I was angry with her because she said that Jarleth doesn't want to marry me anymore and that I was faking losing my memory and I lost control a bit. A vase hit her in the head."

Jaitar sucked in a breath. "My daughter tells us a different story."

"Dakawa is your *daughter?*" That explained her hostility. My stomach sank. If Dakawa was the daughter of an Elder, I was in a lot more trouble than I'd thought.

"Yes. She has a large bruise on the side of her face and a blackened eye. There is also a cut on her head—"

"But she only had the cut on her head!"

She slammed her hand down on the table. "Do not interrupt me! Are you calling me a liar?"

I clenched my fists. "No. I'm calling *her* a liar."

"Be silent! She says that you attacked her without reason. She came to your cave to see how you were doing, as you were good friends before you left, and you screamed at her and used your Gift to hurl things at her. She was so scared when she came to me."

"She's lying!"

Jaitar rose to her feet. "I said be silent!"

Franzen stood. "Calm yourself, Jaitar."

I took an involuntary step back, unsure of what would happen between them, but Jaitar slowly lowered herself to her seat.

I found it difficult to believe that Dakawa and I had been good friends.

I waited for the next question while cursing Dakawa in my mind. Then I hoped that I'd been able to keep my mental shield up. The last thing I needed was for her mother to hear me.

Eredor spoke up while Jaitar still seemed to be struggling with her self-control. "Sifayah. We want your loyalty and respect."

"I *am* loyal."

"You have not proven to be today and you are not respectful."

"But—"

"Hush. Listen to me. This is what we want from you. Unless you can remember everything and adhere to what we say, you will step away from the leadership. We want you to refrain from hurting anyone else in the village. We want you to apologise to Dakawa. And you will complete your training as soon as possible. You are a danger to us all with your Gift out of control like this."

I opened my mouth, but nothing came out.

Jaitar snickered. "She remembers. It's all an act."

"No, it isn't. Look into my mind and see." I let down my mental shield.

They all looked at each other and before they could discuss it, I felt Jaitar's presence in my mind and sucked in a breath as she forced her way around, poking at my memories and finding the wall that was blocking them.

"See what I mean?" I asked.

"She is in your mind?" Eredor asked, looking at Jaitar in surprise.

"Yes."

Jaitar found the other memories of the places I'd been and searched through them. "Look for yourselves," she told the others.

I felt them enter my mind and panicked. Tasha had said that she needed to be careful when looking around in my head. I shouldn't have given them permission.

They were soon looking at a memory that I hadn't seen before of a man giving instructions to a group of people. It had just burst forward. He was telling us to observe the natives and report back to him. We were there to find out as much information as we could. He was speaking Basic, but through my thoughts as I was watching the memory, they were able to understand what was said.

"Traitor!" Jaitar screamed, and I put my hands up to my ears to try to block her out. It didn't help. *"You have been sent by the Jungle People to spy on us! I knew it! You've put us all in danger!"*

CHAPTER 23
You Must Have Lost It

"Get out of my head!" I pushed somehow with my mind and shoved all three of them out. At the same time, I shoved the heavy table back a bit.

They were all shocked, but not as much as I was.

"She will bring the Jungle People upon us!" Jaitar continued to scream. "She is out of control! We need to stop her!"

I didn't know what else to do, so I ran from the cave. Not knowing where to go or what to do, I headed to the little section of beach where I'd first seen Samura, hoping that no one would be there.

———◦———

I sat on the sand, watching the waves with teary eyes. How could I convince these people that Dakawa was wrong, that they were wrong? Why would I want to betray my people? My family?

I didn't even remember the Jungle People. A thought struck me and pierced my hearts. If I didn't remember, then how did I know it wasn't true? What if they'd somehow turned me against my own people and sent me back here? How could I know that I'm *not* a danger to everyone here?

I shoved those thoughts out of my head. Nothing could ever make me betray the people I love. *Nothing*.

The Elders and Dakawa were going to make my life miserable from now on. I could see it.

"Hey."

I jumped and looked up at Samura's gentle face. "You scared me."

She knelt down in the sand. "Sorry. Are you well?"

"Not really."

I told her what had happened and she sat with her mouth hanging open.

"I don't know where the memory came from that they saw. It was the worst time for me to remember something like that. And just because that man told us to do those things, doesn't mean I agreed and did it."

She tucked her hair behind her ears. "I don't believe you would do anything to harm the village. It must be a mistake."

We sat on the sand for a long while, with Samura telling me about things we did as children. I tried to relax, but it was hard. I couldn't help wondering what the rest of the village would think once they knew what the Elders had seen.

One of the things Samura told me about was when we both learned how to make jewellery from shells, seaweed, bone and wood. It sounded interesting and when she offered to show me some of the things she'd made recently, I decided to take a look. Maybe I could get her to show me how to do it. I needed to learn everything I could about life in the village as quickly as possible. I couldn't rely on my memories.

We headed to her home, which I should have known the location of, and I walked in to find a large table full of necklaces, bracelets, armlets, anklets, rings, earrings, and brooches.

"These are amazing," I said.

She pointed out all the different materials used to make them and we settled down to create pieces of art together.

I gauged from her words that she made pieces of jewellery for a lot of people in the tribe, and even took some to the Shinnari sometimes.

So Dakawa was wrong again.

After I'd managed to make a wonky-looking bracelet, Samura fidgeted with a necklace, her hair falling across her face as she looked down at the floor. "Jarleth said you were not wearing any jewellery when you were found."

"No. I wasn't."

"You must have lost it."

I tried to see her face through her long hair. "Lost what?"

"The necklace I made for you. You wore it everywhere."

I felt a pang in my chest. "I'm sure I would have kept it if I could... Whoever captured me must have taken it."

She straightened. "I will make you another one."

"Really? Thank you."

⸻

"Why don't we go to the Dive?" Axiak suggested. "You might remember stuff."

Samura and I had wandered back from her cave after I managed to make another bracelet and a necklace and found Jarleth and Axiak walking together.

"Yes," Samura said. "We've had a lot of good times there, so something may surface."

"And it will be fun," Axiak threw in, looking up at me with hopeful eyes.

I smiled down at him. "Okay. Let's go."

"Yay!" He jumped up and down on the spot and took off running toward the beach.

I laughed as we followed him.

On the way, I noticed Jarleth stealing glances at me. He was probably hoping that the familiar scenery would trigger something. But as usual, there was nothing.

I longed to apologise to him again, but what else could I say? It had been a few days now and maybe it would be better to just say nothing.

When we finally reached the outcropping of rocks, I hesitated. There was something familiar about this place and I hoped it wasn't from when I was found near here.

Jarleth stopped walking. "Are you well?"

"Uh, yeah. I just... It feels familiar, that's all."

His face lit up. "It's working."

CHAPTER 24
Who Am I Really?

We continued to the end of the rock formations and I looked out at the ocean. Waves crashed up against the rocks and it scared me. I stepped back away from the edge.

Axiak frowned. "Don't be scared. We dive off here all the time. You did too."

But I didn't remember doing it. I stepped closer to the edge again and looked down into the water. I couldn't imagine jumping in there, but if I'd done it hundreds of times before, I must have found it fun.

Jarleth suggested that he and Axiak jump off to show me how it's done. I nodded and Axiak shouted that he wanted to go first. They each took a few steps back and ran to the edge, leaping and flipping over a couple of times before disappearing into the waves.

I held my breath as I waited for them to surface and they came up smiling.

Samura waved down to them. "Now it's my turn," she said, and leapt off the rocks at a higher angle so she could flip three times.

I waited until they swam around to the side where it was easier to climb up the rocks.

Axiak hugged me and dripped water all over me. "Do you want to have a turn now?"

My first instinct was to back away and head back to the beach, but I didn't want to run away from this. This was part of my life. I couldn't shrink away from it. It would help me to feel myself again. I needed to get back to my life and move on now that I was home.

I looked down at him and smiled. "Okay. Tell me how."

His smile slipped for a moment — probably because I was the one who taught him in the first place — but it returned and he started giving instructions on how to run up and jump, and telling me about the rocks on the left I needed to avoid hitting.

"Don't worry about flipping, just jump up and out."

I stepped back, hearts pounding, and ran at the edge, thinking I must be crazy. As I got to the edge, I leapt high and my arms and legs flailed about until I hit the water and rocketed under. It felt almost like flying.

I went a long way under and as I was coming back up, I started to panic, thinking I'd run out of air before I got to the surface. But then I remembered that I could breathe under here and felt silly as I breathed in the water.

I came up laughing. "That was amazing!" I shouted up to them, and they smiled.

Of course, I couldn't wait to do it again.

We spent a long time jumping off the rocks and I was eventually game enough to try some tricks. They came pretty naturally to me. My body remembered what to do, even if my mind didn't.

Axiak insisted on showing me the backflip that I'd taught him, of course.

One time when Samura and Axiak had just jumped in, Jarleth stopped me. "Sifayah. Do you remember us being out here together? Just the two of us?"

He came closer to me and I looked up into his eyes. Should I be honest? "Um. I'm not sure."

He stepped closer still. "We came out here a lot."

Those brown eyes were so full of hope. His face came closer. His hands rested on my upper arms. I couldn't look away.

The waves pounded against the rocks and something shifted. This was familiar. That memory burst into my mind again. This was definitely something that had happened before. I could feel it. Could feel something in my chest. The feeling swelled and spread across my chest and it felt warm. Was this what I'd felt for Jarleth before I lost my memories?

"I... There's something... In my chest. I remember standing here with you."

"Yes?" He leaned closer, tears glistening in his eyes.

I jumped as Axiak noisily climbed up the rocks and wrapped his arms around both of us, bringing us closer together. I had to put my arms around Jarleth to stop myself from falling over and he put his arms around me.

Axiak squeezed us tighter. "Mama just called me. We have to go home for dinner."

As I untangled myself from both of them, my first thought was, how did she call him? But in a village full of telepathic people, how else would she call him? I felt so stupid for forgetting these things all the time.

I tore my eyes away from Jarleth. "Okay, Kiddo, let's go."

On the way back, as sand squeezed through my toes, I was almost knocked over by a memory. Axiak and I were sitting on the sand, right in this spot. We'd built ourselves a tall mound of sand with caves carved into the sides. It had some leaves sticking out of the top and a pond full of seawater at its base.

His eyes were bright as he turned to me. He was so proud of his creation.

He looked behind me and I turned to see Jarleth holding a single flower in his hand. He placed it behind my ear and kissed me gently on the lips.

I was brought back to the present when Axiak tugged on my arm. "What's wrong? Are you well, Fayah?"

"Uh, yeah. I just remembered something."

I told them what I'd seen and there were smiles on their faces.

Axiak knelt down and started gathering sand together. "We could make another one now."

Jarleth's smile faded. "We need to go home for dinner, Axiak. Your mama wouldn't be pleased."

"Oh, yeah. I forgot."

He jumped up, dusted himself off, and grabbed my hand. I replayed the memory in my mind as we walked back.

———◦○◦———

After dinner, I felt I needed to be alone for a while. I trudged slowly back to my cave.

The things I'd remembered today and the words Tasha had said about there being more than one person in my head swirled around relentlessly.

Who am I really? How can I have two people in my mind? How did this happen?

It was too hard to fathom how it could be possible.

You shouldn't be here.

Was that what he was talking about? The man who'd said that to me? I didn't belong because I was *not* Sifayah?

I rounded a corner and bumped into someone. I started to apologise and looked up to see Dakawa's red face scowling at me. Those fading bruises on her face could not have come from me.

Chapter 25

What the Hell Just Happened?

"Watch where you're going!" She spat.

"I'm sorry. I wasn't paying attention."

"You never are. I've told you to keep away and to leave Jarleth be, but you just can't help yourself."

I frowned. "I don't need to do as you say."

Her hand went to her hip. "You do. You need to listen to me. You are ruining everything."

"I might not remember everything, but I can tell he doesn't feel the same way about you."

"You're wrong. He loves me. You're just confusing the issue. He was over you long before you returned to the village."

My frown deepened. I knew that wasn't true, especially after what had happened today at the Dive.

"No one wants you here. No one wants you as their leader. You're weird and freaky now and wouldn't know how to lead a baby shellback to water."

"I'm not going to be Zheav. I've told my father and I've told the Elders."

"What?" She put both hands on her hips as if that meant she was serious now. "Who will lead us?"

"Jadidi. He has been preparing for it while I was... while I was gone."

"While you were running around with some other man."

How could she have known about that? Did Jarleth tell her?

Then I caught a thought from her. She'd overheard Jarleth talking to Samura about it.

She lifted her nose higher. "Oh, yes. I know about that."

Another thought. She was upset that he'd confided in Samura and not her.

She was letting her mental shield slip. Or was I getting better at this without even trying to read her mind? Maybe I could see more if I pried.

Tasha had told me how strong I was and according to her, I could easily push past shields and see into people's minds. But Dakawa would know I was there and I already knew it wasn't considered ethical to read someone's mind without their permission. The Waikari took things like that very seriously. They had to have rules in place in a society where everyone was telepathic and some were more powerful than others.

I clenched my fists. "I don't need to explain myself to you."

She tossed her hair over her shoulder, reminding me of her mother. "You are useless. You can't even hunt or cook! How can you be a good wife for him?"

"I will remember how, and if I don't, I'll get someone to teach me." And a little voice inside my head was saying, *but you don't want to marry him anyway.*

She laughed. "A grown woman who cannot cook? It is disgraceful."

I tried to get past her. "I don't have to listen to your rubbish."

She stepped in my way. "At least I was here for him. Where were you, huh? Where were you when he needed you? When he searched night and day and cried for you? You don't care about him! You left him all alone and after a while, he hardened his hearts. He turned away from what you had together. It's too late for you now. Things can't go back to the way they were. You've ruined it. Lucky he had me there to comfort him and to help him through it all.

"Now you've returned and slashed open that wound. It will take him a while to recover, but I'll be there for him. You need to keep away. You're only making things worse."

I stepped back. I knew she had to be lying, but her words still stung. Part of it was true. He *had* gone through hell, but had *not* given up on trying to find me.

My nails were digging into my palms. "You can't see that he still cares for me and I don't think he sees you as anything more than a friend. You have this image of him in your mind that isn't true. You need to stop living in your dream world and face reality. He doesn't love you."

She took a slow breath in. Her face went red and her hands clenched into fists at her sides. "You will see that you are wrong. He will marry me and forget about you! You should leave the village and go back to wherever you've been all this time. Go live in the underwater for all I care. There are whispers about you in the village. People are uneasy. They do not want you leading them. I think you're here to spy on us. We cannot stand by and let this happen. Silurian is sick and is not seeing sense."

So even if I remembered enough to take up the leadership, there were people who would not be happy about it. Just another reason to renounce my claim and let Jadidi take over.

She stepped closer. "I will make sure that you *never* become the first female Zheav."

The first? That would be something new and ground-breaking within the village, but I still couldn't do it. "Uh, have you heard anything I've said? I am *not* going to be the Zheav."

Her eyebrows came together for a second in confusion. "Yeah. Well, that was just in case you were still thinking of doing it. Anyway, Jarleth is mine and you need to stay away."

She was starting to repeat herself. Maybe there was something wrong with her.

I tried again. "I spoke to him—"

"I told you not to speak to him."

"Yes, but—"

"You're just confusing the issue and making things difficult."

"For who? You or hi—"

"You enjoy making people's lives a misery, don't you?"

I ground my teeth. "No. I think you—"

"You're a troublemaker and there's something wrong with you since you got back."

"I'm not trying to—"

"There you go again. Making excuses for your bad behaviour."

"Would you shut up and let me fin—"

"Just stop this nonsense! I can't even have a civil conversation with you." She flipped her hair over her shoulder again.

"What are you talking about?"

She glared at me. "Why do you have to be so hostile?"

"I'm not being hostile—"

"I don't have to put up with this. I'm leaving." She turned on her heel and stormed away.

What the hell just happened?

CHAPTER 26
Surely it Wasn't Possible

As I stood there with my mouth hanging open, someone walked around the corner and almost ran into me. It was my sister. The one that had called me an impostor before. "Oh, sorry...uh..."

"Melina."

"Oh. Yeah. Sorry." I felt terrible. I should at least know her name, shouldn't I?

"Surely you know who I am?"

My cheeks flushed. "Yes. Well, no. I mean, I know you're my sister, but I couldn't remember your name. Sorry."

There was a voice in the back of my mind saying that I wasn't Sifayah, and she was not my sister.

I cringed as I waited for her to yell at me again.

She just sighed. "Look. I don't know who you are really, but I want to get to the truth."

"Me too."

She raised her eyebrows. "What?"

"Me too. There's something to what you're saying. Tasha and I think there's two people inside my head. One is Sifayah, and the other is me."

Her eyes were wide and she looked like she was trying to see inside my soul. "How can that be?"

"I have no idea. But there's memories up here," and I pointed to my head, "that should not be here. There's no way that they belong to your sister."

I had her attention now. "Can we go somewhere quiet?"

That had me worried. "Why?" What was she planning to do?

"I want to see if I can help you. To find out what happened to her." She must have believed me if she was saying 'her' instead of 'you.'

I ran my hand through my hair. "Okay. Where can we go?"

She was still staring intently at me. "To my place."

Should I be worried? She was pretty upset with me the last time I saw her. I brushed my worries aside. She wasn't anything like Dakawa and I was pretty sure she wouldn't hurt her sister. And I needed answers.

It didn't take long to get there. It was close to our parents' cave, but she assured me that no one would disturb us.

She gestured toward a spot on the floor. "Okay. Sit over here."

There was a soft rug on the floor made out of the furry skin of I-didn't-know-what. I sat. Now wasn't the time to be asking about that.

Melina sat opposite me on the floor and took my hands. This wasn't the same as what anyone else had done. Maybe her Gift worked differently.

She didn't bother giving me any instructions, she just closed her eyes and took a long deep breath and let it out slowly.

I closed my eyes too and tried my best to relax. I had no idea what she was doing or how any of it worked, but had to trust that she did.

She sat for a long time and I wondered if she was doing anything at all. Maybe she was fooling me. Maybe she was trying to trick me or make a fool of me. I didn't say anything. I just sat and waited.

I started to think about all those weird memories in my head that couldn't be Sifayah's. An image popped into my head of me in one of those rooms with computers in it and I was a child. Sifayah couldn't possibly have been there.

Then another vision of me looking down at my webbed hands for the first time. A man stood by my bed and explained that they'd transferred my consciousness into another body. I walked over to a mirror on the wall and waved my hand in front of it, shocked at what I saw. This wasn't me. I was someone else before that moment. I used to have light brown hair and blue eyes. Now my hair was very long and black and my eyes were brown.

He told me her name was Sifayah and my breath caught.

This scared me more than any of the other things I'd remembered. How could this have happened? How could my mind be put into someone else's head? Surely it wasn't possible.

I sensed Melina in my mind.

"I don't know how they could have done this." I said. "What happens now? What do we do now?"

"I don't know. Maybe we should see Tasha."

I nodded. "Yes. We definitely should."

Melina and I headed towards Tasha's cave, hoping that she was home. I was half expecting to run into Dakawa again.

You shouldn't be here.

It frustrated me that I still didn't know who'd said that to me and when. I pushed it aside for the moment and kept walking.

When we were almost there, Jarleth approached us. "Sifayah. I need to speak to you."

"Not now. I need to see Tasha."

He frowned. "But we need to talk. To sort things out."

"But this is important." I saw the hurt in his eyes. "Sorry. I didn't mean that you're not important, but this is urgent. Something I remembered."

That got his attention. "Did you remember me?"

"No. It's... just come with us so I don't have to say it twice."

Thankfully, Tasha was at home and invited us in.

Tears were threatening to spill as I thought about how I'd be crushing their hopes of ever getting Sifayah back.

I took a deep breath and told them about what Melina and I saw and waited for their reaction. They were both silent.

"I don't know how they did this. I could tell that I didn't ask for this and neither did Sifayah. I don't know what to do." After a while, I added, "Tasha and I found the memory of what happened to Sifayah on the day that she was captured by these people. They took her as she walked back from the Dive."

The anguish on Jarleth's face was like a knife in my chest. Tears flowed down his cheeks. "Stop it! Stop talking about her like you're not her!"

CHAPTER 27

What Have You Done to Jarleth?

"I'm *not* her. It's becoming clearer now. I don't belong here."

He swiped at the tears on his cheeks. "*No*. Don't talk like that!"

"Look inside my mind and you'll see it's true." I nodded to Tasha to let her know she could look too.

When they'd seen it all, Jarleth let out a tortured moan and ran out of the cave. I turned to follow, to help any way I could, but Tasha told me to let him go. What could I possibly do to help anyway? There was nothing in the universe that could help him.

I realized my cheeks were wet and saw tears in Melina's and Tasha's eyes too. "What do we do now?"

So many things were running through my mind. How would everyone react? What would the Elders say or do to me? What about Tamari and Silurian? He wasn't well and I didn't know what this would do to him. The knife in my chest twisted even more when I thought about poor Axiak.

"I... I have to go." I turned to leave.

"Where are you going, child?" The tears were sliding down her cheeks now.

"I don't know. I need to clear my head." And I practically ran out of there, not really knowing where I was headed.

I found myself back in my cave. I needed to get out of the village, even if it was just for a few hours. I packed a bag with some food that Tasha had brought me and I thought that I should take my fur boots so I can walk in the jungle without hurting my feet. At the last minute, I threw my fur clothes in too. I might need them. I wasn't sure what I'd need them for. Maybe I could wear them in case I ran into one of the Jungle People. I could blend in.

How long did I think I was going for?

I was about to take them back out when Dakawa walked into my cave, dripping wet and white with rage.

"What have you done to Jarleth? He dove into the underwater and swam straight out to sea so fast I couldn't keep up. He wouldn't answer me."

Not this again. "None of your business. Go away."

She clenched her fists at her sides, trembling with rage. "But it *is* my business. I will be his wife soon."

"Jarleth is not yours. I have spoken to him and—"

"I told you to keep away from him!"

"—and I *know* he doesn't love you and does *not* want to marry you. It's all in your head."

"No!" she screamed. "You're lying! I've spoken to him and he renounced his betrothal to you. He loves me!"

She stepped forward and I flinched as she tried to grab my hair and missed.

I pointed a finger at her. "I wouldn't if I were you. You know my Gift is strong. I don't want to hurt you again."

"Yes, but right now you have no clue how to use it."

"Well, that's not entirely true. I've been training with Tasha."

She lifted her chin. "From what I've been told, things aren't going well. I heard that Tasha's house is in ruins."

"That wasn't from training, that was—" I flicked a hand in her direction. "Why am I even bothering to tell you? Just go. Get out of here. I'm done trying to deal with your childish behaviour."

She lunged forward and wrapped her hands around my throat. I was too stunned to react. She'd totally lost it.

I tried to speak, but she squeezed harder and I couldn't breathe in. I was surprised by her strength. I pulled at her wrists but couldn't pull her hands away. I tried to pry her fingers loose, but they were clenched too tightly around my neck.

Her fingers dug in harder and panic seized my mind as my lungs screamed for air. I had to do something. I didn't want to hurt her again, but she'd left me no choice. She was trying to *kill* me. I would have to use my Talent to stop her.

It was hard to concentrate as black spots formed in front of my eyes, but managed to pry her fingers off my throat using nothing but my mind and pushed her back away from me with such force that she flew through the air. I heard a crack as she hit the rock wall, then she fell in a heap on the ground. She lay motionless and I feared that I'd thrown her too hard.

I reached out to her mind to find that she was only unconscious. I was surprised to find that I didn't feel an ounce of remorse for hurting her. The inside of my throat burned and the outside throbbed as I grabbed my bag and ran.

The sun was fading from the sky and I hoped that the darkness could help me slip away unnoticed. I kept my mental shield up so no one could call me.

Walking quietly along the paths that led out of the village, I knew I couldn't stay. I couldn't get the answers here that I needed.

I was already in trouble for hurting Dakawa before, and when they found out I'd hurt her again and that I wasn't Sifayah, I wouldn't be welcome in the tribe. In a weird, twisted way, I *was* an impostor.

I walked to the shore and headed out in the opposite direction of the Dive. It would probably be one of the first places they'd look for me. Heading north into the jungle seemed to be my best option.

I'd been travelling for a while when I had to hide behind some rocks to avoid being seen by a man wearing the clothing of the Waikari. A Waikari scout. I didn't think anyone would be this far away from the village, but I remembered that they had ways of keeping the Jungle People away. The Waikari were paranoid about them, and maybe they had reason to be. I wasn't sure. That part of my brain was still missing.

That was a horrible way of thinking about it — that part of my brain was actually missing — but it kind of felt that way to me.

I kept going, ducking under low branches, skirting around huge tree trunks and stepping over fallen trees. There were also a few more Waikari scouts I had to avoid. I was hoping to make good ground before anyone found out I wasn't just going for a walk. I didn't want anyone to follow me.

Guilt swamped me. Was I doing the right thing by leaving?

But I had to leave. At least for now. A lot of people would think I hurt Dakawa on purpose. She would tell more lies and they'd believe her again. They would... I wasn't sure what they'd do. What did the Waikari do when someone broke their laws? What *were* the laws? Just something else I couldn't remember and another reason why I couldn't lead. Someone would break the law and I'd have no clue what to do with them.

I didn't know any traditions or ceremonies or anything about their culture at all.

I pushed it all aside. I *had* to leave. I had to find Darion. I had to find answers. I needed to find out what happened and how the hell I'd ended up like this. It was slowly driving me insane to think my consciousness had been put inside Sifayah's mind somehow. I guessed that I was a normal person before that. So, what happened to *me?* My body?

My chest felt tight and I suppressed a shudder. I needed to know.

I pressed on. The ground rose and the underbrush grew dense, but I wouldn't let it stop me. Nothing could stop me.

I tried not to think too much while I walked. I sang a song in my head to try to keep my mind occupied. Something Mama used to sing to me. Well, to Sifayah. It was about the ocean and how at one time our people could only breathe in the underwater. The Waikari spent time on land *and* under the sea so that they wouldn't change over time to be stuck on land or stuck in the sea. That made sense to me. They were, in a sense, controlling their destiny; their evolution. They were keeping their amphibian bodies.

Amphibian. Another word that was not Waikari. I sighed. I desperately wanted answers.

A sharp rock made me remember my boots. I stopped and put them on, shaking my head at myself for not remembering them sooner.

I kept pushing my way through the jungle, trying to come up with a useful plan. There were too many gaps in my memories for me to know what to do or which way to go. North just seemed like a good choice because it was away from the Waikari.

Trudging along and thinking hard was starting to wear me out, but I didn't stop. I thought about Samura. I'd told Tasha and Jarleth what I'd found out, but I felt bad that I'd left without seeing her. It occurred to me that I could still talk to her now. I stopped walking, focused my thoughts, reached out with my mind and called her name.

I shouldn't have been surprised that it worked.

CHAPTER 28
I Need to Explain

"Sifayah? Where are you? What's going on? Jarleth has gone into the underwater at night and won't answer me. Tasha hasn't said much, only that they've found out some more news about you. Are you well? Are you hurt?"

"I'm fine. I've gone for a walk. I need to explain."

"Are you sure you are well?"

"Yes. Don't worry about me. I remembered some things. It would be better if I just showed you."

"Okay." She sounded calmer now.

As I ducked under a low-hanging vine and stepped over a moss-covered rock, I recalled the memories and let her see them in my mind and could feel her emotions sweeping through me as she realized what it all meant.

I thought I would probably lose her as a friend now that she knew the truth. It caused an ache in my chest and I thought that was weird considering that I'd only really known her — as me, anyway — for a few days.

I waited for the anger and the words she'd throw at me, but they didn't come. I could feel her sadness and wanted to somehow take it away. But there was nothing I could do. I didn't know what this meant for Sifayah really. There were memories in my mind that belonged to her, but it wasn't like she was present in my mind, talking to me or trying to vie for control. Besides the memories, she was gone somehow.

"I'm so sorry, Samura. I don't know what to say. I didn't want this. I still don't know why or how they did this."

"It... shouldn't be possible."

I narrowly missed stepping into a hole between two rocks. "I know. But I guess it is. I need to find the people that did this. I want to see if they can undo it."

"Oh, do you think they can?"

I stopped walking. "I don't know, but something in my gut tells me they can't." I ran a hand through my hair. "I'm going to see if I can find out what happened, but I don't want anyone following me, okay?"

"What? Where are you?"

The thought that someone might come after me made me start moving again. "I'm pretty far away from the village already, but I don't want Jarleth to come looking for me. Or anyone else. Please tell him not to come. I will find out as much as I can and tell you what happened, okay?"

"No! Don't go! It's not safe!"

"I'll be okay. I have to do this."

"Please come back! We can work this out."

"I can't really come back. Once everyone finds out I'm not Sifayah, I won't be welcome."

"We'll talk to them. To the Elders."

"That isn't going to work. Jaitar is Dakawa's mother and—" I thought I might as well tell her. "—I had a fight with Dakawa."

"When?"

"Just before I left. I will tell you what really happened before she spins her lies again."

I told Samura everything, even how badly I'd hurt Dakawa. I felt terrible that I'd used my Talent to hurt someone on purpose, but she was trying to kill me. I knew that much. I swallowed hard and flinched at the pain.

Samura tried to convince me that things could be sorted out, but I knew it would be futile. I told her to tell everyone what I'd said and *not* to follow me, then I said goodbye and ended our conversation.

It was completely dark now — not that it bothered me — so I was on the lookout for somewhere to stop for the night.

I found myself wandering in darkness, looking for something. It was close, I could feel it. I walked around the trunk of a large tree and there he was. The man who could give me the answers I sought. I opened my mouth to ask him what was going on, but nothing came out.

"There you are," he said, and moved closer.

I looked up into his eyes and he smiled. He gathered me into his arms and our lips met. Instantly, I felt like I was melting and my mind raced and it felt so right and so familiar. He deepened the kiss and when I felt his tongue slide into my mouth, I came undone. I'd waited so long for this...

I opened my eyes to darkness, breathless after the dream. It had seemed so real and left me wanting more. Is that how it felt to be kissing Darion? I sucked in a breath, which hurt my throat. I needed to find this man that evoked such strong feelings in me.

The way I'd felt when kissing Jarleth was nothing compared to that.

I had walked for hours before I'd found a cave to sleep in. I'd carefully made sure there was nothing living in it before finding a spot on the floor to sleep. My bag was a pillow.

Still wondering if I'd made the right decision by leaving, I stretched out my arms and legs, my stomach growling in protest. I'd only had a small portion of food before falling asleep.

I sat up and pulled out some pieces of fruit from my pack and savoured the taste. Being able to see in the dark was handy.

I looked to the entrance. There was a large spiderweb above it that housed an enormous, hairy spider. It would easily take up most of my palm. I would need to crawl under that thing to get out. I probably crawled under it to get in here. I shuddered.

My doubts sprang up again. How was I going to find someone who could give me answers? What kinds of creatures lived in the jungle? What would I do if I found somebody out here? Would they be friendly? Would they know I'm Waikari and will that cause problems? I would have to try to hide my webbed fingers, just in case.

That led to me thinking that I should change my clothing. If I did run into someone, at least I would look like them. I finished eating, wished I had some water, and put the spotted skins on, glad that someone had washed them. They were surprisingly comfortable.

The entrance was small, so I had to crawl — under that giant spider — to get out. My mind kept imagining the spider leaping down onto my back and I shuddered and moved faster. My skin crawled and I shuddered again as I stood up and looked around. It was morning. Time to get moving.

It was hard to work out exactly where the sun was through the canopy, but once I'd found it, I at least knew where east was.

I kept heading north, away from the shore, having no real idea what was in that direction. I just hoped that I could find out what had happened to me and then I could decide what to do. I obviously didn't belong with the Waikari.

I got a real sense of deja vu while wandering through the dense undergrowth of the jungle. Had I been in this part of the jungle before, or was it just that it all looked the same? I was sure it was because it all looked the same. There were no significant landmarks and nothing to let me know that I wasn't walking in circles.

It rained heavily while I walked, and I cupped my hands together to catch some water to drink. It didn't work as well as I thought it would, but I managed to drink some. Once the rain stopped, I saw a plant with cone-shaped leaves that had captured the water, so I tipped it over into my mouth and drank greedily.

I reminded myself to look out for recognisable food. I wasn't sure if I'd find the same types of fruit here as I would along the shore.

There were a lot of crawly things making their way along the forest floor that I tried to ignore and that made me glad I was wearing boots. Some of them I recognized from in and around the village, but some I'd never seen before.

The dragonfly that was as long as my forearm was a scary sight. I stood perfectly still until it had flown away.

It was frustrating, not remembering anything that could help with basic survival out here. If I found a river and caught a fish to eat, I wouldn't know how to prepare and cook it. This really was ridiculous.

I sighed heavily and walked on. Under a low-hanging vine, around a huge tree trunk, over a log that wasn't a log — it was a snake, I realized with a strangled yelp as I jerked away and broke into a run and didn't slow down until I was sure I wasn't being followed or stalked in some way by the giant reptile.

After ducking and weaving my way through the foliage for hours, I felt some cool drops of rain on my arms and face again. The rain was a welcome relief.

Pretty soon, it was raining so heavily that I could hardly see. It reminded me of learning about the Monsoon Season in some parts of Earth. In the tropics.

More proof that I wasn't from this planet.

Once the rain had stopped, I found a tree laden with fruit. I remembered eating some recently with Axak. *Jannu* fruit. It was a new discovery for the Waikari as it hadn't grown so close to the coast before.

I reached the tree with the intent of filling my bag with as many as I could. As I pulled on one of the fruits, there was a flash in my mind. I'd done this before. I saw myself picking and eating the fruit, but then I remembered the flowers. A flower had popped and sprayed its pollen into my eyes and mouth. Seeing the horrific hallucinations that followed had me stumbling away from the tree and falling onto my butt.

CHAPTER 29
They Weren't People

Visions of trees and vines coming alive, snakes slithering toward me, dinosaurs attacking, and some sinister-looking man coming towards me with lots of sharp implements flooded my mind. I struggled to push the memories aside and sat on the forest floor panting.

Once I'd collected my thoughts, the sight of rocks and sticks falling to the forest floor around me had me jumping to my feet, until I realized that I'd caused them to float around while I was reliving those horrible visions. I sighed. I was so relieved that it hadn't happened again.

It would be okay to pick the fruit as long as I was really careful.

I managed to gather some more fruit without disturbing the flowers and put all but one into my bag. I couldn't get away from the plant fast enough.

Chumana.

The word just came to me. The fruit was called Chumana, but what language was that? It wasn't Waikari or Basic. Maybe it was from the Jungle People.

I took a bite and the juice stung my sore throat. I had to ignore it. I had to eat.

As I continued on, I could sense that there was water up ahead. Probably a river or creek. I wished I had a bottle or container to fill with water.

I didn't have any trouble finding the river. I had a long drink and wet my face and arms, but drew back quickly when I saw what looked like a crocodile lurking beneath the surface. I would have to be more careful.

As I moved away from the river, I thought it would be a good idea to walk parallel to it so that I could get a drink whenever I needed to.

The jungle was too entangled at the water's edge so I had to move a certain distance away to be able to walk more freely.

I kept going, ducking and weaving through the dense foliage and keeping a lookout for creepy crawlies and vegetation that wasn't vegetation.

I checked behind me to make sure I wasn't being followed by who-knows-what, and found nothing. As I turned back around, I felt something touch my arms and the side of my face. I took a step back; I'd walked into a spider's web. Flailing my arms around like a crazy person, I felt something crawling from the back of my head to my shoulder and without even thinking, I threw it off me using my mind. I heard a thwack and turned to see a humongous spider fall to the ground after hitting a nearby tree. That thing was bigger than the one at the cave entrance.

I shuddered and started rubbing my hands everywhere to remove the sticky web. It took a lot of effort as it was all over me. I was amazed at how strong the stuff was.

I shuddered again and kept going.

I soon found myself in a cleared area. An animal track. It was fairly wide and my chest tightened as I tried to picture the size of the creature that could easily walk through here. Getting off the track seemed like a good idea.

As I headed back into the foliage, I heard a crashing sound coming from the right. Maybe I was about to see the creature that could easily walk through here. My first thought was to climb a tree to avoid being the next meal of whatever was making about as much noise as a tank.

The nearest tree had low branches and plenty of roots sticking out of the ground that would make good hand- and foot-holds. The ease with which I climbed it and found a suitable branch to sit on told me I'd obviously climbed many trees before.

The noise became louder and either the thing approaching had more than four legs, or there were more than one of them. As that thought entered my head, I saw the head and neck of what looked like some sort of dinosaur come into view, followed by another dinosaur of the same species. They looked like an Anatosaurus from Earth's distant past — a fact that just popped into my head — with saddles made of hide, and had people riding on their backs.

Only, they weren't people. Not exactly. They looked more like some kind of apes or cavemen and seeing their faces sent a chill down my spine. I'd seen them before. I must have encountered them while I was missing. I watched as they passed by below me and realized that I'd been holding my breath. I let it out slowly and sat still, waiting for them to pass. Something bad had happened to me when I'd met up with that race of people.

Were all Jungle People like them? Is that why the Waikari kept away?

The sound of chains clinking made my blood run cold. Walking behind the dinosaurs were four more of the beast-like men holding chains. On the other end of those chains were people — five of them — with shackles at their wrists. They weren't beasts. They looked human like the Waikari.

They were slaves.

Chapter 30

A Fresh Meal in a Tree

I had a flash of chains on my own wrists. At some point, I'd been in chains too. The memory sparked more questions. How did I end up in chains? How did I get away?

I rubbed my wrists, but the memory of the pain caused by the shackles didn't fade.

Another memory flashed into my mind. One of those beast-like men standing over me, holding a huge knife, dripping with blood. *My* blood.

I sucked in a breath, then looked down to see if anyone had heard me. No one looked up. They were making too much noise for me to be heard. I breathed out slowly. I had to bury that memory deep in my mind, along with all the questions it raised. I'd deal with it later.

I had somehow gotten away, and that was all that mattered right now. I had to concentrate on the here and now so I wouldn't be discovered and invited to join the poor souls below.

One of the slaves stumbled and was dragged to her feet and forced to keep going.

I stayed in the tree long after they'd gone.

I wished I could help them, but there was nothing I could do. I might've had a powerful gift, but it was useless when I wasn't trained enough to wield it. I needed to get my memories back as fast as I could.

The memory of the man saying, *You shouldn't be here,* entered my mind, followed by, *You shouldn't be alive,* then, *You don't deserve to live. You have no soul.*

<hr>

As I descended to the last branch, I looked down to see a small dinosaur that was about the size of a chicken stalking around in the leaf mulch. Two small front legs and two long, muscular back legs, long tail — kind of cute really — until you saw the rows of sharp little teeth. I froze. I remembered reading about a similar dinosaur from Earth. Compsognathus. It was a carnivore and was thought to hunt in packs. I didn't know where that memory had come from. It just popped in there.

It looked up and made a weird hissing sound, its strange reptilian eye looking right at me.

Uh oh. There was no way I was going to get out of the tree now. Even though it was such a small creature, those teeth could do some damage. I stayed as still as I could, hoping it would lose interest, and was thankful that I'd spotted it before I'd actually reached the ground.

Of course it wasn't going to leave. It lifted its head higher and sniffed the air, then moved closer to the trunk of the tree. Was it going to try to climb up? *Could* it actually climb a tree? I shrunk back away from where it was trying to find a foothold.

What if it could climb trees? How could I get away? Hearts pounding, I started to move up to the next branch, a loud screechy noise almost making me lose my grip. When I looked down, there were two more of them looking up at me. My chest tightened. I needed to get higher.

I forced myself to look away from them and climbed back to where I'd sat while the slavers passed.

More screeching and some scratching noises came from below. There were more of them now. The branches obscured my view, but I counted at least seven of them. And they were all trying to find a way up.

My hearts pounded out a fast rhythm and I tried in vain to slow my shallow breathing. I needed to calm down or I'd faint and fall out of the tree, giving them a free meal. I shuddered at the thought.

Breathe in. Breathe out. They can't climb this high... At least, I don't think they can...

The screeching was getting louder and it sounded like they were fighting. Looking down, I could see that one of them was clinging to some smaller branches and was close to making it to the lowest branch.

I looked around in a panic, hearts hammering in my chest. Could I make it to the next tree over by climbing from this tree to the other's branches without falling?

A loud roar had me jerking my head around and almost falling off the branch. At first, I couldn't see anything below me, but a thing that looked like a giant version of the little ones stalked along the path, scattering the smaller reptiles. It looked around on the ground, probably looking for whatever the little ones were attacking or eating, and found nothing. I held my breath and willed it not to smell me or see me, but of course it could smell me. A fresh meal in a tree, if it could reach me.

CHAPTER 31

Dinosaur!

It looked up hungrily, sniffing the air, and my hearts skipped a beat or two before galloping full speed again. It was maybe three metres tall but I was well out of its reach. My body was tense though, ready to run. It refused to believe that I was safe.

The reptile stretched its neck and body toward me and could see that it was futile, so it turned and wandered away.

I breathed a huge sigh of relief and concentrated on slowing my breathing and heart rates. What was I thinking, coming out here alone and unarmed? My problems back at the village didn't seem as bad now. I touched my bruised throat. At least Dakawa wasn't out to eat me.

I stayed in the tree for about an hour before I felt I could keep going. Remembering how to use my Talent properly would have been handy for escaping from something like that three-metre monster.

Besides a few creepy crawlies and a large python sitting in a tree, I didn't see anything else that might want to hurt me or crawl on me for the rest of the day.

I couldn't find any caves to hide in as the ground had flattened out, so I opted for sleeping in a tree. Although it wasn't safe, I knew it would be safer than sleeping on the ground. So I found a tree with a wide enough branch for me to lie on, then found some vines that looked strong enough to use as ropes to tie me to the branch so I wouldn't fall out of the tree while I slept.

It wasn't ideal and it certainly wasn't comfortable, but after I'd spent a long time questioning my sanity for coming out here, I managed to doze a few times throughout the night, waking each time I heard a roar or a screech.

I woke in the early morning light to the sight of a large, striped, hairy spider making its way across the branch I was hugging, heading straight toward my hand. I snatched my hand away and tried to sit up, but the vines stopped me. I fumbled to undo the rough knots fast enough to enable me to get out of the spider's path, while at the same time remembering how I'd dealt with the last one and just flinging it out of the tree.

I sat up, hearts pounding, while I tried to calm down. There must be a better place to sleep. How did the natives do it? Once I felt like I was awake enough to climb, I grabbed my bag and headed down to the forest floor.

There were no little hungry critters waiting at the bottom this time, so I set off toward the river for a drink.

I climbed back up the embankment after quenching my thirst and stopped. Did I imagine hearing footsteps in the leaf mulch?

After listening for a few more seconds, I thought I heard something off in the distance, probably travelling down the animal track. My mind raced. I needed to find another tree to hide in.

As I stood staring straight ahead and straining my ears, I noticed two things. The first was that there were voices coming from the direction of the footsteps, which increased my heart rates. The second was that I could make out a shape amongst the foliage in front of me. About ten metres away.

The shape blended into the greens and browns so well that I thought I must have imagined it. Then its lizard-like eye blinked and ice ran through my veins. It was watching me. Waiting for a chance to attack.

The longer I looked, the more I could see of the outline of its body. It was a smaller version of the predator that chased the Compsognathus clones away. This one was only about two metres high. My brain finally supplied the name Allosaurus. It looked like an Allosaurus from prehistoric Earth.

What do I do?

What else could I do but run?

After a second or two I heard the sounds of heavy footfalls crushing leaves and twigs.

My mind scrambled for ideas as I weaved through the underbrush. I knew I couldn't outrun the thing, so I tried to run into small spaces between trees and rocks in the hope of slowing it down. Maybe if I got far enough ahead I could climb a tree or something. Maybe even head back to the river and jump in. I had to hope that it couldn't swim.

Branches scratched my arms and pulled at my hair, but I ignored it and ran faster. A quick glance over my shoulder almost made me scream out loud. It might have been smaller than the other one, but it didn't really matter when I saw all of those long, sharp teeth coming for me.

I kept to the smaller spaces, forcing the creature to go around the obstacles, but I was barely keeping ahead of it. As I burst out of the foliage into an open space, I found to my horror that I was back on the animal track. Before I could even register that there were people there, I'd run straight into a hard, bare chest. The man I'd ploughed into grabbed me by the arms to stop me from falling and without thinking, I blurted out, "Dinosaur!"

I wondered if they understood, but the man pulled me behind him and drew a long knife from its sheath. I was vaguely aware that there were other men around me and took some steps back as the Allosaurus-thing burst onto the track. They were all armed with knives and spears and took the reptile by surprise. It screeched and roared as they stabbed at it, drawing blood and almost severing one of its front legs. It tried to bite a man's arm off, its teeth grazing the skin, but soon realized that it was outnumbered.

It took a few backward steps, then dashed away down the centre of the track, screeching as it went.

I hadn't moved. The shock kept me in place even as the men turned to face me. Five of them were wearing skins like me, but the sixth man was wearing a shipsuit. He also had long white hair that fell to his waist. It had a number of small braids in it and was partly tied back. He was a lot taller than the others.

He definitely didn't fit in. Like me. Maybe we were from the same planet. Maybe we knew each other and he could tell me who I was.

They all started speaking at once, and I realized with a sinking feeling in my stomach that I couldn't understand a word they said. Great. I didn't expect them to know Basic, but I'd hoped that they spoke the same language as the Waikari. Now this made things infinitely more difficult.

"Thank you," I said, using Sifayah's native language, hoping that they knew it.

They all looked confused. So, no.

I looked closely at each of their faces in the hope that I would recognise one of them. When I finally looked up at the tall one in the shipsuit, I gasped as a memory hit me full force.

He was there in my mind, as well as a woman with long white hair like his. We were talking about him. She liked him and was too shy to say anything. We watched him walk away into the jungle. We spoke with another man with short dark hair. Mosuti. I argued with another man who stood at the hatch of our shuttle about Mosuti being a Talent. The man said Talents needed to be controlled. Then the jungle lit up with laser fire. We were pushed to the ground away from the line of fire. I saw a woman with her hair on fire and closed my eyes to try to block it out.

"Do you speak Basic?" he asked.

My hearts were pounding and I looked back up at him. "Uh, yes!" Maybe I could talk to them after all.

He stepped forward. "Who are you? How do you know Basic?"

"I..." It just hit me. "Janssen."

He blinked. "What?"

"Your name is Janssen."

CHAPTER 32
How Do You Know Me?

He frowned. "Yes. The last time I checked. How do you know me?"

It was my turn to frown. "I... I don't know."

"What? How can you not know?"

I shifted uneasily in the leaf mulch. "I... well, I've lost my memory, but when I looked at you, I remembered something."

"What did you remember?"

I told him what I remembered.

"How can you know that? You weren't there. It was just my crew and the pilot. I've never seen you before. Were you watching from the trees or something?"

"No. I was there. I remember. I was talking to a woman with long white hair like yours."

"Larissa? Where is she?"

"I don't know. I don't remember that part." His shoulders slumped a little.

This wasn't making any sense. How could I have been there, but he didn't remember me being there? My stomach sank. It must have happened before I was changed... put into this body.

How was I going to explain that?

He rubbed a hand down his face and I remembered what I'd spoken to her about. "She liked you too," I blurted out.

He half-frowned, then gave me a lop-sided grin. "She did?" He paused. "How could you know that? How can you know any of this stuff when you weren't there?"

"I would have looked different then. I didn't look like this. I had light-brown hair. Blue eyes."

"What are you talking about? You're not making any sense."

"I woke up on a beach a few days ago and couldn't remember anything. I had a head injury. I have been slowly remembering things and I can remember stuff about the village I was in, but also stuff about travelling through space and technology and someone named Darion, and now you and Larissa."

"I don't know any Darion. And you're still not making any sense."

My hearts sank. He didn't know Darion? Then how did *I* know Darion? Who was he?

The other men asked Janssen some questions and he tried to answer them while my mind raced. I knew him. I knew that I'd been there when we were attacked.

"Janssen?"

"Yes?"

"This is going to sound impossible, but somehow my mind has been put into this body. I don't know how or why. I was someone else from Earth. Now I'm a native woman from this planet."

"How could anyone even do something like that?"

"I don't know. I was hoping you could tell me."

He ran a hand over his face, deep in thought.

Maybe he knew me after all. "Can you tell me who you were with when the attack came?"

His eyes snapped to mine. "Why?"

"Just tell me. Please?"

"Okay. I'll try to remember." He scratched his chin. "There was Larissa, Bazeelia, Mosuti, Lanu, Zhenna... and .. I can't remember."

Zhenna!

Hearing that name felt like something had come alive in my chest. I had trouble breathing.

Janssen stepped forward and touched my arm. "Are you alright?"

I looked up at him. "I was Zhenna."

He raised his eyebrows. He thought I'd lost it. I could tell. I would too. Maybe I had.

"Believe me. This happened. They changed me. I was Zhenna and now I am Sifayah. I still have her memories because I keep remembering parts of her life and parts of mine. It's confusing and frustrating."

"That's impossible."

"You think I'm crazy. I can see it in your eyes. But I'm not. You are from a planet called Shakira. So is Larissa. We came here and we were attacked by... Hey, how did you get away?"

"I was near the edge of the clearing and they didn't realise I was there. I crawled away into the underbrush.

"Then I got lost in the jungle, got chased by a bigger version of the dinosaur that just chased you, was nearly eaten by a sabre-toothed cat of some kind, somehow avoided being swallowed by a python, and met up with these guys, who, as far as I can tell, are looking for these beast-looking men that are travelling around the jungle catching people and turning them into slaves."

"Oh..." The memory of my wrists in chains hit me again. "What is it?"

"I... I remember chains... on my wrists." I started rubbing them.

"Are you okay?"

"Yeah."

He gestured to a nearby log and we sat down. The other men kept alert, holding their weapons at the ready.

"I think I was a slave at one point. And I've seen the men that you're looking for travelling along this trail. They look like beasts and they had about five people in chains."

"That's them. How long ago?"

"Yesterday afternoon. Then I had to stay in the tree I was hiding in for a bit longer as there were these little dinosaurs wanting me to join them for dinner."

"What?"

"They wanted to eat me."

"Oh."

"They were trying to climb the tree I was in, but they were scared off by the same type of dinosaur as the one that was just here. I was glad that it couldn't reach the branch I was on."

The other men interrupted us again.

Janssen spoke to them for a while, then turned back to me. "They want to know what's going on. I told them that I know you and that you saw the slavers. Now they want to get going. Will you come with us?"

I shuddered at the thought of catching up to the Beast-men, but staying out here by myself was not an option. "Okay. As long as they don't mind," I said, waving my hand in their direction. "I left the village I was in to find answers and I'm hoping you can help me."

Janssen introduced me to the other men. The first two, Mazaak and Nakano, were from the Charan tribe, and Rihyan, Rinaru, and Shadrak were from Chandra. They were all well-muscled, long-haired young men that looked the same as the Waikari, minus the webbed fingers and toes. I greeted them as best I could and they didn't seem surprised that I couldn't understand them.

Janssen turned to me. "You don't speak their language?"

"No. Sifayah's tribe don't speak the same language as the other natives."

"That is a problem. I can barely understand them and was hoping you could translate."

I rubbed my upper arm. "Sorry."

"It can't be helped. We'll just have to make do." We started walking along the track. "The reason I've stayed with these guys is because there's safety in numbers out here and because they know what's safe to eat. I want to help them get their people back too."

I'd only been relying on fruit I recognized and didn't know how to hunt. And the fact that they'd just saved me from being that dino's dinner proved how right he was.

As we walked, I noted how alert the men were. Armed and ready for an attack from any direction. That eased my worries a little.

Janssen asked me what tribe I was from. He said the others had asked too.

"I can't really tell you. These guys might know them by name."

He gave me a sideways glance. "Why is that a problem?"

"Sifayah's tribe are different from the others and keep to themselves."

He frowned. "Define 'different.'"

"They are amphibious and..." I hesitated. "Telepathic."

CHAPTER 33
Egg Stealers

His eyes widened. "So, can *you* do these things now?"

"Yes."

"So, you know what I'm thinking right now?"

I stiffened. "*No*. I don't just read peoples' thoughts just because I can. It's not ethical."

I hadn't had much practice at it anyway.

He looked relieved. "Oh. Yeah. Sorry."

"That's why they keep themselves separate from the other tribes. People would fear them."

"Yeah, you're right."

We were silent for a while, then I asked him what he knew about the different land tribes. He explained that the natives collectively called themselves the Darsana. There were six different tribes that lived in the jungle and out on the plains. Some held slaves and some were against it. The Beast-men were not Darsana and were called the Bahadori. I felt a chill at the word, so I'd probably known them by name before. I wondered again how I'd gotten away from those chains.

All five of the Darsana we were travelling with were looking for their friends or relatives that had been captured by the Bahadori. Rihyan and Rinaru were brothers and they were looking for their younger sister. I remembered the young woman who had stumbled and been dragged back to her feet and could understand their hurry to get to her. She may not have been their sister, but I was sure that they'd all be treated the same.

I wondered how they were going to get them away from the Bahadori and asked Janssen about it.

"I'm not sure exactly what their plan is because of the language barrier."

"Well, two of them were riding on dinosaurs and four of them were walking behind them holding chains."

"How many slaves?"

"Five, I think. They weren't being treated well. A girl stumbled and they just pulled her up by the chains and made her start walking again."

Janssen spoke to the others with lots of hand gestures, presumably telling them what I'd seen. A lot of angry words followed. Then their tone changed to what I assumed was determination. I hoped that my information had helped them form a better plan for when we did find them.

I jumped at the sound of rustling in the underbrush, followed by some awful screeching noises. Everyone around me assumed a defensive stance with weapons at the ready. My first thought was that the little dinosaurs I'd seen before were about to attack, but what burst out of the foliage was much larger and was carrying an egg in its 'hands.'

It darted out onto the track and saw us, screeched loudly and held its egg closer to its body. It was a rusty-brown colour, the same general shape as the little Compsognathus look-alikes, but minus all the sharp teeth. It looked back into the jungle and screeched again, then rushed into the foliage on the other side of the track, heading toward the river. It was quickly followed by two more of the lizards. One held an egg and the other looked to be trying to steal it from him. They followed the path of the first one, only giving us a cursory glance as they passed.

My hearts were hammering in my chest as the men slowly lowered their weapons.

"Egg stealers." Janssen said.

I looked up into his dark eyes and couldn't see where the pupil ended and the iris began. "Oh, so they weren't carrying their own eggs?"

"No. They steal the eggs from other dinosaurs and eat them."

I guessed that was why they didn't really pay that much attention to us and was relieved that they didn't attack.

We kept walking until dark, stopping only to eat, drink and rest. I couldn't help wondering where we would sleep. I hoped that there was a better solution than tying myself to a tree.

Eventually, they veered off the track into a spot closer to the river and started setting up camp for the night. Rihyan collected twigs and branches for a fire while the others used their knives to cut some large, broad leaves from nearby plants. The teamwork was quite impressive. I felt out of place and didn't know what to do.

"Is there anything I can do?" I asked Janssen.

He looked around. "No. Not really. They seem to have everything under control."

I felt like I needed to contribute, but didn't know how.

When everything was organized, we all sat around the fire on rocks or logs and I tried to relax. The distant roar as I shifted my position on the log made it impossible.

As we ate fruit and shared fur bags full of water, Janssen asked me how I ended up in the jungle, so I told him some of the things I'd been through and some of the things I could remember from before I hit my head.

He listened intently, deep in thought. It was a hard story to believe. I had trouble believing it myself.

"That was a dangerous move, coming out here."

"I know. But after what happened with Dakawa, I thought that they'd lock me up or something, and then I'd never get any answers."

He nodded.

I yawned.

That's when I found out that the large leaves were for us to sleep on. The fire had died down a bit, so they added more logs to it. One of the men, Shadrak maybe, took up a position near the edge of our campsite, spear in hand, to watch for predators while we slept.

I was invited to sleep on a leaf next to Janssen, which was closer to the fire. I was on edge about sleeping so close to six men I didn't know, as well as the possibility of being attacked by any number of things during the night. I forced myself to calm down. It was infinitely better than tying myself to a tree and hoping for the best.

⁓◦⁓

I looked through the branches of the bush I was hiding behind and could see an animal that looked like a deer from Earth. The Darsana called it a meeru.

It was a dappled brown colour that helped it to blend in with the jungle, but the colouring of its fur would not help it today.

I wished that I could jump up and scare it away, warn it somehow. I didn't want to see it die. Which was stupid, of course. The fruit we'd been eating wasn't enough. We needed the extra energy that the meat's protein would give us to keep going at the pace we'd been walking — and there was enough meat there to feed the seven of us and have some left over.

Although I didn't want to watch, I couldn't look away. Rihyan slowly pulled his spear back. It was so slow that I would have missed it if I wasn't paying such close attention.

I turned back toward the deer — meeru — and in the blink of an eye, the spear hit it square in the chest. It let out an awful cry of agony as it fell to the ground, writhing around. I had to stand up to see it through the bushes and I kept watching until it lay still.

CHAPTER 34
I Don't Remember You

I couldn't help feeling sorry for the poor thing and I turned away when the men walked over to start preparing it for our meal.

"You don't want to watch?" Janssen asked.

"No. I don't have the stomach for it. Sifayah didn't have a problem with it, but I don't know how to hunt, how to kill and dress an animal or how to cook it. When it comes to all of that, I'm clueless."

"You will get used to it."

"I doubt it..." But these skills were important if I was going to survive out here. "Maybe I could start by learning how to cook it."

"Good idea."

My stomach roiled at the thought.

We had to wait until they'd taken the meeru back to camp and finished carving it up. It was hard for me to hear the sound effects and I saw some of what they were doing, but I was determined. I couldn't keep turning away from something I needed to know for survival.

Once I'd learned how to put the pieces of meat into the right position in the fire and was able to tell when it was cooked through, it became easy.

I noticed that while the food was being prepared and cooked, a few of the men were on guard. Well, more than they usually were while we were stopped. When I asked Janssen what was going on, he explained that the little dinosaurs they called meat stealers were always waiting out there in the bushes, hoping to get some of the meat.

I looked around us and could see movement. The Compsognathus look-alikes were out there, waiting and hoping.

As we ate and I tried to forget we were eating that poor deer, I tried to talk to the others more, asking them about what things were called. Well, mostly pointing at things so they would tell me what they were called.

I learned, quite by accident, that I could see into their minds as they said some of the words and knew what they meant because of the mental image I saw there. That could make communication a lot easier. I kept doing it until I remembered what I'd told Janssen about not reading his thoughts just because I could. Then I felt guilty, even though what I was doing wasn't quite the same. I was only reading images and was using it to translate their language. The line was blurry here. I thought I'd better stick to learning the language the same way that Janssen had to.

Once we'd eaten, we packed up and walked back to the track, leaving the carcass of the meeru behind. I looked back as the meat stealers moved in. They didn't even wait till we were out of sight.

My feet hurt and I was tired of all the walking, but the Darsana were determined to catch up to the slavers. We'd wasted a lot of time hunting and eating the meeru, but Janssen told me that they hadn't eaten meat for days and couldn't keep going on fruit alone.

The men at the front of our group stopped suddenly and I nearly ran into Rihyan. I was about to ask why they'd stopped, but the sound of footsteps ahead answered my question.

The Darsana raised their weapons and I moved so I could see past Rihyan's broad shoulders. A group of men emerged from the undergrowth with their arms up to show they were unarmed — only, that wasn't true. They had weapons partially hidden in holsters around their waists. They may have been dressed in skins, but they definitely weren't natives.

My heart rates sped up.

A man with broad shoulders and a short, neat haircut stepped forward and said hello in Darsana. "We mean you no harm," he added in Basic.

My hearts pounded now.

Janssen stepped forward cautiously. "Greetings. I am Janssen Malakua. Are you from Voyager Division?"

"We've been looking for you, son. I'm Commander Totino Kozienko. Voyager Division sent me."

Janssen managed to get the Darsana to lower their weapons.

I stared at the commander's face. Did I know him?

He looked at each of us, probably watching for signs of danger. His gaze landed on me and there was recognition in his eyes. "Tamisan?"

I opened my mouth to speak, but nothing came out.

A man with short, dark hair stepped out from behind the commander. He looked around wildly and when he saw me, his face lit with excitement. It was Darion.

"Tamisan?" His voice cracked on the single word. He rushed forward and crushed me to his chest. "I thought you were dead!"

"Darion?"

"Are you okay? Where have you been?"

I was vaguely aware of Rihyan and the others moving around us, but Janssen must have stopped them from interfering.

Being in Darion's arms had a strange effect on me. My hearts sang. It was like coming home. Like a missing piece of me had been found and melded back into my soul.

He bent down and kissed me hungrily and instead of pulling away, I melted into him. I became lost in him. Everything faded away to nothing and I couldn't get enough. My hands ran up and down his back. He deepened the kiss and I let him in, tasting him and...

Something clicked in my brain. What was I doing? I could barely remember this man and I was kissing him like he was the air I breathed. My hearts obviously remembered more than I did, but I needed to get my head straight.

I pulled away from him, suddenly aware that everyone was staring. There were tears on his cheeks.

"What is wrong?"

How well did I know him? Were we in a relationship? Were we married?

"I..." *How do I even explain this?* "Um, I can't really... I mean... I don't remember you." *Yep. That explains everything*

He frowned. "What? What do you mean? You know my name. You..."

Kissed me.

CHAPTER 35

Him

"I know. I remember *some* things... but I hit my head and lost my memory."

"How? What happened?"

"I don't remember. I woke up on a beach with a head injury and no idea how I'd got there."

"That part makes sense. You fell into a river. You must have been washed out to sea."

Something wasn't adding up. "Wait, who is Tamisan?"

"*You* are Tamisan."

There was another weird sensation in my chest. "I thought I was Zhenna."

"You were. You changed your name."

This just kept getting more confusing. "Why?"

"It is a long story."

I crossed my arms. "I've got time."

He told me that my name was Zhenna Rhodarma. I was originally from Earth and had applied to work out here on Althar 3 as a computer programmer. He confirmed that Janssen and I were in the jungle with the other members of our team when we were attacked.

The attackers didn't see Janssen escape and the rest of us were taken to an underground base called Station Maztec, where we were subjected to illegal experiments. The scientist, Dr Leonard Starrick, used a procedure called the Eibhlin Process to transfer my consciousness to a native — Sifayah.

Some more puzzle pieces clicked into place.

I told him about being found by the Waikari and them thinking I was Sifayah. My mind was reeling, trying to make sense of it all.

Janssen stepped forward. "What about Larissa? What happened to her? Is she okay?"

Darion's face didn't show sadness and I dared to hope that what he said next wasn't bad news. "She is okay. She has gone back to Shakira. Dr Starrick did perform experiments on her, but like Tamisan, they were successful."

"What did he do to her?" Janssen and I asked together. There were too many horrible possibilities racing through my brain.

Darion looked at me. "He was able to transfer the Talent that you'd gained from Sifayah's mind into Larissa's. She has some telepathic and telekinetic abilities and will need some training on how to control and use them."

"Yeah, me too."

"What?"

"I've had some issues because I didn't even remember I had any abilities."

He frowned. "That must have been difficult."

"Yes. I've caused myself a lot of trouble."

Rihyan interrupted then and Janssen spoke to them, probably trying to explain that we knew each other. I picked up a few words and could see that they wanted to keep moving. I understood their urgency. They couldn't afford to waste any more time. They had to get their people back.

Janssen was soon thanking them and they said their good-byes to us all.

What would happen now that Darion and the commander had found us? How long would it take us to walk back to wherever they'd come from? It didn't really matter if it meant that we'd get out of the jungle.

Janssen explained to the others about the Darsana's quest to rescue their friends and family members, but I'd tuned out. I was watching one of the men because he wouldn't make eye contact with me. He wasn't a wall of muscle like the commander and some of the other men. He was shorter and had the appearance of someone who usually spent his time indoors. He was standing so that he was almost completely hidden behind another man and it seemed odd. And suspicious. Why would he be hiding? Did I know him? Did he know Janssen?

As soon as he looked me directly in the eye, I felt like I'd been kicked in the stomach. I couldn't breathe properly. There was something really wrong here.

Darion moved forward. "Tamisan? What is it?"

For a few seconds, all I could do was point.

"What's wrong?"

I kept pointing at the man and he grew uneasy. "Him."

"That is Nykolar Taarel. He is part of our team. Do you remember him?"

"No. Yes."

Darion's eyebrows drew together. "What?"

"He..." My mind faltered. I struggled to remember. The ice flowing through my veins told me it was something bad and something important and it involved this Nykolar.

Nykolar seemed to realise that I couldn't remember and lifted his chin defiantly. I glared at him. He knew why I was reacting this way.

You shouldn't be here.

I closed my eyes for a few moments and concentrated. It was there in the back of my mostly blank mind. I knew it.

My waiting paid off as it burst forward into my brain so fast it was almost painful. My knees buckled and I would have fallen to the ground if Darion hadn't grabbed my arm. Everyone's voices sounded far away as I saw Nykolar in my mind, pointing a stunner at me. The back of my neck stung as he told me he'd disabled my tracker. I saw him flick the stunner to the highest level. Heard him tell me I shouldn't be here. I shouldn't be alive.

He gave me a creepy smile. "I've disabled your tracking device."

"*What?* Why?"

His eyes filled with hate and his voice became flat and hollow. "So no one can find your body and bring it back to base for further study. You're an abomination. Made in a lab. You don't deserve to live. You have no soul."

I relived the pain of the stunner blast and the pain of hitting my head below the surface of the water.

I opened my eyes and reality came sharply into focus. Darion and Janssen were holding my arms and as I looked around, I could see that Nykolar was starting to retreat into the jungle. I pointed at him again. "Stop him!"

Some of the men went after Nykolar as Darion and Janssen asked me what was going on but I couldn't find the words yet.

He was caught and brought back to the group.

"I haven't done anything," he was saying as two men held onto his arms.

"Then why were you running?" One of them asked him.

Darion turned to me. "What is it? Did you remember something?"

I was trembling all over. "He... tried to kill me."

CHAPTER 36
Enigma

Nykolar started to pull against his captors. "No! She's lying! I saw her slip and fall! And I saw the croc go after her!"

Darion stalked over to him and grabbed him by the shirt. "You told me a croc came out of the water and took her!"

Nykolar winced. "I... She slipped and fell first. Then I saw the croc."

"Did you actually *see* it attack?"

"No."

Darion punched Nykolar in the face and his head jerked violently to the side. "*You fucking bastard!* You said she was dead!" His voice cracked on the last word. "We could have gone after her!"

Kozienko took Darion's arm. "Back off, Andiyar. He'll get his. He's not worth it, son."

Darion turned to me and the anguish in his eyes undid me. I moved forward and wrapped my arms around him. "I'm here now. I'm okay."

He squeezed me tighter and kissed the top of my head.

I thought I should tell them more about what happened. "He used his stunner to disable my tracker while I was washing the blood off my legs, then he switched it to kill."

One of the men removed Nykolar's stunner from his holster. Blood dripped from Nykolar's split lip.

"She's lying! She hit her head! She's not thinking clearly! If I'd done that, she'd be dead!"

"No. I managed to switch it back with my mind just before you pulled the trigger. It only stunned me, but I hit my head when I fell in the water."

He was trying harder to get away and managed to kick one of the men in the shin. "No! I wouldn't hurt her!"

"You did." I spat. "You said I was an abomination. You said I shouldn't be alive."

Darion started toward him again as Nykolar managed to pull an arm free and it looked too easy. Like the guy had let him go. Nykolar grabbed his stunner back and shot Darion, the commander, and the guy on his right before anyone could react.

I lunged forward. "Darion!"

Janssen was next to join the others on the ground. I struggled to process what I was seeing and hoped the weapon was set to stun.

As my brain started to work again, I tried to hurl the stunner from Nykolar's hand with my mind and nothing happened. I knew I wasn't in complete control yet, but I should have been able to do something that simple. I tried again. Nothing. Why couldn't I do anything?

Before I could try again, the guy on Nykolar's left reached forward and grabbed my arm, pulling me down as I heard stunners buzz above us.

Dizziness swept over me and I suddenly found myself being wrestled to a hard floor instead of the leaf litter. It took a few seconds to realise that we had teleported out of the jungle.

The guy that had lunged forward was now on top of me and I struggled to push him off. He took his time getting up and I panicked, trying to push him with my mind, but my Talent had failed me again.

Once he was standing I noticed that Nykolar had been transported too.

"What...?" was all I could manage.

Nykolar turned to the other man. "Nice work, Braydac. Good timing, too."

I looked from one to the other. They'd planned this? "What do you want?"

"You, of course," Nykolar said, wiping his mouth with the back of his hand.

I got to my feet, not wanting them to be towering over me anymore. It didn't help that Sifayah was so short. "But, why?"

"You, my dear, are valuable, apparently."

"To who?"

"Lots of scientists, for one. You are quite the anomaly. An enigma. Doctor Starrick's big success."

"Who?"

"Oh, you don't remember him? The brilliant scientist that Darion told you about, who successfully transferred your brainwaves into that body without messing anything up, and keeping the Talent that the Althari woman possessed. It was pure genius."

He seemed to be impressed with Dr Starrick's success, but his facial expression told a different story. And then there were the things he'd said before he'd tried to kill me. He believed that I was an abomination and that I had no soul.

I cringed. He'd wanted me dead.

Braydac stepped forward. "You cost me a very large amount of credits with your stupid stunt."

I thought for a second that he was talking to me, but he was looking at Nykolar.

Nykolar raised his eyebrows. "What do you mean?"

"We were supposed to deliver her alive, and you tried to end her. Everyone thought you'd succeeded." Braydac's hands were clenched into fists.

"I... Yes. I did it. She is an abomination, created in a lab, and so are the other natives on this forsaken planet. Our people are trying to play God. Meanwhile, the real gods are growing angry. They will retaliate and we will pay the ultimate price."

"Really? You believe in the Old Gods? You Korovskans are crazy! There *are* no gods."

Korovskan? Nykolar wasn't human? Or was Korovska a human settlement? I tried to remember anything about a race called the Korovskan, but failed.

Nykolar was clearly insulted, but managed to keep his temper in check. "You are blocking her?"

What?

"Of course. You think I'm stupid?"

"Good." He pointed his stunner at me, no doubt set on the highest setting again, and things happened too fast for me to comprehend.

Before he could press the trigger, it disappeared from his hand. Did Braydac do that?

He stepped closer to Nykolar and swiped a hand across Nykolar's throat. Nykolar gasped and his eyes went wide as his hands went to his throat. Blood spurted between his fingers and I felt a warm spray across my face and chest. His knees buckled and he fell to the floor.

I couldn't move. Couldn't breathe. I watched as more blood spurted and ran across the floor in a growing puddle.

Braydac grabbed my arm and pulled me back out of the way so my boots wouldn't be soaked in it.

Once I started breathing again, I took in fast, shallow breaths. I couldn't believe what he'd done. Flashes of someone killing a jungle cat by slicing its throat open sped through my mind. I couldn't look away.

Braydac grabbed my upper arms and turned me to face him but my eyes were fixed on Nykolar. His eyes were wide and glassy. "Tamisan."

I looked from Nykolar's eyes to Braydac's. Was he Korovskan too?

His eyes looked wild and for a moment I thought I was next. He still held the small knife in his hand and I could feel its handle pressing against my arm as he held me. My hearts were pounding their way out of my chest. I looked down at the knife and saw the blood on it. Saw the blood smeared on my arm...

"Tamisan!"

Was I supposed to answer him? I felt light-headed and fuzzy all over.

"Slow down your breathing."

I couldn't. He'd just killed someone in cold blood right in front of me. My legs started to give way.

"Tamisan! You stupid girl! Calm down or you'll—"

Too late. The blackness swallowed me up.

CHAPTER 37
Five Minutes

I opened my eyes to darkness. I was lying on a bed that wasn't made of leaves or skins, so that made me instantly alert. I was in a room with modern furnishings. A table. A chair. A small stand next to the bed. A toilet and sink. A humming noise came from a large archway separating the room from the unfurnished part at the other end, causing my stomach to sink. I was in a cell. The humming was from an electrical field at the archway that prevented me from walking out of here.

I was on my feet and moving toward the field before I could think and had to stop myself before I got too close. My mind scrambled to remember what had happened and how I'd ended up in a cell.

We'd been found. I remembered Braydac killing Nykolar.

My stomach churned. I needed to sit down. All that blood. It was everywhere. How could he just cut someone's throat and stand there watching them die?

I looked down to see that I still had spots of blood all over me.

It was unbelievable, but true. Nykolar had tried to kill me, and was about to try again, but Braydac could have stopped him without *killing* him. Could have teleported us or him somewhere else. Could have knocked him unconscious. Could have even put him in a cell.

I went to the front of the cell again. I could see the faint line of light marking the electrical field. I knew touching it would be similar to a stunner blast. It would knock me unconscious and alarms would let Braydac know that I'd attempted to escape.

Who was he? Why was he keeping me here? What did he want from me?

I struggled to remember what he'd said to Nykolar. Something about Nykolar's actions costing him a lot of credits. Someone *paid* them to take me? But who? Who were the — what did they call them? Koroska? Or something...

My head hurt. I wanted to lie back down and get some more sleep and just block all of it out, but my brain had other ideas.

How long is he going to keep me in here?

I was tired and frustrated. Where *was* he? Didn't people like him like to come in and stand on the outside of the cell and taunt their prisoner?

Ugh! I watch too many HoloMovies!

Maybe I could use my Talent somehow to get out. I could pick something up and throw it through the field or short circuit it somehow or make a hole in it with my mind.

I tried to decide which thing to try first. Pushing a piece of furniture through sounded like a silly idea. How would that be helpful? Unless it formed a shape that would hold back the electrical field while I stepped through, it wouldn't be useful. So I stood in front of the field and concentrated, trying to make a hole in it. I had no idea what I was doing, so of course nothing happened. My brain felt... heavy, each time I tried. I'd felt the same heaviness before we ported here, when I was trying to use my Talent to stop Nykolar.

I tried to lift the chair. The table. Nothing. I tried a few more times. Just heaviness. It was like there was a weight on my brain that was stopping it from working.

My headache worsened, so I stopped and lay down on the bed. I would have to try something else. Or try again once I'd rested.

•◦•

I opened my eyes and stared at a wall. Memories flooded in to tell me where I was. I must have fallen asleep at some point, but it felt like I'd only been asleep for maybe an hour. I was still really tired, so I wondered what had woken me.

I got the eerie feeling that I was being watched. The hairs on the back of my neck stood up and I rolled over to see that Braydac was sitting backwards on a chair on the other side of the field staring at me. He had both elbows casually leaning on the back of the chair and I could see he'd washed Nykolar's blood off.

I sat up. "What are you doing? Why are you watching me sleep?"

"They want to see you."

I frowned. "Who?"

"Your creators." He chuckled to himself. "Well, that's what they call themselves."

"Creators? What are you talking about?"

"The Korovska. They've been playing with the genetics of all kinds of creatures on this planet for centuries, and the Waikari were their biggest success, until you came along."

"Me? Why?"

"I told you."

"No. You didn't. Nykolar did. Right before you *killed* him in cold blood!"

"He was going to kill you. Right then and there. I couldn't let that happen. He would have killed me if I tried to arrest him or some equally-lame thing. He really was insane."

"You didn't have to kill him."

"Yeah. I did. He would've killed you the first chance he got. Haven't you ever wondered how Doctor Starrick was able to escape custody so quickly and easily? Nykolar let him out, knowing that he wanted to kill you."

"What? How?" I was struggling to remember the things he was talking about.

"He worked in security. He gave Starrick the syringe that he used to drug you. The one that made you blind and paralysed."

My blood ran cold, the memory almost choking me. I pushed it aside and tried to deal with the here and now.

"Why?" I asked him.

He frowned. "Why what?"

"Why did you save me?"

"Because if you die, I don't get paid."

I crossed my arms. "That's it?"

"Yep," he answered casually, making the 'p' pop.

"How did you know for sure that he was going to kill me?"

He smirked. "It was right there in his mind."

"You're a Telepath?"

"Yep." Another pop.

"But you can also teleport?"

"You're fast."

"Shut up."

"You don't get to tell me what to do." He stood up. "Okay. You have five minutes to use the facilities and then we're outta here."

"Where are we going?"

"Five minutes." He stalked off and left me alone.

I 'used the facilities' as fast as I could as there was no privacy in the cell and cleaned as much blood off my hands, face, and arms as possible. I tried unsuccessfully to push thoughts of Nykolar's blood from my mind. I wished I had a mirror so I could see to get the blood off my face properly.

I waited for him to come back, wondering where he was planning to take me.

I didn't have to wait long. He strolled in and casually held up a pair of handcuffs. I cringed, memories of being in heavy shackles popping into my mind.

He smiled. "Now, don't try anything, or you'll regret it. I'm a T1 rated Talent in telepathy, teleportation, and telekinesis *and* I have a stunner."

I didn't answer. He pressed a button on the outside of the cell and the field crackled and disappeared.

I needed to be ready as soon as he stepped into the cell. I planned to use my Talent to push him across the room and make a run for it.

I would have to be quick. As he raised the cuffs, I tried to push with my mind, but that heavy feeling was back. I tried harder as he grabbed my arm and he started to laugh.

I looked into his eyes. *What's so funny? And why can't I use my Talent?*

"Because I can block Talent."

I gasped and his smile turned to a smirk.

"That's right, girl. I stopped you all from using your Talent back in the jungle, and I'm stopping you now. There won't be any way for you to escape." He snapped the cuffs on my wrists. "Now, let's go."

CHAPTER 38

You Are the Property of the Dekora Corporation

One moment we were standing in the cell and the next we were in a hallway facing a large metal door with writing on it that I didn't recognise. Dizziness swept over me for a second, like it did the last time Braydac teleported me, but this time it was more intense.

Braydac waved a hand in front of a sensor next to the door and a few long seconds later, the door swished open and he pulled me inside.

The office had a large desk in the middle and a couple of chairs facing it on this side. On the other side was a huge intimidating man with bright orange eyes that had black vertical slits for pupils. Other than that, he looked pretty-much human with broad shoulders and large midsection.

I sucked in a slow breath.

He smiled widely and gestured for us to sit. Braydac pushed me into a chair and sat down casually in the other one.

The man behind the desk kept smiling as he turned to Braydac. "Good work. Are you sure this is her?"

He had a deep voice and spoke with a stilted accent.

Braydac raised his eyebrows a fraction. "Yes. Positive. She suffers memory loss after Nykolar's previous attempt on her life, but is otherwise unharmed."

He looked me up and down and I managed to not cringe. "Are you sure she isn't injured?"

"Yes. It's not her blood."

"What about her throat?"

"Only bruised."

"Hmm. And Nykolar?"

"Dead."

"I see."

Didn't he care?

Braydac was all business. "He intended to finish the job. I had to take immediate action."

"I see." He turned to me. "Do you know why you are here?"

"No."

He blinked slowly. "I am Lundahl Saizen and you are the property of the Dekora Corporation."

I sat forward in my seat. "What? You don't *own* me! It is illegal to own a sentient being."

His eyebrows went up. "According to whom?"

"According to Intergalactic Law."

He waved a hand, dismissing my statement. "We have worked on this genesis project for centuries. No imbecile in a suit or robe will tell us what we can and cannot do."

"What do you want with me?"

"That is not something you need to be concerned with right now."

"Yes, it is! This is my life you're talking about!"

"You will be kept alive. You will further our studies. That is all you need to know." He turned to Braydac. "Take her to Madhur."

I tried to protest, but Braydac grabbed my arm and pulled me to a standing position. We were suddenly standing outside another metal door. The dizziness wasn't as intense this time.

I turned to him. "Why are you helping them?"

"Money."

"You're disgusting."

"I know."

He waved his hand at the sensor and we went inside. This room wasn't set up like an office and it chilled me to my core. There were two hospital beds on the back wall of the room, with weird contraptions bolted to the edges and straps across the mattresses. There were various pieces of equipment around the room and an assortment of strange and deadly-looking instruments on trays on a bench top.

I felt lightheaded. Even Braydac looked a little pale. What were they going to do to me?

A door on the right-hand side of the room swished open and a man with the same creepy orange eyes as Saizen strode in. I instinctively took a step back. He was taller than both of us and seemed to have an ice-cold air about him.

"I am Doctor Jozean Madhur. I will be running some tests today." He looked at Braydac. "You will sit there," he pointed to a chair in the corner, "and block her so I can get on with my work."

Braydac looked annoyed at being treated like a child, but nodded.

Madhur kept staring at him. "Well, go on!"

Now Braydac looked like he wanted to hit something, but he turned and sat down.

I tried not to cringe when Madhur looked at me. "Well. There you are. We'll see what makes you tick."

My blood ran cold as my mind conjured up all sorts of terrib e scenarios.

His eyes were intense and there was no hint of a smile. "Now. Sit on the bed."

I hesitated.

"NOW!"

I quickly scrambled onto the nearest bed and sat facing him.

"First, all the boring stuff." He looked at Braydac. "You. Take the cuffs off her, and keep blocking her." To me he said, "You'll not try anything stupid."

He glanced over his shoulder and I could see two guards standing just inside the door armed with stunners, and laser pistols at their hips.

Braydac removed the cuffs. Madhur took my blood pressure. My temperature. Took blood. Tested reflexes. Tested hearing. Tested eyesight.

He was right. It was boring. I couldn't stop thinking about Darion and Janssen and the others, and Braydac sat there casually, blocking my Talent. I'd push against the sludge in my mind every now and then to see if it was still there and I couldn't help wondering how long he could keep it up. Surely it would take a lot of energy to keep going for such a long time.

He looked across at me with narrowed eyes. Maybe he could hear my thoughts. I pushed my mental shield higher to keep him out.

Why could I still do that? Wasn't he blocking me?

Then I realized that creating a mental shield in your mind didn't require Talent. Anyone could do it. A lot of non-Talented people were trained in how to create a mental shield because Telepaths were one of the most common types of Talent. Some were totally paranoid, of course, thinking that Telepaths just go around reading people's minds at will, but there were laws against that. They had to have permission, unless they were members of law enforcement.

That was just another thing I'd remembered without any effort. But why couldn't I remember important things about Jarleth or Darion or what Dr Starrick had done to me?

It was beyond frustrating.

"Doctor?"

"What?" he snapped.

I almost changed my mind with the tone he'd used, but I needed to know. "What do you want from me?"

"I want you to lie down and shut up so I can check your blood pressure again."

"No, I mean, what do you want me for? Why am I here?"

"Saizen didn't tell you?"

I shook my head.

"I thought he'd want to gloat." He scratched his chin, those orange eyes creeping me out. "We want to duplicate Starrick's work."

Was that it? He wasn't going to say any more?

"What do you mean?"

"Are you thick? He managed to transfer your mind into this body without damaging your brain, but then, the pinnacle of perfection, he transferred the psychic abilities *only* across to another patient without damage."

"Who?" I'd been told it was Larissa, but I wanted to hear it from him.

"It doesn't matter. She now has the same abilities as you, but has retained the rest of her own mind. With a little intensive training, she will be battle-ready in a short period of time."

CHAPTER 39
Should I Have Let Him Kill You?

"Battle-ready?" I couldn't keep the waver from my voice.

"Yes. This venture started off as a 'see what we can do' kind of thing. Then it was a 'see if we can develop these psychic abilities for our people.' Now the military have taken it upon themselves to up this into a way to create the perfect soldier and the perfect first class of citizen. For the elite of our species only, of course. We are ready to begin the next phase of our plan now that you are here."

I couldn't speak. I was shocked beyond words. They were absolutely insane.

"The other specimen went back to her home world of Shakira, but has been found. She will soon be here."

"No!"

That confirmed it was Larissa. And now she was on her way here to help them create these super soldiers too. I hoped that we could get through this somehow. And I hoped that Darion and Janssen were alright.

"You have no say in it. She will further our research."

No...

I had to get out of here. I had to warn someone. But how could anyone find me? Where would they even start? We'd just disappeared right in front of them, and I'd been teleported a second time to this place.

"Where are we?"

"You don't know?"

I shook my head.

"We are at Dekora Corporation."

"Okay, but where is that?"

He laughed loudly. "The planet Korovska."

Wait, what? Braydac could teleport to *another planet*? How was that even possible?

There was a smirk on his face. I quickly looked away, not wanting him to see the awe on my face a second longer.

Madhur straightened. "Right. I've had enough of you for now. Get out of my sight."

Braydac took me to a place to get something to eat. I was so hungry. I couldn't remember the last time I'd eaten.

It looked like a small cafeteria and brought back a memory from my childhood on Earth at the Academy, sitting with a room full of children, all eating, hardly talking, all wearing the same clothing, all the same expressions on their faces. My childhood was ordered and sterile and... boring.

The food here wasn't recognisable, but most of the goopy stuff tasted okay. It was easy on my sore throat, so I guess there was that.

Braydac ate about half of what was on his plate, so maybe he didn't like it that much either.

"Where are you from?" I asked him.

"Not here," was all he said.

I rolled my eyes. "Okay, but where?"

Silence.

Okay. Whatever.

I finished eating and he took me to a room with an en-suite bathroom and told me to wash up and put on the clothes that were folded neatly on the shelf in there. He left the room and the door's lock clicked in place.

I showered, scrubbing at my skin to make sure there was no dried blood left on me, the images of Nykolar's vacant eyes and bloodied body replaying in my mind.

I hesitated to put on the drab, dark grey, pyjama-like sleeveless top and long pants. Even the undergarments were grey and there were grey shoes and socks on the floor. I didn't want to wear clothes doled out to me by these people, but there wasn't anything else to wear. And I wasn't about to put my bloodied skins and boots back on.

Afterwards, sitting alone in the room, it hit me that I really was stuck here. No one was coming to get me. No one would think to look for me on another planet.

I tried to lift one of my boots with my mind, but there was nothing but sludge in my brain. I wondered how long he could keep this up and whether he had help. Then I started to wonder if he had to be close to me for it to work. Probably. This stuff would be good to know if I was going to get out of here.

And I needed to get out of here.

I didn't know how long they were going to keep me here, so I decided that I should try to keep fit by doing some exercises and practice some of the self-defence techniques that I'd learned.

I had only been doing the exercises for a few minutes when I felt a wave of exhaustion hit me. I stopped and sat on the edge of the bed. I knew that I'd had a rough day, but it was weird that the tiredness had hit so suddenly.

I gave in to it, kicking off my shoes and lying down. I fell asleep almost instantly.

It took me a while to remember where I was when I opened my eyes, panting and panicked. I'd been dreaming about being trapped in the dark, not being able to move or see, and the blanket was twisted around my legs.

Braydac showed up right after I'd gone to the bathroom and changed into some clean clothes. They were the same dark grey colour, but the pants looked more like cargo pants. He took me to eat breakfast, then back to that horrible room.

The testing lasted for hours.

They took me to another part of the facility to a swimming pool so I could swim around underwater. I'd done this before, I realized. I remembered the tank at Station Maztec and being stared at by Dr Starrick and his scientists.

Some were physical fitness tests; some were for intelligence. Some brought back memories, others didn't.

I spent a long time sitting with a wiring harness on my head that had a web of wires coming out of it while Madhur watched the screens for the results and took notes on a Palm-pad.

I needed to get out of here, but how?

I needed help to escape, but didn't have any credits or anything of value to offer Braydac, so he wouldn't help me. In any case, I'd never be able to match the large amount of credits they'd be paying him.

I needed a plan. I wondered if I could strengthen my mental shield enough to stop Braydac from blocking me. If it could block thoughts and intrusion, I didn't see why it couldn't block a block. There was only one way to find out if I was right.

That was at least part of a plan.

———◦———

When we finally went to the empty cafeteria for our evening meal, I tried to get some answers out of Braydac.

"What's in it for you?" I asked, "I mean, besides the money?"

"Nothing." He looked across to me. "Just the money."

"They must be paying you a lot to babysit me all the time."

He smirked. "Yes."

I tried to sound casual. "Are there other Blockers here?"

"No. Blockers are extremely rare."

I'd thought so because I'd never heard of them. But then, what would I know? I stirred my goop. "How did the Korovska find you?"

"I contract out."

"You kidnap people for money?"

A smile crept across his face as he leaned back in his seat. "I do a lot of things for money. Things that would make your hair stand on end."

The hairs on the back of my neck did stand on end. "Why?"

"For the money."

"Yeah, I know that, but... don't you care about the people you hurt? Didn't you care about Nykolar?"

"Should I have let him kill you?"

"No!" I ran a hand through my hair. "I mean, doesn't it bother you that you killed him?"

"No. He was a crazy Korovskan with a death wish, going against his people like that."

"Korovskan? How come he didn't have orange eyes?"

"He did. Contacts."

"Oh."

"And if I had to listen to him complain about how uncomfortable they were one more time, he probably would have been dead sooner."

We ate in silence for a while.

"What about these experiments? Aren't you worried?"

He sighed. "About what?"

I looked him in the eye. "About what they'll do once they've got their army of super soldiers."

"It won't affect me. I'll be outta here soon."

"What if they try to take over the galaxy or something?"

"I don't live in this galaxy."

"So, you don't care about anyone but yourself."

"You're so observant."

"What if—" I decided that maybe the rest of our conversation should be private. There were cameras everywhere, and our guards were standing near the door to the cafeteria. I thought my next words, knowing he would hear them and could *send* thoughts to me in return. *What if they decide that they want your Talent?*

He quirked an eyebrow. *"What do you mean?"*

You said that your Talent for blocking is very rare.

"Yeah, so?"

They might decide to add that Talent to mine. It would make their super soldiers even more powerful and deadly.

"No. They won't do that."

How do you know that for sure?

He was silent.

Chapter 40
We Always Have a Choice

The next day, after the usual physical tests, Madhur asked me about my memories and how much I could remember about my life. He looked very unimpressed when I told him that most of it was still blank and that recalling memories seemed to give me a headache — which was true some of the time. I didn't add that each time I remembered something traumatic, I'd damaged any nearby objects. He didn't need to know that. Plus, with Braydac there to block my Talent, it shouldn't be an issue.

"Right," he said. "We want to know the extent of your Talent. I was told that you were T1 material, but I never believe what I hear."

"Um, I'm not sure how you can test that." I looked at Braydac.

"It is quite simple. The boy here will drop his hold on you long enough for you to be tested and if you try anything, you will be punished." He didn't need to point out the guards in the room.

My stomach dropped. I remembered the horrible pain from the stunner blast and every muscle contracting. I'd lost control of my body and couldn't stop myself from falling backwards into the river.

I tried to focus on the conversation. "Uh, I don't know how accurate the tests will be."

"What are you talking about?"

"I forgot everything and have just started training again. I can't do much yet." I felt small and useless.

Madhur pinched the bridge of his nose and sighed heavily. "You're giving me a headache." He paced the room and came back, waving a hand impatiently. "Just do it."

He put the wiring harness on my head and told me to lie down. "Now, I want you to have a telepathic conversation with each other."

"Okay," I said. I took a deep breath and let it out slowly. My head seemed to clear.

"Tamisan?" Braydac ventured.

"Yes."

"So, what do you want to talk about?"

I scowled at him. *"Oh, that's funny. I don't want to talk to you."*

"Yeah, well. We don't have a choice, do we?"

I sighed. *"We always have a choice. We could just pretend to be having a conversation. They wouldn't know any better."*

"Yes, they would. They are monitoring your brain activity right now. If we stop talking, the readings will show it."

I looked over at the screen showing graphs and lines moving up and down. *"Great."*

"Well, we just need to communicate for a while about whatever."

"Like, the reason why I'm here? That's your fault. You're the asshole that brought me here."

He crossed his muscular arms. *"Yep. And I told you, it's nothin' personal. Just the money."*

I glared at him. *"In my books, no amount of money justifies ruining a person's life — probably ending it."*

His eyebrows rose. *"Ending it?"*

"Yes. What do you think happens when they've gotten what they want from me?"

"They will wipe your memories of this place and let you go."

"Really? Is that what they told you? You don't even know if they are capable of wiping selected memories. And it would be easier and quicker to kill me." My blood ran cold just thinking it.

He shook his head.

"And as I've said, you'll be next. And maybe they'll just get rid of you too, just to make sure you don't change your mind or maybe tell someone in exchange for money. They know you'll do anything for the right price."

"No. You've got that wrong."

"Have I?"

"Right, that's enough. Block her."

The heaviness returned. *I should have tried to do something while he wasn't blocking me... But what?*

"It wouldn't have worked," Braydac said. *"I would have blocked you faster than you could blink."*

His smirk was infuriating.

Madhur typed furiously on a touchpad before turning back to us. "Now for telekinesis." He pulled a small table with wheels on it over to the bed and placed a ball on it. "Move this. Lift it up into the air."

I hesitated. "I'll try."

"No. Don't *try*. Do it!"

I didn't answer. I knew there was no point in trying to make him understand that I might not be able to do it. I took another deep breath, feeling the heavy feeling disappear and resisting the urge to look at Braydac.

I concentrated on the ball.

Nothing.

It was hard to focus with Madhur standing there with his arms folded.

It took several attempts to make it move and several more to lift it off the table.

"Finally," Madhur said, moving to his computer and reading the data, all the while muttering about what a weak display I'd given.

The guard by the door looked at me with an expression of awe. I wondered if Talent was rare with the Korovska, or maybe it was non-existent and that was why they were doing all of these experiments in the first place. That would explain a lot. If there were Talented people in their race, they would probably be using them as test subjects instead of me.

Once Madhur had finished, he glared at me. "Right. What else can you do?"

"What?"

"Are you deaf?"

"No. I'm not sure what you mean."

"You're rated as a T1. You are a Telepath and a Kinetic. What else?"

There was nothing else. I started to shake my head, but then Braydac decided to blurt out that I could teleport as well.

Chapter 41

I Don't Care What They do to Me

If that was true, then he'd just let them know one more of my secrets. I wanted to punch him in the face. "How do you know that?"

"I worked at Jannali. I heard Darion talk about it. How you teleported yourself out of harm's way when you were trapped by two battling dinosaurs. You ported Darion to you when you were in those caves and he was a prisoner of Doctor Starrick. You even helped him port people back to Jannali from the jungle."

I stared at him. "But I don't remember doing any of that."

Madhur groaned. "This memory thing is slowing everything down." He looked at me with those intense, creepy, orange eyes. "So now you're going to tell me we can't test your teleporting abilities because you don't remember how to do it?"

"Yes. That's exactly what I'm going to say." The fury was written on his face. "I didn't even remember that I could do it."

He turned on his heel and growled like an animal, disappearing out the door. "This is not acceptable! Take her away!"

That afternoon, they were finally ready to attempt the transfer of my brainwaves to someone else. Well, only the part that was responsible for my psychic abilities. They called the procedure the Eibhlin Process. From what I understood of it, it wasn't painful, but the thought of it terrified me anyway.

They would map out my brainwaves and transfer them to a machine, then they'd be able to transfer the data held to the minds of as many people as they wished. If it worked, these people would inherit my Talent.

This was the procedure they'd used to transfer my consciousness to Sifayah. They'd transferred all of my thoughts and memories and my whole consciousness, and somehow replaced her thoughts, but not her memories.

They were not aware that Sifayah had any psychic abilities, so that area of her brain had remained intact afterwards. It was an accidental stroke of genius.

I was worried about something going wrong, both with me and with whoever they tried to transfer part of my mind to, but I was also worried about the end result if it was successful. They were about to give a whole bunch of people powerful psychic abilities that they didn't know how to control. I'd been in that situation with forgetting my training and the chaos I'd caused still made me feel nauseous.

I looked around me. We were in another room with two beds side-by-side and a huge machine humming in the corner. Braydac lay on the other bed, but he wasn't part of the procedure. He was just there to keep control over me.

I wondered how he could keep blocking me all day. No wonder he looked tired.

And how did he know when he could let go and get some sleep? What would happen if I woke up before he did? Could I escape?

Probably not. I'd forgotten how to teleport and trying blindly would be dangerous. I imagined porting to outer space and dying before I could get myself away from there. I shuddered.

I focused on my mental shield. Blocking him out might be easier while he was tired.

The wiring harness was placed carefully on my head and I was told to lie back and relax. Easy for them to say.

I didn't want to be here and I really wanted them to fail at this. Could I do something to mess this up for them? I tried to come up with things that could block them or mess with the signals going from my brain to the machine, but what if I somehow damaged my own mind in the process? I couldn't risk it. This whole thing was scary enough without me trying to tamper with things. I decided that it would be safer to do everything they told me to do.

Then I thought about whoever they would be using for this experiment. What if I deliberately messed it up, and it messed up the other person's mind when they did the transfer? What if it was irreversible? I couldn't do that to someone else — even if they were someone I didn't know.

My hearts pounded. My breathing sped up. Just because I'd been told that it wouldn't hurt, didn't mean that I actually believed them. They'd tell me anything to get what they wanted.

So I laid my head down against the uncomfortable pillow and tried my best, but could not fully relax.

"I can't get a proper read," Madhur said. He wasn't talking to me, I realized. He was talking to Braydac. "You'll have to stop blocking her."

Braydac nodded and I felt my mind clear. I also saw the guards step closer.

The time dragged on and I found myself wishing they'd play some music or something to help ease the boredom. They were obviously interested in what they were doing, but I just wanted to go back to that stupid little room. That seemed like a silly thing to want, but anywhere else would be better than here.

"That's it," Madhur announced. "You, block her." He pulled the wiring harness off my head and turned to the guards. "Get her out of here."

That's it? Good. I was beyond relieved that it had not been painful. I turned to Braydac. "I'm hungry."

"You're always hungry."

<hr />

Braydac looked uncomfortable sitting on the bed next to mine with a wiring harness on his head. He'd refused to talk to me and he looked at me with a scowl.

"Hey, don't look at me like that. This wasn't my idea," I told him. I realized that he wasn't blocking me.

His scowl smoothed out a fraction. *"I know."*

Madhur had informed us of a change in plan when we'd arrived that morning.

"What do you mean?" I'd asked.

"I think that these results would improve if we removed your memory block."

I felt my body tense up. What did he have in mind for that?

Braydac tensed when he turned to him. "You will solve this problem for us."

"What? What do you want from me? I'm already stuck here babysitting her for you."

"Be quiet. I don't pay you to complain. You will do one of those Mind-link things and start mining her memories and bringing them out."

"What?"

"Are you deaf?"

"No."

"Then this is what you are going to do. We start now."

So we'd been wired up together.

"Okay," Madhur said cheerfully, "let's get on with it. You do your Mind-link thing and be quick about it."

"You know that it's risky to do this," Braydac said. "Playing around inside someone's head can cause damage if you're not careful."

"Well, *be* careful." His tone left no room for argument.

I stared at Braydac, worried about what he was going to do.

He lay back on the bed and clasped his hands together over his stomach. "Sit back and relax, Tamisan. This is gonna take a while. Might as well get comfortable."

I cringed and lay back as well. There was no way I could relax. I didn't want him poking around in my head. I'd had enough of that back at the Waikari village. And I would've preferred Tasha to do this. At least I could trust her.

As I took a deep breath and let it out, I could feel Braydac's presence and my first instinct was to push him out.

"Hey, don't push me away. You know we have to do this or the consequences will be bad."

"I don't care what they do to me."

"Oh, you will. And they probably won't do much to you. You're their prized monkey. They'll probably take it out on me and make you watch."

"What? No!"

CHAPTER 42

Rylar

"Yeah. They will. So let's just do this." He paused. *"Besides, if I can bring your memories back, that would be a good thing, wouldn't it?"*

"Yes."

"Okay, so get out of my way."

I sighed. He was right. I needed to let my shield drop completely if I was going to get my mind back. But letting him in was hard. He was the enemy.

He started to dig around for my lost memories and found something from my childhood. I was sitting in a classroom with a lot of other kids my age. Each of us had a computer screen in front of us and we were all reading the same words at the same time.

Then we were all sitting down at long tables eating food and drinking red liquid from white cups. We were all dressed the same and all the girls had their hair the same. Shoulder length. The boys all had short back and sides, just like in that other memory I'd seen.

It was like I was watching a Vid screen and I just sat back and watched parts of my life go by. Learning, playing, eating, sleeping, rinse and repeat. Boring.

It changed to Sifayah's memories of her growing up in the village with her family and friends around her. Learning how to hunt and prepare food, playing, diving off the rocks at the Dive, climbing rocks up the sides of the cliffs surrounding the village, climbing trees, discovering her Talent and being trained by Tasha.

It was hard work going through my past and some parts were emotional, especially when I thought about how Sifayah's friends and family had lost her all over again.

Then I reached the memory of the death of little Rylar, and things slowed down as if my mind wanted to torture me.

I had been told to take Rylar and Axiak across from the small island not far from Akilina Cove back to our village, but I hadn't wanted to do it. Sometimes they felt like a burden to me when I had to look after them instead of doing whatever I wanted to do.

We were swimming in the open ocean and they were going too slow. Of course they were slower than me. I'd accepted that — they were only four years old — but they were playing around and twirling and flipping over in the water and wouldn't listen to me.

"Come on!" I scolded. *"We need to get back home before dark."*

They laughed and kept playing around.

I'd had enough of their games. *"Fine. You keep playing. I'm going home."*

I swam away from them, thinking they'd soon stop their nonsense and catch up to me.

I kept going, waiting for them to call out for me to stop and wait. It didn't happen. I looked back to see where they were and my hearts stopped. In the shadowy depths, I could see the dark shape growing bigger, heading straight for the boys.

I started swimming back to them. *"Rylar! Axiak! Come here right now! You need to swim really fast!"*

"Why?" They both asked.

I was getting closer to them, but so was the Water Dragon. *"There's a Water Dragon. Behind you. You need to come here now!"*

I could see the panicked looks on their faces. They started to swim toward me, but the distance was too great. I needed to reach them before the deadly creature so I could use my Gift to force it away. I couldn't do that until I was holding the boys, or I'd push them towards it.

My hearts pounded as I swam. Adrenalin surged through me, propelling me forward. I reached out my hands for them. I grabbed Axiak first as he was closer, and as I reached for Rylar, the dragon's jaws closed around his legs. He let out a scream in the water and a scream with his mind and it almost deafened me. It mixed with mine and Axiak's screams and all I could do was watch the dragon take Rylar away into the depths of the ocean and out of sight.

I couldn't hold it together any longer. I ripped the wiring harness off my head and leapt off the bed.

"What are you doing? Get back there and keep going!" Madhur roared.

"No!" I screamed, and his body flew backwards and hit the opposite wall. That was what I needed to do to the Water Dragon, but it was too late. Rylar was gone. As Madhur crumpled to the floor, I ran out of the room, not even stopping to wonder why it was unlocked.

I could hear Madhur's voice as I ran down the hallway. "Stop her!"

CHAPTER 43
You Will Pay for This!

Tears ran down my face as I tried to find somewhere to go to escape them. I could see Rylar's face in my mind. I could hear Braydac running behind me, and although I didn't know where I was going, I was determined to outrun him.

"Tamisan, wait!" he called, but I kept going, trying to escape the memory. The guilt.

I darted around a corner to the left, wondering where my room was or if I even wanted to go there and ended up running into a body that felt like hitting a brick wall. I fell backwards onto my butt and hurt my left wrist when I tried to stop my fall.

I cried out in pain and was almost trampled from behind by a burly Korovskan guard who was twice as wide as Braydac as he tried not to fall on top of me.

I looked up to see who I'd run into and it was Braydac. *What?*

He must have teleported ahead to stop me.

The guard glared at me and turned to Braydac. "Get her under control, Azaeli scum, and get her back to the lab."

Braydac tried to pull off a smirk, but it didn't quite work while he was looking up at the guard. He turned back to me and scowled. "What are you trying to pull?"

My mind was still in the memory. The guilt was eating me from the inside out. "Poor Rylar! It's my fault! It's all my fault! He's dead because of me!"

"Calm down! It's just a memory, and it's not even *your* memory. You weren't there. It was Sifayan."

"But—"

"No buts. You weren't there. You didn't do it. Just stop."

"Rylar—"

"Wasn't even your brother—"

"But it *feels* like he was. Don't you understand? You saw what I saw!"

His eyebrows tilted upward. He knew. It probably upset him too, but he wasn't about to let me know that.

I sighed. "She blamed herself for what happened."

"I know. But you can't do anything about it now. We have to go back."

"No!" More tears streamed down my face. *"Can't you get them to stop, just for today?"*

"I can try, but you shoved him across the room." He cringed. *"How did I do that? I thought you were blocking me."*

His face hardened. *"I was distracted. It won't happen again."*

"You were *upset by those memories."*

"Shut up!" "Get up. Let's go."

He grabbed me by the arm and I winced and gave a little yelp. Maybe I'd sprained my wrist or something. It wouldn't have surprised me.

He marched me back to the lab and the closer we got, the more nervous he became. Sweat beaded along his forehead. I started to wonder what he had to be nervous about. I was the one that threw the douchebag across the room. But then I remembered what he'd said about them not wanting to damage me because they needed me for their experiments.

We walked into the room and Madhur was standing there with a hand pressed to the back of his head. His face was pure hatred as he stepped forward. "Look what you've done to me!" he shouted, pulling his hand away to show a bloodied cloth. "You will pay for this!"

I cringed and tried to step back away from him, but Braydac held me in place. Madhur slapped me across the face, hard, and my head jerked to the side. Pain exploded in my cheek and tears filled my eyes.

The doctor turned to Braydac. "And you!" I felt Braydac tense up. "You're supposed to be stopping her from doing this sort of thing! What are we paying you for? I've a mind to tear up our contract right now!"

"It was a minor distraction—"

"Minor? She could have killed me! You better start doing your job right! Now get back on the cots, both of you!"

We headed over and the uncomfortable wiring harnesses were put back on our heads. Just when I thought the doctor was going to get on with what we were doing, he turned to Braydac and pulled out a stunner. Up close, I could see that there was something different about the Korovskan design.

"You need to learn a lesson, Novak."

He pulled the wiring harness back off Braydac's head. My eyes went wide as he pointed the stunner at Braydac and fired.

A stunner blast usually made every muscle contract before you lost consciousness. This stunner was different. Madhur kept his finger on the trigger, which caused Braydac's whole body to keep convulsing. The seconds ticked by and it didn't stop, and when I looked at Madhur's face, he was enjoying it!

You bastard! "Stop it!"

In my anger, I pushed the stunner out of his hand and onto the floor. He turned to me with a look of horror on his face and I realized that Braydac wasn't blocking me. The doctor was an idiot. How could Braydac keep blocking me while he was being electrocuted?

I pushed the wires off my head again. "Leave him alone!"

The fear on Madhur's face was priceless. "Guards!"

Two men in uniform entered the room and I pushed them away from me with my mind. One of them fell backwards out the door and the other fell on top of him.

"GUARDS! GET IN HERE!"

I couldn't help the smile that spread across my face at how terrified he was.

"Braydac! Stop her! That's an order!"

I glanced at Braydac. He was still recovering from the stunner and was only now becoming aware of the situation.

I *pushed* slowly so that Madhur had to walk backwards to avoid falling over until he was standing up against the wall that he'd smashed into before. "You need to stop trying to play God with people's lives."

CHAPTER 44
Chaos Reigned

His eye twitched and he looked to Braydac for help. "I will have you tortured and killed if you don't stop her now!"

As the two guards got to their feet and three more entered the room, I felt the block return. "No!"

Two of them grabbed my arms and held me in place. "What do you want us to do with her, Doctor?"

He slapped me across the face again. My head jerked to the side again and the pain was unbearable. "Get her out of my sight! Take her back to her room." He gestured towards Braydac. "Him too."

Braydac was still dazed, but was somehow able to keep a hold on my mind.

We were taken back to my room and I was shoved inside. I heard the door lock behind me.

I lay down on the bed and fell asleep before I could even start to think about what had happened.

<hr />

Braydac was standing outside the door the next morning when it swished open. I'd woken up wondering how I'd even fallen asleep after what had happened the day before. And my stomach was reminding me I'd skipped dinner.

The left side of my face had looked terrible in the bathroom mirror. A bruise the shape of Madhur's hand had formed across my cheek and my eye was slightly swollen. I imagined both sides looking like that and was glad that he'd slapped the same cheek. Well, *glad* was probably the wrong word.

Braydac looked at my face and winced. "Come," he said gruffly. He turned on his heel, expecting me to follow him.

I wanted to protest. I wanted to tell him to drop his hold on my mind and help me get out of here. But I didn't. What else could I do? He was the enemy. He was one of them, even if he wasn't Korovskan. What did that guard call him? Azaeli scum. That must be where he was from.

The guards waited for me, but Braydac walked ahead.

As I entered that horrible room, I couldn't help feeling uneasy. The last time I was in this room was disturbing. It wasn't just the memory of losing poor Rylar, but the way Madhur treated Braydac, who was supposed to be on their side. He'd enjoyed torturing him. I resisted the urge to touch my bruised face.

Madhur was there to meet us and I cringed inside. How was I going to do this again? I needed to somehow find the strength to endure this until all my memories returned. After that, I wasn't really sure what they were going to do to me. The Eibhlin Process didn't hurt before, so it was safe to assume that it would be the same the next time, but after they'd done it, then what? Do I just wait around in that cell they called a room and wait to see if it worked?

"Sit down, both of you," Madhur said. His tone was deadly.

I looked around. There were two guards inside the room and four outside. One of them looked human. That was odd, I thought.

We had no choice but to obey. I sat and waited for the wiring harness.

He looked at me. "You will be trained so that you are battle-ready. You may be needed. After all, you have an advantage over the other soldiers that we are creating."

"Yeah? What's that?"

"Your ability to breathe underwater."

My hearts sank. They were going to add that too? "But that isn't something you can just transfer with a machine."

"That is true, but that is not included in this phase of our plan. That is part of a long-term goal. And we are a patient people. We have been doing this for centuries."

My chest felt tight. I hoped that the genetic experiments on the Altharian natives had not been painful. If the scientists responsible were anything like Madhur, then they probably were.

It seemed like he was waiting for something. Did he want me to comment on that? I didn't know what to say, so I stayed silent.

He grabbed the wiring harness, quickly put it on my head and looked at Braydac as if he expected him to put his on himself. I doubted Braydac knew how.

Madhur sighed and put it on. "Now, hurry this up. You're wasting time."

We settled down onto the beds and the whole thing started again. More memories of my past were dug up, and it was mortifying when Braydac could see the times I — I mean Sifayah — spent alone with Jarleth, walking along the beach, swimming through the ocean and standing together at the Dive. All the times she was in his arms, kissing and making plans for the future. The love she felt for him swirled through me. The way she melted in his arms when he kissed her. It was like how I felt when Darion kissed me. I could really see now how much they loved each other. No wonder Jarleth was so hurt.

Things shifted to the moment I woke up in this body and Dr Starrick was explaining everything to me, then shifted to when I found out that it was all a lie. There were no pirates. It was a group of men working for Starrick. They made it look convincing, but were only there to capture us and fake our deaths so we could be used for Starrick's experiments. They killed the pilot straight away in case he recognized them. And a few more of my friends were killed when the experiments went wrong. I felt the loss of those people like a sharp knife in my chest.

I remembered talking telepathically to Darion while walking along in chains after the Bahadori had captured me. I wondered how I'd gotten away from them, but my mind wouldn't go there. It took me to the moment I'd met Darion, which I didn't want Braydac to see, and to us getting back to Station Jannali. Then there were more moments with Darion that I wished could be private, but I couldn't stop them from coming and couldn't stop Braydac from seeing them.

And I had to put up with it if I wanted to remember.

There was Darion helping me get through the nightmares after I'd made it to Station Jannali. Lying together in the night, kissing him and feeling all the wonderful emotions running through both of our hearts and minds. Him standing by me when we were surrounded by Starrick and his men.

A lot of things flashed through my head too fast to work out what they were and where they fit, but it all slowed down when

I got to one of Starrick bursting through a door and stabbing me in the neck with something sharp. The horrible thing about remembering everything was reliving all the pain and emotion all over again. I felt the contents of the syringe spread through my body, relived trying to escape him and then me chasing him, full of whatever drug he'd given me. I was crazy and out of control. I wanted to hurt him.

Then I saw the things that happened in the generator room. I started to become paralysed and the generators were going to overload. It was still hard to believe that I'd done all of this, but it had happened. Then I'd lifted myself up in the air. I'd been basically flying and didn't even realise it at the time.

Things turned horrific when I ended up back in that place where I couldn't see and couldn't move. The source of my nightmares. My breathing was shallow and I couldn't help panicking.

Braydac's voice burst into my mind. *"It's just a memory, Tamisan. Calm down."*

"I can't! I can't move! I can hardly breathe! I've gotta get out of here! Help! Someone help me!"

"Stop! It's a memory! It's not happening now!"

I opened my eyes to see that chaos reigned. Various pieces of equipment were flying around the room and people were running and ducking out the way.

CHAPTER 45

They Won't Let You Walk Out of Here

"Tamisan! Stop!" Braydac yelled.

I could feel him trying to block me and pushed my mental shield up. "No!"

I wanted the things to stop flying around because I didn't want to get hit by a flying scalpel, but I didn't want Braydac to take over again. I fought against him and the heaviness started to clear. Me practicing blocking him was paying off.

"Stop her, Braydac! Do you hear me?" roared Madhur.

Braydac was standing next to my bed now. "Tamisan!" *"Stop this! Remember what happened yesterday?"*

Everything in the room fell to the floor with a loud clatter. I remembered. I didn't want to see him hurt again.

Madhur stood up straighter. "Guards! Get them out of here! Now!"

We were both man-handled out of the room and marched down the hallways that led to my room. Things were getting crazy. The more I remembered, the more traumatic the memories got. What kind of life did I have? What horrors would I remember next? Maybe it would be better to leave them buried. But I knew that wasn't an option. Madhur was going to make Braydac keep going until there was nothing left to dig up.

The door slid shut behind me.

I sat on the bed and thought about all the things I'd just dug up. It was amazing. The things I could do were amazing. No wonder they'd hired a Blocker.

My thoughts shifted to Darion. I was so in love with him, but felt guilty about Jarleth. It wasn't like I'd cheated on Jarleth. He was Sifayah's love, not mine, but knowing that didn't make me feel any better.

My stomach growled. I hadn't had any dinner last night and hadn't had any breakfast either and it was probably past lunch time now.

I walked over to the door and pounded on it with my fist. "Hey! I'm starving! I need some food!"

No response.

"Hey! You haven't fed me all day! I'm no use to you if I'm dead!"

A shiver went down my spine at the thought.

I kept yelling and pounding until the door slid open and Braydac stood there glaring at me. "When are you going to learn to shut up?"

"I'm starving! I didn't have dinner last night and I haven't eaten all day!"

He turned to one of the guards, who gave a curt nod. "Let's go."

———◆———

Once we'd started eating, I tried to relax. My stomach was in knots, making it hard to swallow, but I was too hungry. I had to eat.

Battle-ready. What did that even mean? Were they going to teach me how to fight, how to shoot, or just how to use my Talent to hurt and kill? Whatever it entailed, I wanted nothing to do with it.

Yes, I needed to learn how to defend myself, but I didn't want to fight whatever battles they had in mind. I didn't even know who they intended to fight against. It was all too much.

I looked across at Braydac. By the way he was eating, I'd say he hadn't eaten since lunch time the day before either.

He wasn't blocking me, so I asked him if he knew what they meant by 'battle-ready.'

"What do you think it means?"

"It could mean a lot of things. Do they mean hand-to-hand combat? Weapons training? Using my Talent?"

"Probably all of the above."

I cringed. *"I don't want to be turned into a soldier."*

"You don't have a choice."

"Yes, I do. You can help me escape."

"No can do."

"Really? All you care about is the money? After the way he treated you?"

"That wouldn't have happened if you hadn't lost your shit."

I stood up. *"So it's my fault? That's just pathetic."*

"Sit down! Don't draw attention to yourself."

The guard at the door was glaring at me. I reluctantly sat back down again and stirred my goop. *"It's not going to get better, you know. Next time, it will be something worse."*

"You better make sure there isn't a next time."

"I couldn't help it! He was torturing you! You should have seen his face! He was enjoying it!"

Braydac winced, then he frowned. *"Why did you defend me?"*

"Because it's not right. You looked like you were in agony."

"Yeah, but I'm the enemy. I brought you here. Why do you care what happens to me?"

"Because I'm not like them. And because there's good in you. I know it."

He straightened. *"No there isn't."*

"You can't fool me with your attitude. I know."

He gave a snort.

I could tell by his reaction to my memory of Rylar and could sense it when our minds were linked. He could say he didn't care a million times over, but I knew better.

I took a sip of my water. *"So, what are you gonna do when they decide they want to use you too?"*

"They won't."

Not this again. *"You don't know that. They're going to use me for as long as they can. They're going to transfer your Talent too. Maybe if they find out that your teleportation skills are better than mine, they'll use that instead. Once they've finished with us, they'll kill us."*

"No."

"Yes. We know too much."

"How do you know that my skills are better?"

"I can't remember how to do it, but I'm pretty sure, from my patchy memory, that no one else can teleport to another planet."

He went quiet.

"I'm right, aren't I?"

No answer. I knew it.

"I want you to help me get out of here. We both need to escape before it's too late."

Nothing.

"If you don't help me, I'll tell them your little secret."

"What secret?"

"About your porting skills."

"No, you won't. I'll make you regret it."

"I don't care anymore. Do what you want. I need to get out of here. Help me escape or I'll tell him."

"Blackmail. I thought you said you weren't like me."

"I'm not. But this is life and death."

"You don't know that for sure."

"I'm ninety-nine percent sure that neither of us is getting out of here alive."

"You're so melodramatic."

"You know I'm right."

He shook his head. "No. I'm gonna hurry up and get your memories back, then I'm outta here."

"They won't let you walk out of here."

He shoved the block back in place and looked away.

CHAPTER 46

Turak

The next morning, I moaned when I remembered where I was and what I would be forced to do as soon as we arrived at that room. I wanted my memories back, but I wished there was an easier way.

I just want to go home... But where is home? Station Jannali? It's definitely not Akilina Cove...

Thinking about the Waikari just made me sad. I felt so terrible about how I'd just left them. They were probably looking for me again. I wished I could go back there and explain things now that I knew more about what had happened. It would break their hearts. It would be like Sifayah was dead and in a way, she was.

My cheeks warmed when I thought about how many memories I'd recovered in front of Braydac. He had no right to intrude on my privacy and to see every little detail, feel what I'd felt. It made me feel vulnerable.

I pushed those thoughts aside and forced myself to get up and get ready before Braydac arrived. I hoped that we were going to be able to eat something first.

Once I was ready, the door swished open and Braydac stood waiting.

"Why do you turn up just when I've finished getting ready? Is there a camera in here or something?"

I'm an idiot. Of course there is. I looked around the room. So they were watching me get dressed? My face flushed red.

"Yes. Of course there is. What did you expect?"

My anger welled inside me. "But why are you watching me?"

"Don't worry. There's no camera in the bathroom." "So I can know when to pick you up."

But I hadn't been getting dressed in the bathroom. He'd been watching me get dressed. "Oh. That's not creepy at all." I suppressed a shudder. "You pervert. You could have told me!"

He smirked. "You didn't ask."

My face heated and I clenched my teeth. I slapped him on the arm. "Arsehole."

He chuckled.

There wasn't anything I could do about it except get dressed in the bathroom from now on.

I pushed those thoughts away as my stomach grumbled. "Well, can we eat first today? I really felt ill when I was so hungry before."

"Yes. Hurry up."

It was so hard to walk into that terrible room again. My hatred for Madhur would have been written on my face, so I kept looking at the floor.

We stood near the doorway and Madhur turned to face us. "Right. Today, you are both going to behave, or there will be dire consequences. I am on the brink of not caring if you lose fingers or limbs as punishments. We only need your minds after all."

The malicious grin on his face made my blood run cold. He was serious. And he'd probably enjoy hacking off arms or legs—

I had to stop my mind from conjuring up visuals for that scenario. I trembled as I continued to stare at the floor.

I could see him in my peripheral vision putting his hands on his hips. "Now. Get to it."

We didn't hesitate.

Once we were set up, I closed my eyes and tried to mentally prepare myself for whatever I would remember.

Braydac seemed determined to get this over with and plunged into my memories.

My mind didn't mess around this time. The first thing I remembered was the bulb of the Chumana flower popping in my face and the horrific hallucinations that followed. I'd already remembered this, but my brain went into more detail this time around. Somewhere in the distance, I could hear Madhur's voice telling Braydac to keep a hold on me. Did that mean that things were moving around the room again already?

Things shifted to me being held captive in chains and being sold like an animal. My breath came in short bursts and I was both terrified and outraged.

Then I saw Turak. He was terrifying and totally vulgar and disgusting and my hearts nearly stopped with the things he did to me. Things shifted past everything that happened with Anjou and I and the jungle cat that tried to kill me, then I was being chased through the jungle with Turak on my tail.

I heard voices in the distance again that weren't part of my memory. I ignored them. I was too caught up in trying to outrun Turak. He'd caught up to me and pinned me to the ground and was trying to kiss me and take off my clothes and I couldn't escape. Suddenly I was standing in the middle of the lab with total chaos all around me. The objects in the room that I was levitating seemed to be moving in a circular motion and the guards were using trays as shields to protect the doctor and everyone was yelling at once. I heard a shout from the corner of the room. One of the guards was actually floating in the air!

I was grabbed from behind and my first thought was that it was Turak. I struggled and thrust my elbow backward, connecting with hard abs, but before I could do any more damage, I heard Braydac's voice next to my ear. "Stop it! Right now!"

Everything raced through my mind. Memories from my life and Sifayah's life flashed by so fast I thought I was going to be sick. Braydac's grip on me was the only thing keeping me upright.

Madhur drew his stunner and we were both hit with the blast. Pain radiated through my body and I instantly lost all control. We both fell into a writhing, convulsing heap together on the floor. The heat I felt through my body was so intense, I felt like it was melting the flesh from my bones.

He kept his finger on the trigger and somewhere faraway I could hear him laughing.

The agony kept on going. There was no end to it. All I could think about was the pain and the feeling of utter helplessness as my muscles spasmed uncontrollably.

Finally, the pulse stopped and my body went limp, but every muscle burned. Like they'd been fried. I couldn't move. My body wouldn't obey me. I was positive he'd electrocuted us for a lot longer than what he had for Braydac.

Far above me, I heard Madhur's voice, but couldn't understand what he was saying. I was vaguely aware of being lifted up and carried, probably back to my room.

And the last thought that swirled through my brain before I blacked out was that it had finally worked. I could remember *everything*.

Chapter 47
You're Next

Regaining consciousness was a very unpleasant experience. My whole body ached and if I tried to move, it hurt even more. It was worse than how I'd felt when I'd woken up on that beach. I knew it was because of how long he'd kept his finger on the trigger. All the stunners that I'd ever seen didn't work like that. This one must have had a lower power setting that allowed him to keep the electrical surge going indefinitely. It was a form of torture. It wasn't right.

I tried to lie as still as possible to avoid causing more pain. What was going to happen to me now? He'd warned us about being punished and now we'd paid the price. I winced.

But it wasn't like I did it on purpose. Reliving the horror of what Turak almost did to me was too much. A sort of half shudder ran through me just thinking about it. My muscles weren't working properly.

Whether I meant it or not doesn't matter to him. He enjoyed torturing us.

I couldn't help wondering if there was more punishment to come. Thinking about that didn't help me feel any better.

I pushed all that aside for now. I had to get used to the fact that there were no giant holes in my memories anymore.

Everything was clear. The puzzle pieces matched and it felt good to be able to see the whole story.

It was impossible to remember every single thing that had ever happened to me or to Sifayah, but I could feel that everything was back the way it should be.

I concentrated on some of my more pleasant memories, but some of them made me sad. I missed my friends back on Earth, Oliana and Kaliya. They weren't missing me though, because — as confusing as it was — the original me had gone back home to them.

I wondered if Zhenna had been compensated in any way for the things she'd had to endure. I should have gone down that route. I'd had a much worse time of it than her. Maybe I still could. If I ever got out of here.

I thought about happier things. Darion had helped me while I was stuck in the jungle before he'd even met me. He never gave up on me. He'd found me and taken me out of the jungle.

The time we'd spent together since then had been so good. We shared an apartment and worked together on the base. He'd bought me an Artmedia device that I used to draw and paint digital pictures in my spare time. It was so relaxing to be creative, but the best times were spent with Darion. The things we could do in the underground base were limited, but we did spend a lot of time together watching HoloMovies and playing games and catching up with friends on the base.

I'd been taking the self-defence classes so I wouldn't be so helpless if I ever ended up in a dangerous situation again. Yes, I had my Talent to help me, but I was told that if I was ever in a situation where I didn't have my Talent to rely on, I could use tactics that the non-Talented used.

So it was ironic that I'd ended up in a situation where my Talent was being blocked and I couldn't remember my training. Before I'd met Braydac, I didn't know that Blockers existed.

If they expected me to be up and ready early today, they would be very disappointed. They would have to drag me to that room, screaming, but probably not kicking. My muscles weren't functioning properly.

I wondered if I should tell them that I'd remembered everything. I sure as Hell didn't want to. Braydac would be able to see that there was nothing blocking my memories now and tell them. I didn't care. I wasn't going to give them anything. They could all go to Hell.

My pulse raced. What were they going to do when they found out? Take what they needed from my mind and then kill me? They would probably kill Braydac too. After they'd taken his Talent, of course.

I lay there for a long time with thoughts racing through my head, not knowing what would happen to me next. My stomach let me know that I needed food. My bladder let me know that I needed the bathroom. I groaned. How was I going to manage that?

I slowly rolled over to the side of the bed and let myself slide off onto my hands and knees on the floor. My muscles were jelly and I crawled to the bathroom. Taking care of my needs took forever and caused me a lot of pain, but I managed to do it and to crawl back to bed. I seethed at the thought that they were probably watching me through the camera in the room. They probably thought it was funny.

As I started to drift off to sleep, the door swished open and a guard walked in carrying a tray of food. He left it on the small table and stalked out the door without a word.

I was too hungry to ignore it. I had to push myself to get up and eat. It was a slow and painful meal, but I somehow made it through and crawled back to bed.

How could I get out of here? I needed to escape. I needed Braydac's help to teleport off-planet, but there was no way he'd help me when there were no credits involved. He'd made it perfectly clear. He was only in it for the money. I thought that the only way he would help was if I could give him more than the Korovska were paying.

I had to find another way. I could remember how to use my Talent and could teleport again, but I couldn't teleport to somewhere I'd never been and couldn't go as far as another planet. But how could I use my Talent when Braydac was stopping me at every turn? I needed to keep fighting against that block.

My thoughts turned to Darion. I'd found him and lost him again on the same day. My chest tightened and tears sprang to my eyes. I could remember him now and knew what we'd been through together. And what he meant to me. That made my imprisonment so much harder.

I still didn't know if Nykolar's stunner had been set to kill or stun. Something twisted inside me as I remembered Darion crumpling to the ground. What if he was dead? What would I do? How could I deal with that, knowing that he'd found me and I'd lost him?

I turned toward the wall and curled in on myself. I let the tears come and didn't hold anything back. I hurt all over, but I didn't stop. I sobbed into my pillow.

I'll never see him again, even if he did survive.

I cried harder. I couldn't bear the thought of losing him.

Why did I think I could make a difference to Braydac and the way he thinks? Why did I think I had any chance at all of escaping? I'm so stupid!

There was no way out. No one was coming to get me. They had no way of knowing where I was. I hadn't known that it was even possible to be teleported to another planet.

I would have to stay here and endure whatever punishments Madhur doled out. I'd have to let them transfer my brainwaves into other people and use my DNA in experiments. I'd be trained to fight a battle I knew nothing about. One that I wanted nothing to do with. I could even be forced to fight against my own people.

It was hopeless. There was no way home.

I resolved to refuse to fight. I didn't care what they did to me, I wouldn't fight in their stupid war.

I didn't know how long I'd lain there for, but I thought it was strange that I hadn't fallen asleep quickly this time.

There was a small spark of hope when I remembered that Braydac wasn't able to stop me when everything was flying around the room. He'd grabbed me and practically begged me to stop. I'd somehow pushed past the block and I didn't think it was only because of my mental shield. My Talent was stronger than his.

<hr />

At breakfast the next day, I decided to try again to convince Braydac that he would be next. Now that my legs would actually hold me up, we were going to go to the lab straight after our meal so that they could repeat the Eibhlin Process and try to record my brainwaves again. Of course Braydac had told them that my memories were restored, and they were confident that it would work without any problems this time.

I knew he would tell them. I was seething inside, but then I thought that if he hadn't told them, we'd be forced to keep mining my memories, and I never wanted to go through that again.

So I tried to be civil to him. Tried to talk to him.

The guards at the door must have thought it strange the way we just sat and ate in total silence, not realising that we were having a conversation with our minds. I smirked at the thought.

"What's so funny?" Braydac asked.

"These guards. They think we're ignoring each other or something."

"We are."

"Oh, you're so funny."

He just smiled. He didn't do it often and I realized that he was quite attractive when he did.

"So. When are you going to realise that you're next on their radar?"

The smile faded. *"I'm not. It would be total chaos if they stole my blocking ability."*

"All the more reason for them to do it."

"They won't. I won't let them."

"Then you won't get paid."

"I need that money."

"What for?"

"None of your business."

"You won't be able to stop them."

"You just watch me."

We continued to eat in silence.

We were taken to the room where they performed the Eibhlin Process last time and Madhur met us at the door. "You will both need to be thoroughly checked out after being stunned the other day."

His smug expression made me want to hurl.

"What do you mean?" I asked. "What did you do to us?"

He laughed. "You were there, and you don't know what happened? And I thought you were intelligent."

"You know what I mean."

He squeezed the bridge of his nose and sighed heavily. "I want to make sure all your neurons are firing the way they should after your punishments. I don't need you to ask questions and I certainly don't need to tell you any more than that." He stepped away from the doorway. "Now, get in your positions and shut up."

I resisted the urge to roll my eyes.

We got into our 'positions' and didn't say anything more. There was no point in talking to this man.

All the worries from the day before that had me feeling so defeated flooded back into my mind, but I didn't want to give in to them again. I had to be strong. I had to somehow get through this.

But it was hard when I didn't know how I was going to get out of there or what was going to happen next.

I thought about Darion. *I can't just give up. Not now. Not after all the things I've been through.*

They hooked Braydac up with the wiring harness first and ran some 'routine' tests, which took some time, then it was my turn.

After they were done with that, they repeated the procedure for the Eibhlin Process and I lay there trying not to think about what they would do to me now.

Once they were finally finished, I couldn't get out of there fast enough.

We walked down the corridors with one guard in tow, who kept staring at me with a creepy smirk on his face.

I suppressed a shudder and kept walking.

I could feel the familiar heaviness that told me Braydac was blocking me. Why did he bother anymore? What was I going to do? Where would I be able to go when I couldn't teleport to an unknown place like he could? Maybe he was worried I'd attack him now that my memories had returned. Maybe I would. But as soon as I used my Talent for anything, we would both get punished and my muscles hadn't fully recovered from the last punishment.

As the door to my room opened and I was about to ask if we could go for something to eat, the guard pushed me in through the doorway and forced me up against the wall to the left of the entry.

I tried to get around him. "What are you doing? Get away from me!"

His hands were suddenly all over me and he leaned his head down to my ear. "You're a pretty one."

My stomach lurched and I struggled to get away from him. Turak's face flashed into my mind and I sucked in a breath.

"That's it. Do I turn you on?" He started licking my neck and I struggled harder.

"No!"

CHAPTER 48

You Expected Them to be Honourable?

He pushed me back to the wall. "Don't be like that."

It was no use. He was too strong. I would've had more luck moving the wall behind me.

How could he do this? Why wasn't anyone stopping him? Surely the camera in the room would pick up what he was doing.

I heard a voice. Maybe it was Braydac. Maybe he would help... Or maybe not. There wasn't anything in it for him. He only seemed motivated by credits.

I was on my own. His breath was hot against my cheek and I couldn't stop his hands from wandering and I wanted to scream.

No! I couldn't just stand there. I had to do something.

The guard's hands went up under my shirt and as he reached my breasts, I pushed him away with my hands and my mind and flung him across the room, almost ripping my shirt. He hit the wall with a crack and fell to the floor, dazed, but still conscious.

"You little *suka!*"

As he scrambled to his feet, Braydac stepped in front of me and I felt the block in my mind come back down. I hadn't realized it was gone. "Steady on, there. You need to be more careful of where you walk. You don't want to trip over again."

"I didn't trip, Azaeli scum! She did this! You're supposed to be blocking her. That's what we pay you for!"

"Sorry, man. My concentration slipped. It's not easy blocking her all day."

I couldn't stop shaking, but kept my head held high as the guard glared at me. "You will pay for that," he spat.

Braydac folded his arms across his broad chest. "I wouldn't do that if I were you."

"Why? What you going to do about it?"

"I won't have to do anything. Madhur will decide what to do with you."

The guy flinched. He knew what Madhur would do.

He stepped up to Braydac. "Get your worthless ass into your room."

Braydac laughed. "After you."

The guard glared at him with his creepy orange eyes, then shoved Braydac out ahead of him. Braydac looked right at me as he passed, his face expressionless.

The door swished shut and I let myself slide down the wall until I was sitting on the floor. Tears streamed down my face.

Braydac?

"Yes?"

Thank you.

"For what?"

Helping me.

"I don't know what you're talking about."

A short laugh burst from my chest. Of course he'd say that. But I knew what he'd done. He didn't just stand up to the guard for me. He'd stopped blocking me so I could defend myself.

I mean it. Thank you.

They'd left us in our rooms for hours before we'd been allowed to go and eat something and I was still shaken up over what had happened with the guard.

Later that night, Braydac called me. *"Tamisan! I need to talk to you."*

"What is it?"

"You were right. Oh, fuck! *You were right! I should have known! That checkup they gave me? It wasn't a checkup. They lied. They did the Eibhlin Process thing on me and are going to start transferring my blocking ability to their people straight away. I teleported around and overheard them talking about it. If they succeed, there will be chaos. I didn't mind them handing out your abilities. I thought that it would be a good thing to have more people with Talent in the universe. But how can anyone with Talent function if there are people everywhere who can block them?"*

I sat on my bed with my back against the wall and hugged my pillow. *"I knew they would do it."*

"Don't rub it in."

"I did tell you. You wouldn't listen."

"I was determined not to let them, but they lied to me. I shouldn't have fallen for it. They knew I'd be worried about that stunner doing damage. Dammit!"

"You expected them to be honourable? Seriously? After all they've done?"

"No. I was going to make sure they didn't get my Talent."

"Well, I guess it's safe to say that you failed." A spark of hope lit in my chest. He would have to help me now. "We have to stop them."

"Yeah, but how?"

He was *agreeing* with me? Finally?

Focus!

"We need to get back to Jannali, but we have to find and destroy their research first. We can't let them continue."

I could almost feel him nodding. "We need a plan."

I lay down while we talked about what we would need to do to destroy the data and Braydac said that he would find out where their servers were kept. Once we were satisfied that we had a rough plan in place, he said goodnight and I fell asleep quickly.

The next morning, Braydac came in as usual and we went to the cafeteria with a different guard. I was relieved that I wouldn't have to face the one that had attacked me.

"I have been looking around the base." Braydac told me.

"How? Surely they don't just let you wander around."

"I can teleport, or have you forgotten?"

"You've been just porting all around the place? How do you do that?"

"What do you mean?"

"How can you teleport to a place you've never been?"

"I can travel there first in my mind, then once I can see that it's safe, I port myself there."

"Wow. Okay. I don't know anyone who can do that. And how do you travel between planets?"

"I tap into a power source, like the power generators for this base, and add it to my own power."

"Do the Korovska know that you can do these things?"

"They know I can teleport just about anywhere. They just don't know the physics of it and I'm sure they don't really care."

We'd talked about this before. But that was only about him porting to other planets. *Do they know that I can't just teleport anywhere?*

"Probably not. It doesn't matter now anyway. If they find out, they'll just use my Talent instead."

"Yeah." I tried to eat the goop from my plate while I longed for real food. The freshly-cooked meeru was so much better than this crap, even though I'd watched them kill the meeru beforehand. *Did anyone see you?*

"I don't think so. I was careful. I have looked around the base before, but last night I was more thorough. During the night there's hardly anyone about. Usually just a few guards."

"What did you find out?"

"I found the armoury. They keep all sorts of goodies in there, even a few little explosives. I don't know what they'd need them for here, but that doesn't matter because we need them. I've located the mainframe computer and where they store the backups and I have just enough explosive devices to blow them both up."

My muscles were still stiff from the stunner and the pain made me more determined to get out of here. *What if they have off-site backups?*

"If they're smart, they will have, but there's really nothing we can do about that. We can only deal with what's here and hope we slow them down until the authorities can stop them altogether."

"Okay. Then what? Can we leave?"

"Yes. We get our butts out of here. I will port us to Jannali."

"*Really?*" My hearts were in my throat. The thought of getting out of here, coupled with the thought of seeing Darion again left me breathless.

"*Tonight.*"

"*What?*"

"*We go tonight. I've stockpiled everything we'll need and if we go in the middle of the night, there'll be less people about, so less people to deal with if we're spotted.*"

Deal with? You mean kill? "*What time then?*"

"*Eleven forty-five is when some of the guards go on a break, so I'll come and get you five minutes before that.*"

"*Okay. I don't have any way to tell the time, so I'll just wait.*"

I thought about how I always fell asleep as soon as I lay my head on the pillow. "*Wait, how am I going to stay awake? Every time I lay my head on the pillow, I fall asleep instantly. Something isn't right about that. It's not normal.*"

"*That's because they set it up so that they put you to sleep with an odourless gas.*"

CHAPTER 49
We Have a Problem

"What? Why?"

"So I can get some sleep or just rest from blocking you."

"What? I can believe this!"

"I had to be able to rest. Do you know how hard it is to block someone's abilities all day long?"

"No, and it's a violation of my rights."

"You haven't had any rights since you got here, so what's the problem?"

"Everything!" I sighed. *"So how do we stop them from gassing me tonight?"*

"I won't turn it on."

"You have been doing it?"

"Yes."

"You're such a jerk!"

"I told you. It's necessary so I can rest and sleep."

I clenched my fists and took in a slow, deep breath. I had to put my anger aside for now. We had to escape. *"Alright."*

I knew that it was the Korovska that had organized everything, but Braydac was the one who had kidnapped me and given me to them. He was the enemy, but also my ticket out of here.

"So, you don't turn the gas on and you come and get me when it's time?"

"Yes. You will have to lie down and pretend to sleep, so the cameras won't show anything suspicious. I can come get you in the darkness."

The day dragged on and Madhur didn't send for us. I was glad, but the waiting was eating at me. I had to try to act normal and not pace up and down in my room like I wanted to. I did some exercises and practiced some self-defence moves, which wouldn't arouse suspicion because I'd done it a few times before. It helped to work some of the stiffness out of my body.

I wished I had something to read or something to draw with, but there was nothing to keep me occupied.

I spoke to Braydac a few times during the day, but he wasn't a big talker, so our conversations were brief.

I didn't know what time it was, so I had to keep waiting.

"Tamisan?"

My hearts leapt in my chest. *"Yes?"*

"We have a problem."

I got a sinking feeling in my stomach as my mind thought of all the things that could go wrong. *"What is it?"*

"I did some more snooping and found someone else here."

"Who?" Had they brought Darion here?

"Larissa. They said that they were bringing her here, remember?"

"Oh, crap! Is she okay?" I'd forgotten all about that.

"She is in good health. I spoke to her and she has been here for a while. Almost as long as you. She was kidnapped while on her way home back on Shakira and brought here."

"We can't leave her here. They brought her here for her Talent. They'll use her too. They probably already have."

"It makes things a bit more difficult."

"We can't leave her!"

"I know. I told her to pretend she's going to sleep. I'll have to collect her when it's time."

I went into my bathroom and was about to get dressed for bed when I decided to just stay in what I was wearing. There wasn't much difference between the grey clothing I wore during the day and the grey pyjamas I wore to bed. It shouldn't seem too suspicious as I'd slept in the day-time clothes before. I did brush my teeth though.

"Didn't they see you on the cameras?"

"No. I ported into her bathroom."

"How are they blocking her Talent?"

"Her tracker is modified, just like Darion's and Lazuli's. Just like yours was until Nykolar fried it."

I turned off my light and got into bed. "How can she use her Talent to help us if she's being blocked?"

"I still have a controller. I turned her blocker off. She is free to use her Talent as much as she likes, although I don't think she has mastered it yet."

"Oh. Okay. I hope she knows enough to get out of a danger-ous situation."

"We'll have to keep a close eye on her."

I lay on my back, staring up at the ceiling. "So, is it time yet? I'm in bed."

"*Yes. Turn off your light. Don't be alarmed when I appear in your room.*"

"*Okay.*"

One second, I was alone, and the next, he was crouching next to my bed. Even though I was expecting it, it still made my hearts pound in my chest.

"*Okay,*" he said, "*get out of bed so that you're crouching on the floor.*"

I crept out from under the covers until I was crouching next to him.

"*Give me your hand.*"

"*Why?*"

"*What do you mean, why? You can teleport too. You know how this works.*"

"*Yeah, but I don't have to be touching the person I'm teleporting. Neither does Darion.*"

"*Well, I do. Now that I think about it, you're right. Darion doesn't always touch the person he's porting. I hadn't really noticed before.*" He put out his hand. "*Let's go.*"

I hesitated just a second before putting my hand in his. I had to take the chance and trust him if I wanted to get out of here.

The dizzying swirl of the teleport was disconcerting. We were crouching on the floor next to a different bed in the darkness.

"*Larissa. It's me, Braydac. Get out of bed so that you're crouching on the floor, then grab my hand.*"

As soon as she hit the floor, we appeared inside a storeroom of some kind. The light was bright compared to our dark rooms and I squinted as Braydac stood up. I stumbled as I stood, the dizziness still affecting me.

Larissa jumped up and wrapped her arms around me. "*Tamisan! It's so good to see you!*"

I hugged her back and Braydac said, *"We don't have time for happy reunions. We need to get moving."*

CHAPTER 50
Intruder Alert

Braydac rushed to a corner cupboard that had a door with broken hinges and pulled it aside. He grabbed two back-packs and shoved the door back in place.

He held one of the bags out to me. *"Here. Put this on."*

"What's in it?"

"Explosives."

I grimaced. *"Okay."*

"What's wrong?"

"Now I have to make sure I don't blow myself up."

"There's not much chance of that. They aren't really that dangerous without their trigger."

"Oh."

He pulled a stunner out of his pack and handed it to me. *"Take this. It's set to stun."* As soon as I took it, he pulled out another one for himself. *"Sorry, Larissa. I didn't have time to get one for you."*

Braydac looked down at my hand and gently pushed it down and away from him. I frowned before realising I'd been pointing the stunner right at him. *"Don't worry. I won't shoot you. I'd never get out of here if I did that."*

He smiled.

I felt bad that Larissa didn't have a way to defend herself. I held the stunner out to her — handle first, of course. *"Here. Take it. You'll need it more than me."*

She smiled at me. *"Thank you."*

"We need to stick together in case something goes wrong and I have to port us out of the base completely." Braydac said. We nodded.

Braydac grabbed our hands and took us to a huge room full of computer terminals and what looked like lots of cupboards. The mainframe.

He unzipped his backpack, pulled out some small rectangular devices and handed them to us. *"Put these near the storage drives and press the green button once they're in place."*

I nodded and got to work. Larissa wasn't sure where the storage drives were so I pointed them out.

We only took a few minutes to place the explosives and Braydac whisked us away to another smaller room that I could only assume was where the back-ups were stored.

He looked at me. *"I've been watching the patrols. We only have ten minutes before the guards come down this way, so let's make it quick."*

We took the explosives from my backpack this time and made quick work of placing them around the room.

Just as Braydac pulled the trigger mechanism from his pack and told us to come closer, there was a click and the door started to open. We weren't within his reach so I ducked behind a desk in the corner, hearing laser fire as I hit the floor.

Sticking my head out to see what had happened, I could see that Braydac's shoulder was charred and he was crawling across to Larissa. The guard at the door fired again and Braydac's only choice was to teleport or be shot. The shot passed through the space he'd just occupied and I managed not to shriek as the blast hit the wall near me.

A second guard walked in and they started looking around the room with their torches. I wondered if they recognized Braydac, then realized how dumb that was. The fact that he'd teleported would've been an instant giveaway.

The first guard grabbed a Com from his pocket. "Intruder alert. The Blocker has been sighted in the Backup room. Please advise."

They mustn't have seen us.

A crackle emitted from the Com, followed by a male's voice. "Check the room thoroughly and report. We'll have Unit Six check his room. All available units will be put on High Alert."

"Acknowledged."

I tensed. If they searched this room, they'd find us and the explosives. Had Braydac left us to be caught? Had this been the plan all along? No. I didn't think so. He'd had no choice but to teleport.

Now Larissa and I had to get out of here, and fast. And I just remembered that I didn't have to be touching her.

The lights flickered on. The second guard came close enough and saw me crouching in the corner. Guard number one found Larissa at the same time.

The guard looked down at me and smiled. "Looks like he's deserted you. He's not here to teleport you away." The smile became a smirk.

I smirked too. "I don't need him."

I reached out with my mind and teleported Larissa and I back to the first place I could think of that wouldn't have anyone in it: my room. I wished I could've seen the look on the guard's faces once we'd vanished into thin air.

I looked around my room, checking for threats. There was no one there. *"Larissa? Are you okay?"*

"Yeah, but I can't see. Where are we?"

I stepped forward and touched her arm in the darkness and she flinched. *"I teleported us to my room."*

"Oh. Thank you. That guard found me." She sucked in her breath. *"Do you think Braydac is okay? He got shot."*

I ran a hand through my hair, hoping that he was alright and that he hadn't abandoned us. *"Braydac. Are you okay? We're back in my room. Where are you?"*

"In that storeroom again. We can't leave yet. We need to trigger the explosions."

Relief flooded my body. He hadn't abandoned us.

An alarm started up in the hallway outside. *"We need to hurry."*

He appeared in front of us and a split second later, the door started to open. Braydac grabbed us as a guard came in and fired his pistol. I watched as the laser blast headed toward my chest and the next second, we were in the storeroom again.

I cried out. I looked down and saw nothing and rubbed my chest. "Oh!"

CHAPTER 51
Take Her to My Lab

"Be quiet! You'll get us killed!"

"Sorry! I couldn't help it. I was almost hit."

"Almost hit? How do you think I feel?"

"Oh, I'm so stupid! Sorry. Are you okay?"

"I'll live."

I looked at his shoulder and tried to imagine how much pain he was in. *"You need medical attention."*

"Yeah, later. Now I need you to focus. This trigger has a limited range. We need to be nearby when we set it off, but not close enough to cop the blast."

He paced back and forth. *"We'll go to an office near the server room and blow the explosives, then before they know what's going on, we blow the backups. There's an office near that one too that we can use."*

I looked at Larissa's pale face. *"Alright. Let's do this."*

We teleported and I found myself looking at a desk, chair, and computer in a dark room. My eyes quickly adjusted and I could see a shelf full of HoloMovies of varying colours. A digital display on the shelf behind the desk was running a slideshow of photographs of a family of Korovskans. Whoever owned this office hadn't turned it off before they left for the day.

My attention was torn away from the images as Braydac pressed the button on the trigger. A loud explosion came from somewhere beyond the other side of the wall and before I could see if the wall would hold out, we were in another dark office.

I instinctively covered my ears with my hands, even though it was too late, but I left them there for the next blast. Braydac switched something over on the trigger mechanism, but before he could press the button, the door to the room burst open and Larissa was hit with a stunner blast. Ice raced through my veins and I ducked down behind a desk, hoping that it was set to stun. Surely they'd want to keep us alive.

A familiar voice pulled my attention away from her still form on the floor. "Cease fire!" Madhur stood in the doorway. Everyone froze. "Do *not* shoot to kill."

The man who'd shot Larissa mumbled something about his stunner being set to stun only and Madhur glared at him.

He turned to Braydac. "We had a deal, Azaeli scum. Don't you want your money?"

Braydac stood straighter. "You dishonoured our deal by taking my abilities for your twisted experiments."

Madhur smirked. "There was nothing in our deal to say I couldn't."

A man came around the other side of the desk and gestured for me to stand up.

I glared at Madhur. "Who cares about deals? What you're doing is against Intergalactic Law. You can't get away with it."

"Says who?"

"Says me."

It occurred to me at that moment that I wasn't just the result of cloning and all the different experiments by the Korovskans and Dr Starrick.

The whole is greater than the sum of its parts.

Just because these things had happened to me, they didn't make me *less*. I was *more*. And I was *me*. And I could use all of those qualities against them.

"What are you going to do about it?" he asked.

"We're gonna take you down."

Madhur laughed loudly. "There's nothing you can do, little girl. You are on our home planet. No one knows you're here and no one is coming to save you."

"Then I guess I'll have to save myself."

He laughed again.

Braydac tossed the detonator to me. *"Get yourself out of here!"*

I caught it easily. Braydac ducked down and ported himself and Larissa out of there then I pressed the button on the detonator. I was too far away for him to reach, but he knew I could teleport now.

I was about to follow when a stunner blast that was meant for Braydac hit me instead.

The pain shot through me. As my muscles convulsed and the floor started getting closer, I thought that there would be no escape from this hellhole for me. Then the blackness engulfed me.

Opening my eyes was too difficult. They fluttered open just enough to see Madhur's orange eyes glaring at me.

"Finally," he said. "Now, where are the others?"

I wished I could control my muscles so I could spit in his ugly face.

I was jostled around a bit and realized that I was being held in an upright position and wasn't capable of standing on my own.

"Where are they?" He demanded.

How could I get away from him when I couldn't even stand up? How long had I been out? Were Braydac and Larissa safe? Were they still on this planet?

Pain burst along my cheek and jaw as Madhur slapped me. My vision blurred and my cheek seemed to ignite with flame. Why did he have to keep doing that? The bruises were never going to heal.

I had to get away from him, but how? There was no way I could pull myself free of their grip. Then it dawned on me: I didn't have to. I just had to teleport without taking them with me. Simple.

Yeah, right.

I realized that Madhur was yelling at me. "I don't know!" I shouted.

Another slap sent my thoughts scattering. "Do *not* yell at me!"

I had to concentrate if I was going to get out of here. I closed my eyes and tried to relax.

"Take her to my lab."

His lab? I almost opened my eyes. *No. Concentrate.*

The guards holding me started to march me through the base with my feet dragging along the floor and it was hard to ignore what was happening. I kept telling myself that whatever he wanted to do to me in the lab wouldn't happen if I teleported away from them.

Okay. Where should I go?

The only places I could think of were my room and the storeroom. There could be guards in or near my room hoping to catch Braydac and Larissa, so I decided on the storeroom.

We went around a corner and I blocked everything out. *Just breathe.*

I pictured the corner of the storeroom in case Larissa and Braydac were in there standing in the middle of the room.

We swung around another corner and dizziness swirled through me. I took a deep breath. *Concentrate.*

I focused again. The corner of the storeroom...

The sudden stop had me opening my eyes. We were in the lab and the fear turned my blood to ice. I tried to struggle, but my limbs wouldn't obey me.

"Put her on the bed and turn her on her side."

I could see a number of instruments and small gadgets on a tray next to the bed, which had my hearts pounding faster. What was he planning to do?

They had some trouble getting me into position as I weakly struggled against their strong hands. "*No!*"

"Hold her still."

It was useless. I couldn't move. I felt something cold on the back of my neck and heard the hiss of an injector gun and my heartbeats skyrocketed. What was he doing?

My neck started to feel numb, then I felt a pushing sensation. Was he removing my tracking device?

Then my brain followed the logic. If he was removing my broken tracking device, then he would most likely be replacing it with a new one. Probably one with the blocking technology. Which meant that he would be able to block my Talent. He no longer needed Braydac.

CHAPTER 52
There is No Escape

My brain went into full panic mode. I couldn't let them do that. I tried to struggle. To get away. To stop them from taking my Talent from me. I even tried to teleport, but nothing worked.

I felt more pushing, then he said, "There. All done. Now you won't be going anywhere."

I tried to struggle, but they were too strong. Even when they used the stunners the way they were meant to be used it still rendered my muscles useless.

The guards rolled me over onto my back and I stared up into Madhur's freakish eyes. He was smiling, of course. He had me right where he wanted me. I couldn't teleport to the storeroom. I couldn't even call Braydac to tell him where I was or what had happened. I was in big trouble. I could only hope that he'd gotten Larissa out.

"Nykolar wasn't totally useless," he told me. "He modified the tracking devices to block Talent. We'd been using your friend Larissa's tracker as a blueprint to build our own. We have two of them ready to go and as soon as we find that Azaeli bastard, he will have one implanted. Then there'll be no more problems with the two of you."

I glared at him.

"You are our property. You will further our studies. No one will come to rescue you. There is no escape."

He turned on his heel and walked from the room, barking orders for them to take me to my room as he strutted down the hallway.

Tears slid silently down my cheeks once they'd dumped me on my bed and left the room. We might have blown up their data, but they would rebuild or relocate and use my mind again to transfer Talent to more of their people. It was only a hiccup in their plans. As Madhur had pointed out — more than once — they'd been doing this for centuries.

I just had to hope that Braydac and Larissa had made it to Jannali. Then I could at least be happy that they'd escaped this nightmare.

Each minute that passed meant my chances of escape were dwindling away. The whole place was alert now, so it would be extremely difficult for Braydac to come back for me.

I was tired, but couldn't sleep. I was also very hungry, but did not want to eat. What was the point? Maybe I could just refuse to eat. How long would I last?

I tossed that idea to the side. They'd force me to eat. They'd keep me here as long as they needed me. Then they would either make me battle-ready, or kill me.

I squeezed my eyes shut and a tear escaped. I would rather be dead than be forced to hurt and kill people.

Staying here indefinitely would be so much harder now with my full memories of Darion to torture me. I thought about the first time I'd heard his voice in my mind, telling me he'd help me rid my body of the poison from the hallucinogenic plant and help me escape the slave traders.

I relived the moment I met him. The way he felt. The way he held me. The first time we kissed was something I'd never forget, which was a weird thing to be thinking when that's exactly what happened. I'd forgotten everything about him.

More tears fell to my pillow at the thought that I would probably never see him again.

I didn't know how long I'd been lying on the bed feeling sorry for myself, but I noticed that the lights had faded to nothing, as if the sun had gone down.

A noise behind me made me jump and I turned around to see Braydac crouched on the floor next to my bed.

"Braydac!"

"Shhh!" *Do you want to get out of here?*

Yes! It was frustrating that I couldn't send the thought back to him, but I knew he would hear me.

He'd touched my arm before I'd even answered, and I felt the weird sensation and dizziness of his teleport before hitting a soft surface as if I'd been lifted up off my bed and dumped back down again. He'd actually ported me onto a bed in what looked like the Medical Facility at Jannali.

"Are we at Jannali?"

He smiled. "Yes."

I looked around the room as Darion and Dr Aimery walked in, followed by a couple of guards.

Darion rushed forward. "Are you okay?"

I somehow managed to sit up and fling my arms around him. "Yes. It's so good to see you," I told him. I squeezed him tighter. "I remember *everything*."

CHAPTER 53
You Keep Telling Yourself That

He pulled me closer and I could feel a sob escape him. Tears slid down my cheeks. It was so good to be in his arms again and I didn't ever want him to let me go. He gave me little kisses on my cheek and I was reminded of how I'd felt the last time I was in his arms. Like I was home. This time, I really was home, and to be able to remember Darion fully left me feeling complete.

I started to cry and felt like I could just fall to pieces right there, but I had some things I had to do first. I could fall apart later.

I took a deep breath, forcing myself to calm down. "It's okay. I'm okay. I'm back. But there's a problem. They gave me a new tracker that blocks my Talent."

"We can turn it off," he told me. "Braydac gave us a controller."

Relief flooded through me and I reluctantly pulled away from him so I could see Braydac. "Thank you so much, Braydac. I thought I'd never get out of there."

I tried to suppress a sob and failed and he looked uncomfortable. "I... I couldn't leave them with a source of Talent."

I smiled through my tears. "Yeah. You keep telling yourself that."

He tried to stop it, but a smile crept onto his face.

"Tamisan?" Lazuli had just arrived and stared at me with his mouth hanging open.

My mind went back to the jungle and to the image of him lying on the ground with his shoulder ripped open. "Lazuli! You're okay! I was so worried."

"You've been missing — again — for days and you're worried about me?"

"Of course," I said. "You were attacked by a freaking jungle cat."

"That was weeks ago and we have a Healer now."

"Oh, really? That's great."

Commander Kozienko stepped forward from behind Lazuli and nodded a greeting. "He was bad. When Andiyar brought him in, we thought we'd already lost him. He somehow got through the surgery and was recovering slowly. Then we finally got ourselves a Healer, and he's been fully healed." He ruffled the hair on the top of Lazuli's head as he turned back to me. "How are ya, Tamisan?"

Tears made my eyes blurry. "I'm good now that I'm back."

I told them all what had happened to me after Braydac and Larissa got away, then Kozienko pulled the controller out of his pocket and deactivated my tracker. It was such a relief to be normal again. Normal for me, anyway.

"We'll have those modified trackers removed as soon as possible," the commander said.

Before I could say anything more, a nurse came into the room and asked everyone to step back so she could check me over. She released a Bio-scanner from its bay at the head of my bed so it could check my vitals as it floated up and down above my body. She asked me a few questions about how I was feeling and I told her that I'd been stunned, but wasn't sure how long ago.

She checked the stats from the bio-scan. "Everything looks okay. Normal brain function — well, normal for you — and both hearts are beating a little fast, but that's understandable given the circumstances."

"Okay... Thank you."

She put some cream on my left cheek and neck, which made them feel so much better.

I laid there thinking of the Korovskans. The fact that they were experimenting with the genetics of the different species of Althar 3 was not new information. They were being investigated by The Six Star Alliance as it was against Intergalactic Law. My story left no doubt as to exactly what they were up to. I would make sure everyone knew what was going on.

I was told that Larissa was in the Medical Facility and Janssen was visiting her. I was relieved that she was okay.

Braydac had brought Larissa back here and told them part of what had happened. He said he'd go back for me. I guess it didn't really matter if they'd given him permission to go back or not; they couldn't stop him.

Kozienko turned to him. "Braydac, what's the state of your injury?"

"Laser hit to the shoulder, Sir. It's cauterized."

"Okay. Medical can take care of you too. And another thing. You're registered as a T1, but nothing in the records show you can teleport to another planet."

CHAPTER 54
There Was Just Him

"I didn't tell anyone."

Kozienko frowned. "Why, son?"

"If you give too much away, people abuse your power."

I huffed. "The Korovskans are proof of that."

The commander had a lot of questions for me, and I told them about what had happened from the moment Braydac teleported us from the jungle.

Once I'd finished, Dr Aimery ordered Braydac be taken firstly to another part of the Medical Facility for treatment on his shoulder, then into custody. I felt bad for him, he had really come through for me, but he was a gun for hire, which made him untrustworthy. And I couldn't let myself forget that he was the one who had taken me to Korovska in the first place.

Braydac turned to me as they led him out the door. "Goodbye, Tamisan. And thank you."

I frowned. Why was he thanking me? And why did that goodbye sound so final? Did he think I wouldn't see him again? I hadn't even thought about whether I'd visit him in his cell. "Thank you for coming back for me," I said, and I meant it.

Walking down the familiar corridors towards our living quarters brought a warmth to my hearts. Being kept in the Medical Facility until they'd finished checking me over had been its own form of torture. I'd just wanted to get out of there and go home.

The only good thing about how long it had taken was that I'd regained control of my muscles enough to walk.

We walked in and the door swished shut behind us. We were in each other's arms in an instant and our lips met. Darion's kisses were desperate and hungry and I returned them with an urgency I had little control over. I couldn't get enough of him.

One hand was pressing against the small of my back and the other was in my hair at the back of my head, holding me in place. It wasn't like I was going anywhere. There was nowhere else I would rather be than right here with him. It was so good to be home. I was home in his arms.

My hands slid under the front of his shirt and I ran my fingers over his bare chest. I'd missed him so much and for most of that time, I didn't know who or what I was missing. There was just an empty feeling inside me.

Then those thoughts faded away and there was just him. His scent. His taste. I wanted to melt into him and join our bodies together.

Something hit the back of my legs and I realized that we had somehow reached the bedroom. I let myself fall back onto the bed and dragged Darion down with me.

Thoughts and memories bombarded my mind, but I pushed them away with a vengeance. This was not a time for thinking. This was a time for feeling.

———◦———

When I woke, I knew that something was different. I was surprised to find that I was home in my own bed. Darion was asleep beside me and it reminded me of the first memory of him that had surfaced when I was still with the Waikari. I smiled and soaked up the moment, but I kept thinking about Jarleth and how we'd left things. How I'd left things with all of them.

I felt bad about just leaving them without any answers. They'd lost Sifayah all over again. I couldn't just forget about them and go back to my life.

Darion opened his eyes and smiled. "Good morning, Beautiful."

"Hey."

"How are you?"

"Fantastic. It's so good to be back home with a comfortable bed to sleep in... and you to snuggle up to." I moved closer and put my head on his chest.

"I'm glad you're happy. I still cannot believe you are really here." He kissed me gently on the lips, which stirred a fire in my belly.

I returned his kiss and ran my fingers through his hair. We melded together and I knew that this was where I was meant to be. I wanted to be in his embrace forever.

"I love you and want to spend the rest of my life with you." I told him, and I meant every word.

He kept kissing me. *"That's good to know."*

"Good to know?"

"Yes. Because I love you and want to spend the rest of my life with you too."

I smiled against his lips.

We stopped and just held each other close.

He gave me a little squeeze. *"I thought you were dead. I thought I'd lost you forever."*

I hugged him tighter. *"I can't imagine what that was like. But I'm here now. I'm okay."*

When I cupped his cheek with my hand, I could feel the wetness there and realized that I was crying too. The Korovska had a lot to answer for.

He looked into my eyes. *"I want us to be together forever. Will you form a Union with me? Marry me?"*

CHAPTER 55

My Hearts Knew

My hearts leapt in my chest. *"Yes!"*

I rolled over so that I was straddling him and kissed him until I couldn't breathe.

As we were lying in bed a little while later, I told him about how they made Braydac force my memories to the surface.

"Braydac saw a lot of private things that I didn't want him to see." My face felt warm just thinking about it. "There were the times we spent together, but also things between Sifayah and Jarleth."

"He needs to pay for his crimes."

"I know. But he did come through in the end."

"That doesn't excuse what he did."

"Yes, I know. But it makes me wonder if maybe he has changed that I-don't-care-about-anyone-but-myself attitude. He could have left us there to rot."

We were quiet for a while. "Seeing the memories of Sifayah with Jarleth makes me feel almost like being here with you is cheating on him."

"But it's—"

"I know it's not. Don't worry. It's just hard when the memories are right there in my mind. And because I've seen how much pain he's in." I paused again. "When I was in the village, I couldn't understand why I wasn't in love with Jarleth. I was so confused. I'm glad I remember everything now, but I wish there had been an easier way to get my memories back."

"Sounds like it wasn't a pleasant experience."

"Not when almost everything I remembered was traumatic. Like Turak and being paralysed."

He gave me another squeeze and kissed my forehead. "I wish I could've been there for you. I feel so bad."

"Don't do that. How could you possibly know that I was on another planet? There was no way you could've found me."

"I know, but—"

"No buts. There was nothing you could've done."

We stayed there together, just letting our emotions flow through our mental connection. I was just thinking about everything.

It was weird, but I'd spent a lot of time worrying about what all the experiments had done to me; the fact that I was a genetically engineered clone and the transfer of my consciousness to an alien who was also the result of genetic engineering. I had wasted a lot of mental energy trying to figure out if I was worthy as a person. Whether I had a soul. Whether I was just a freak of science. Where I fit in in the universe.

I'd come 'round to Darion's way of thinking on one point; that he didn't think someone could live and function without a soul. But I'd never really been able to deal with the rest.

The thing was: all those things added up to who I was. This was who I was now. I had finally accepted me for *me*. It was funny that it had taken another crazy scientist to make me see it.

"I've decided that I don't care about being the result of all those experiments anymore." I told Darion. "I won't let it dictate who I am. All these things have made me who I am and made me powerful enough to have the Korovskan scientists willing to kill to get it from me. But it's not who I am deep down. They can't take that away from me."

"You're damn right, they can't," he said. "And I don't want you to change, either. I love you just the way you are."

I rolled over and kissed him till I had to stop for air.

We lay back on the bed, side-by-side. "Admit it. You missed me," he said.

"How could I miss you if I didn't remember that you existed?"

He chuckled. "Deep down, you missed me."

He didn't know how right he was. "I felt like there was this hole in my chest. Like something important was missing. I thought there was someone in the village I hadn't met yet, but Jarleth told me that there was no one else who meant a lot to me."

"See. Told you."

I smiled. My hearts knew.

His fingers made swirling patterns on my arm. "It's finally over," he said.

"No. It's not. I have to go back to the Waikari village. They deserve to know what happened to Sifayah. It's the least I can do after they lost her again — this time for good. So... I have a request."

"Yes?"

"I want to visit the village and explain things. They deserve to know."

Darion kept the swirling patterns going. "We will have to get permission from Doctor Aimery. We are not allowed to interact too much with the natives, but I think you broke that rule already."

"Broke it and threw it on the ground and stomped on it until it was a bloodied pulp is more like it."

He chuckled. "Yes. That you did."

Once we'd finally climbed out of bed and dressed ourselves, there was a knock at the door to the apartment. Darion pressed the button next to the door and it swished open.

There was a guard standing at attention in the hallway. "Sir, you're both wanted in the conference room."

I exchanged a look with Darion and he shrugged. "Okay. Lead the way."

When we entered the conference room, Dr Aimery didn't waste any time. "I've called you here because Braydac has disappeared. Probably teleported off-planet."

"So that's why he said goodbye like he really meant it," I said.

"He had no intention of facing the charges," Darion mused.

Dr Aimery rubbed his beard. "Unfortunately, we have no way of tracking where he went, but he did provide the names of the employees here and at Maztec who are working for the Korovskans before he left."

My eyes snapped to him. "Really? That's good. They can't spy on us now."

"Yes, and we'll be putting security measures in place to stop it from happening again."

I was disappointed that he'd gone, but also kind of impressed. There probably wasn't a prison in the universe that could hold him. I hoped that he really had changed. He'd gotten us out of the base when he could've saved himself and avoided being shot, so that was a start. He could have blown up those computers and disappeared without a trace.

I realized Dr Aimery was speaking to me. "Sorry, what?"

"You want to go to the Waikari village?"

Darion must have said something while I was distracted thinking about Braydac. "Yes. They had just gotten Sifayah back, or so they thought, and now they've lost her again. They deserve to know what really happened to her."

"As you know, there are certain things that you can't tell them, but I think we could arrange it."

"Thank you!" My hearts leapt and tears welled in my eyes. "I'd like Darion to come with me."

He looked to Darion, who gave a nod. "Done."

There was silence for a few moments and I took the opportunity to speak. "I've been thinking and I've decided that after my contract here is up in a couple of months, I want to resign and go to live somewhere where no one knows about me and my Talent."

"Are you sure that this is what you want?" Dr Aimery said. "Your knowledge of the natives is a great asset to us, and you could stay out of the jungle."

A shiver ran down my spine when I thought about the jungle. I didn't ever want to go back there.

"I'm sure." I turned to Darion and couldn't quite read the expression on his face. "I was hoping that Darion would come with me when I leave."

He smiled. "I'd love to take you to meet my parents. We will work out what we want to do from there."

My hearts melted and I threw my arms around him. "I'd love that." *"I love you!"*

"I love you too!"

**This is the end of this story, but not the end of this book.
Keep reading for some extra goodies:**
An excerpt from a companion novella in the *Tamisan Series*,
SHAKIRAN: LARISSA'S STORY
An offer of a free book
Acknowledgements
A list of other books by Susan McKenzie
About the author

Did you enjoy this book?
Help the next reader to enjoy it too.
Reviews are such a fantastic way for people to express the way a
book made them feel. A way to share it with the world.
Indie authors don't have the huge budgets that the big New
York publishers have, but we have something more powerful.
We have loyal readers like you.
It would be so awesome if you could share what you thought of
this book by leaving a review on the site where you purchased
it.
Thank you so much.
Sue

Keep reading for an excerpt from a companion novella in the
Tamisan Series, ***SHAKIRAN: LARISSA'S STORY***

Excerpt: Shakiran: Larissa's Story

Chapter 1: I Thought You Shakirans Were All Bloodthirsty Warriors

Concentrating on what someone was saying wasn't usually this hard.

Focus, Larissa.

They'd given each of us a Palm-pad to take notes on, so I thought I'd better take notes, or at least look like I was.

The presenter droned on about the natives of the planet we would be studying, but this wasn't new information. Everything he'd said so far was in the reports I'd received after being accepted for the job at Voyager Division. But I wouldn't be studying the natives. My job revolved around the plant life and Althar 3 was teeming with it.

I needed to get up and walk around the room. If I sat here any longer, his monotone voice would put me to sleep.

The only interesting thing in the room was the Shakiran sitting on the opposite side of the table and to my right. It was hard to keep my eyes from drifting back to him. White-blonde hair almost as long as my own, and those piercing dark eyes. With so many people from different planets here on the space station, another Shakiran stood out. Our height difference was one of the main reasons, being head and shoulders above the average race.

The only other person here that was as tall was the Ziflarian sitting to my left. She was amazingly beautiful with her dark skin and long, black, curly hair flowing over her shoulders. Most Shakirans had fair skin and blonde hair, so our races were polar opposites when it came to colour.

I looked around at the other new employees of the Voyager Division and my eyes found the Shakiran's again. He was looking straight at me, his brown eyes almost black. I quickly looked away and tried to concentrate on the presentation.

My heart rate picked up. He'd been stealing glances at me the whole time. I assumed it was because we were both Shakiran, but maybe there was more to it. I hoped there wasn't because I was here to work, not socialise, and that meant no relationships.

At all.

I didn't want all the hassles that came with it.

I tried to see what he was doing by keeping him in my peripheral vision and he was staring at me. Again.

I wanted to look, but I managed to keep my attention on the blue eyes of the presenter, who stopped abruptly and announced that we would be going around the room introducing ourselves to the group. I took a deep breath. I would find out his name.

Stop it.

We were sitting at a long table with three people on each side and one sitting at the end.

The presenter, Fenrick, looked at the woman to his left. She sat on the opposite side of the table from me, but to my left. She was short and had shoulder-length sandy-brown hair and excitement flashing in those blue eyes.

She cleared her throat. "I'm Zhenna Rhodarma and I'm a computer programmer from Earth. I've never been off-world so I thought I'd sign up to see the universe and I will do what I can to keep the computers running smoothly at Station Jannali."

The presenter smiled warmly. "Thank you, Zhenna." He turned to the man to her right. "Next?"

The man was taller than Zhenna and had a rugged appearance and broad shoulders. "I am Mosuti Kyah. I'm a Linguist from the planet Moftar. I have extensive experience in first-contact liaisons with new races."

The presenter raised his eyebrows. "You're the Talent sent to study the Altharian languages, yes?"

"That's correct."

"Hmm. Fascinating." He looked to the Shakiran. "And you are?"

"Janssen Malakua. I'm a botanist from the planet Shakira." *A botanist?* I sucked in a breath and his eyes darted to me as he continued. "I aim to study many different plant species in the universe in order to take that information back to Shakira to improve the crops we grow in my family's business. In the meantime, my priority is to offer my expertise to your company."

A botanist. What were the chances of two people from Shakira applying for jobs as botanists on a planet out on the edge of the Known Universe at the same time? Especially since Shakirans usually choose careers in the military.

His eyes met mine again and I closed my mouth and looked away. I'd been staring too long.

"Very good. Yes," Fenrick said. He turned to the portly man at the end of the table. "Yes?"

"The name is Kami Olion. I'm a sociologist from Setlur. I offer my services to you, but I have some questions."

"Mmm-hmm. Yes?"

"Will we be expected to go out into the jungle? I mean, I have my health to consider. There would be diseases that we aren't immune to and then there's the dangers of the wildlife—"

"Don't worry, Mister Olion. Your position will involve indoor work only. It's in the job description and in your contract."

"Hmm. Well. Yes. I was just clarifying this before I fully committed myself. You understand?"

Fenrick nodded. "Yes, I understand. But you do understand that you have already signed the contract, thereby fully committing yourself to this position, yes?" When Kami didn't answer, he looked to the man next to me. "Now to our next candidate—"

"And there's also the question of the two week's travel," Kami said. "Surely the company can use a better class of ship to get us there faster than that?"

Fenrick pursed his lips. "Voyager Division is paying for your tickets and providing you with accommodation and all meals aboard the ship, sir, so I'm sure you will be—"

"Voyager Division is a large company. Surely they can afford a faster ship."

He sighed. "Mister Olion, the Acronis is a well-equipped Class IV cruiser and it is the ship the company uses. If you have a problem with it, I suggest you take it up with my superiors. I am merely here to give you the information you will need before you set off for Althar 3."

Kami grumbled under his breath for a while.

A person who complained about everything and behaved like a child was without honour or integrity.

Fenrick looked again at the man on my right. "I'm sorry. Please continue."

This man was probably the shortest person in the room, but his eyes were bright and alert. "Hey everyone, I'm Lanu Ricksha. I'm a sociologist from Vanitha. I'm so excited to be joining you all on this journey and to be studying newly-discovered races."

Fenrick smiled and I could see he was as relieved as I was that he was nothing like Kami. "Thank you, Lanu." He smiled at me and nodded.

I sat a little straighter. "I'm Larissa Malinya. I'm a botanist, also from Shakira." Now it was Janssen who sucked in a breath. "I'm interested in the use of plants for their medicinal qualities and look forward to studying the new plant species on Althar 3."

Kami turned to me. "I thought you Shakirans were all bloodthirsty warriors and here we have two of you who are plant lovers."

Chapter 2: I Meant No Dishonour

My fists clenched and I glared at him. "We are not *bloodthirsty*. Do not make assumptions."

Janssen's eyes were fire. "You understand that a society cannot function without food, yes? Other professions are needed."

Fenrick spread his arms wide. "Now, let's calm down here. Let's channel peace. I will ask Mister Olion to refrain from making any derogatory comments about fellow workers. It's part of company policy, which forms part of the contract you have signed."

Kami mumbled under his breath again, but didn't say anything more.

I hoped that he decided to cancel his contract so he wouldn't be going with us.

Fenrick turned to the Ziflarian. "Please go ahead, dear."

She smiled and looked around the room. "Hi. I am Bazeelia Shamari and I am a scientist from the planet Ziflar. I am looking forward to working with you all. The discoveries we will make together will be awesome."

A scientist. I smiled. It fit her well.

I looked around the table. We had a mixed bag from across the universe, which would make things interesting.

I tried to imagine us working together as a group. I'd spent my whole life surrounded mostly by Shakirans and the occasional alien, and my grandmother was Taonese, but to see so many diverse races in the same room was different. And *exciting*.

Most Shakirans had a very narrow view of the universe and our history was marred by many wars with other races on nearby planets, but with my grandmother being from Taon, I had a somewhat wider view than other Shakirans.

I was looking forward to this job. I would be able to observe people from so many places — without getting personally involved with their lives — while learning as much as I could about the flora on the planet.

I had to remind myself that I was here to work, not to make friends.

My heart grew heavy. This wasn't what I'd originally planned to do after my graduation. Things changed in an instant as soon as the news of my grandmother's death had come through to the university. I needed to get away from my life for a while and get over losing the last member of my family. I needed to somehow heal my broken heart and move on with Gran's plan to use plants to heal instead of the usual Shakiran way of war and death.

I tried to smile. This would be a perfect distraction until I had my emotions under control and my head sorted out. Once my contract was up, I would put all my efforts into finding new uses for my plants and healing as many people as I possibly could. I couldn't get rid of my heartache, but maybe I could prevent someone else's.

———◆———

I waited impatiently near the airlock of the shuttle that had taken us from the Acronis down to the surface of Althar 3. After two long weeks aboard the Acronis, I needed to get out. I wanted fresh air and to see the sun.

Where is everyone? Don't they want to see this?

The shuttle, the Outrider, had developed a mechanical fault, forcing us to land for immediate repairs before we could reach Station Jannali, the underground base we would be working from. We'd had to land in a tropical jungle.

An *actual* jungle.

And we were going outside to see it first-hand.

Sure, we had forests near my house on my home planet of Shakira, but this was nature at its wildest.

I could hardly stand still. I'd studied botany for the last two years, so to see the plant life on a newly-discovered planet would be exciting. I'd seen the reports and photos of course, but nothing would compare to the real thing. Up till now I'd only ever had the chance to study plant specimens from my home planet of Shakira and a select few from Earth.

Excitement buzzed through my veins.

Where are they?

I resisted the urge to start pacing.

Of course the rest of the crew wouldn't be as excited as I was to see the wild flora just outside these doors... But there was one person. The only other botanist on the ship. The only other Shakiran on the ship.

As if fate had heard my thoughts, Janssen rounded the corner and stopped in his tracks as my heart stuttered to a halt.

His dark eyes widened as they found mine. "Larissa. Hi." He inclined his head.

I returned the nod. "Hello."

Please don't ask about last night.

His eyes never left mine. "Can I talk to you?"

No. Not now. I can't talk to you now. Maybe not ever. "Uh, we don't have time." I looked both ways down the corridor. "Everyone will be here shortly..."

He looked around to make sure we were alone and lowered his voice. "*Please.* I need to know what I did to upset you."

My chest tightened. "Nothing. You did nothing wrong."

"Then why did you run off?"

"I—" *I can't tell you.* I took a deep breath. "It's not you. It's... something I can't talk about right now."

"I'm sorry if I was too forward, or if my kiss offended you, but you seemed to be responding..." He looked like he was in pain. "I meant no dishonour."

"I..."

He ran a hand through his long hair. "Why won't you talk to me? Is there something you're not telling me?" His eyes widened. "Are you betrothed?"

I cringed. "No."

"Are you — have you formed a union with someone? Have you lied to me these past weeks?"

"No!"

"Please don't dishonour me. If that's what it is—"

"It's nothing like that. There's no one. I—"

Voices and footsteps abruptly ended our conversation and I saw the hurt in his eyes as the room filled with people.

Guilt wrapped itself around my chest and squeezed. "We'll talk. Later."

He gave me a sad smile that I could easily see over everyone's heads. I turned away so I couldn't see his handsome face. I should never have become close to him. I should have kept my distance during our journey.

No relationships. No entanglements.

Why couldn't I stick to my plan?

The shuttle's pilot made his way through the small crowd and stood in front of the airlock doors. He reminded us that the air was breathable and ran through the procedures for exiting through the airlock — and what we were required to do once we were outside.

Once he'd reported that we had no choice but to land, one of the scientists at Station Jannali had suggested we make ourselves useful and collect some plant and soil samples. I'd opted for a plant sample — naturally — and they'd given me the job of finding a type of fungi called Aatrox.

As the pilot spoke, images of the prehistoric wildlife I'd seen in the reports played in my mind on repeat. It had me a little nervous. There were some dangerous creatures here. Even dangerous plants. We needed to be vigilant.

We stepped into the airlock and it sealed itself. Once it had finished depressurising, the outer doors opened with a hiss and sunlight poured in through the gap in the canopy high above. My heart pounded. We'd landed in a small clearing caused by a fallen tree. A few of my fellow crew members filed out ahead of me and I padded down the ramp to the jungle floor. Humidity closed in around me in total contrast to the cool interior of the shuttle.

We stood gaping at the giant trees that formed the canopy. They were covered with moss and had vines intricately woven around their trunks and branches. The small creatures jumping around in the higher branches looked like monkeys. Birds flitted through the treetops and swooped down toward the ground.

The smaller trees boasted many shades of green. The wide variety of fungi growing on rocks and tree trunks displayed so many colours that they rivalled the countless flowers.

Some of the aromas from the flowers were almost familiar and one definitely smelled like an Airlea Blossom. The scent of nutrient-rich soil was hard to ignore and was so welcome after the sterile air we'd breathed for the last two weeks.

The undergrowth was so thick here and I wondered how any of the larger animals could find their way through. It was fascinating to see how plants formed when they were left to their own devices.

I closed my eyes and listened to the sounds of birds, crickets, and frogs, but I was startled by the sound of flapping wings high above us. Something scurried amongst the underbrush to my right. This was no time to be closing my eyes. Images of the many carnivorous dinosaurs and huge cat-like predators that inhabited this jungle flashed in my mind again. We were vulnerable out here in the open. We were not armed. If we were attacked, there would be no way to defend ourselves.

Surely our new employer wasn't stupid enough to send us out of the ship and leave us defenceless.

I looked to the people around me. At how unprepared and clueless they were.

Yes, they *were* that stupid.

I searched for any possible threats and noticed Janssen was on high alert too. Our combat training had been instilled in us from an early age and was impossible to switch off. Shakirans prided themselves on being a warrior race and all citizens were trained in the art of combat. No exceptions.

Being thrust into the jungle unarmed on the first day didn't sit well with me.

Our eyes met and Janssen nodded. We'd been thinking the same thing, but guilt over last night had me turning away.

People started to spread out toward the edges of the clearing and I remembered we had a job to do.

I squared my shoulders and headed for the nearest fallen log. The information contained in the PocketPC I'd been given said that the Aatrox was purple and grew on the underside of logs, but I planned to approach each log with a great deal of caution. Any number of creatures could be sheltering underneath.

Bazeelia strode purposefully toward some red flowers, her long black hair swishing back and forth from its ponytail. It seemed she'd found her target already.

She pulled out a sample case and a pair of clippers. She would be finished in no time and I hadn't even started.

The thunderous sound of flapping wings drew my attention and a huge winged reptile swooped down from the trees. Its screech hurt my ears and I instinctively ducked and screamed.

Bazeelia's scream was comical and mine was embarrassing. I *never* screamed.

Eli would've scowled at me for being such a coward...

I clenched my jaw. I couldn't be thinking about him now.

Janssen and Lanu had both given a shout when the reptile swooped, but were now laughing at us.

Bazeelia scowled. "Don't be laughin' at me. That thing was a monster! And it scared you too!"

Janssen turned to her, his hair falling fluidly over his shoulder as he moved. "Hey. Take it easy. We're just messin' with ya."

That may have been true, but she was right. Its wing-span was about three metres and its long, pointed beak was full of razor-sharp teeth.

Lanu strode over, smiling as he approached. "You've got to admit it was amazing though."

Bazeelia glared down at him, her mouth hanging open. "Amazing? No. It wasn't. It was terrifying!"

Lanu kept smiling, and I recognised that look of awe on his face. I had a photo of me back at home, taken after I'd created a new plant species in our nursery, and my face had that same look. That same light shone in my eyes.

He rubbed his chin. "But that thing is so similar to the Pteranodon from Earth's past and it flew within a few metres of us. It's like going back to the Cretaceous Period and getting a first-hand look."

"Well, you can go look at it and admire its beauty if you want. Pat it. Study it. Although I'm not sure being a sociologist will help when it comes to dinosaurs. Me? I'm glad I'll be working indoors once we get to Jannali." She flipped her long hair over her shoulder and went back to retrieving the red flower.

The fact that we weren't going to be interacting with the natives while we were here probably meant this would be our first and only time in the jungle. Maybe that was why they were okay with us being out here now. We were getting a taste of the environment these people lived in.

It was still dangerous out here; we needed to finish quickly and return to the safety of the ship.

I continued to monitor our surroundings.

Kami, who had continued to be a nuisance to us all since our first briefing, called from the doorway of the shuttle, asking Zhenna what the screaming was about. As she explained what had happened, I tried to ignore the conversation so I could get back to my search for the fungi. Kami had refused to come outside, saying the mechanical failure was a bad omen or some such nonsense.

He told her again that we should have stayed in the ship and kept insisting that Zhenna go back inside. What was his reason for only inviting her? That was odd. And it got my attention.

Zhenna and I had become friends on the trip out here, although I'd kept a certain distance between us.

I wandered over, feeling the need to protect her. If she agreed to go back in, I was ready to stop her. I did *not* trust the man. He was from Setlur, so there was a natural distrust for his whole race — Shakira had been at war with Setlur about two hundred years ago. Kami had shown his dislike for Janssen and I openly from the start, but there was more to my distrust of him than our races' shared history. His behaviour was suspicious and I wanted to keep Zhenna safe.

"Umm, I can't," she told him, the sunlight making her hair look almost blonde. "Jannali wants the samples. It's going to give a bad impression if we refuse."

I was relieved that she was staying out here.

His bushy eyebrows drew downward and his mouth became a straight line, but then he turned quickly and went back into the ship.

Good.

"Don't worry about him," I said as I reached her side. "He's just a superstitious old grump." *And a creepy old man.*

Old was a bit of a stretch. He was probably about thirty, but he acted like my grandfather.

She laughed at that, then cringed.

I shrugged. "I don't care if he hears me."

She giggled.

Zhenna was one of the few people I'd gotten to know on my way out here and although she had no interest in botany, we shared an interest in art and music. She was easy to talk to and it made me forget that I was only out here for work, not to socialise. She made it easy to get distracted from my goal, and so did Janssen. He'd been a *big* distraction.

I pushed those thoughts aside. I had a job to do.

We turned our attention back to the edge of the clearing so we could get the samples before the pilot finished with the repairs. I didn't want to turn up to Jannali empty-handed. How would that look? *"You're a botanist and you couldn't find a plant?"*

No. That wouldn't do. I would not shame myself.

I chose another log over where Zhenna was standing and headed straight to it, but my attention was drawn to Janssen's voice, as it often was. I couldn't help myself. He was reaching up to a low-hanging vine, and I tried to guess what his target was — the moss or fungi growing on the vine, or the vine itself?

I scolded myself for watching him and took another step toward the log. Every time he spoke, I looked over. What was wrong with me? I needed to exercise some self-control.

He caught me looking and my cheeks flushed. I needed to stop this and get back to work.

I checked to see if Zhenna had seen me; she was watching me and smiling. Those blue eyes missed nothing.

She pursed her lips as she tried not to laugh. "I saw you looking at him."

Chapter 3: Stay Down!

Dammit. "No, I wasn't."

She raised an eyebrow.

My cheeks heated even more. "Okay. I was."

When I looked back, the vine was hanging down lower and Janssen ducked under it, his long hair falling over his broad shoulder.

"You like him," she said.

The jungle suddenly seemed a lot warmer. She didn't know the half of it. "I... Uh... maybe. I don't know."

I couldn't tell her the truth.

"Well, you'll have plenty of time to find out since you'll be working together."

And that was the problem I was trying to ignore. Janssen and I would be studying the flora of this planet together while I tried to pretend I didn't have feelings for him.

How was I going to do that?

Getting to know him had been a mistake. I wasn't supposed to get close to anyone out here. Relationships led to heartbreak. I needed to keep away from him.

Somehow.

After checking our surroundings for any movement in the jungle, I watched him pack his sampling gear away and crouch down to look at a lavender flower. "Is he unattached, do you know?"

Why did I ask that? What is wrong with me?

Of course, I knew the answer to that question only too well.

"It has taken you two weeks to even ask that?" Her mouth hung open and she quickly closed it. "I heard him telling Mosuti he doesn't have a girl. Or boy."

I sighed and tried to look relieved and she chuckled.

I wasn't sure why I didn't want anyone to know how well Janssen and I knew each other. Maybe because I was ashamed at how easily I'd broken my own no-relationship rule. We'd met in the ship's hydroponics garden every night after everyone else was asleep where we talked about life in general and our interest in plants. And then last night things changed. He'd kissed me. And I'd kissed him back.

And then I'd run out on him.

Mosuti approached us, sweat from the humidity causing his dark curls to stick to his forehead. "Hey, girls."

"Hey," we answered in unison.

Mosuti's head reached my shoulder and Zhenna's only came to halfway up my upper arm. I was still trying to get used to the fact that most people I'd met since leaving Shakira were so short.

Mosuti smiled. "Found your specimens yet?"

We both said "no" at the same time and laughed. He was the one with the gift of telepathy and Zhenna and I were sounding like we were able to read each other's minds.

I glanced around the area and into the jungle again.

Zhenna looked toward the shuttle and I followed her gaze. Kami's stocky frame filled the doorway again. She kept her eyes on him as she whispered, "Mosuti. Kami doesn't like you, does he?"

Mosuti frowned. "I'm afraid not, Zhenna. Says he doesn't like my 'kind.'"

She glared at Kami. "Don't let it worry you. He's a douchebag."

Mosuti remained calm. "He doesn't worry me."

Kami called out again in his whiny voice. "Zhenna, dear, why are you talking to *him?*"

She shifted her feet in the leaf litter. "Uh, because he's my *friend.*"

"His kind can't be trusted. He's probably reading our minds right now."

Mosuti squared his shoulders. "I would *never* do that. It is against the Talents' Code of Conduct to read a being's mind without consent."

The Code of Conduct was put in place to protect people from telepathic intrusion and to protect the rights of the Talents themselves. It was a well-known fact. One that Kami would have knowledge of. He was just being difficult.

Why did he have to continually stir up trouble? He was such a bigot. He'd taken every opportunity over the last two weeks to argue with everyone and complain about the food and the conditions aboard the ship. He was disrespectful and self-absorbed.

I stepped toward him, fists clenched at my sides. "You're a jerk! What would you know about Talents? You're so narrow-minded!"

He dismissed me with a wave of his hand. "They are nothing but freaks. Mutated beings that taint our genetics."

Zhenna took a deep breath. "What do you suggest we do with these 'mutants'?"

He didn't waver. "We need to keep them under control. They shouldn't be allowed to wander free where they can manipulate our minds and wreak havoc across the universe."

"So, we should enslave them?"

"I... wouldn't use that exact term... but what else can we do? They're freaks of nature and they are a danger to us all."

This man had no honour. Someone needed to put him in his place. I looked to Mosuti, who seemed unaffected. He was probably used to such ignorance.

Mosuti's voice floated into my mind. *"It's okay. Don't worry about me. I'm fine."*

I gave him a nod and thought, *As you wish.*

On the trip out here, he'd shown me how to hold a telepathic conversation with him without possessing any Talent so I knew that he was able to read my response from my mind.

As long as he was okay, I would try to ignore this insult, not only to Mosuti, but to all Talents throughout the Known Universe.

Zhenna clenched her fists. She wasn't willing to let it go. "I'm glad I won't be working with you when we get to Jannali. You're such an arrogant, narrow-minded, backwards hick!"

I stifled a laugh.

Kami didn't get the chance to respond before laser fire burst through the jungle. I ducked my head instinctively, confused as to where it could be coming from.

"What was that?" Zhenna squeaked as she looked around wildly.

Mosuti threw us to the ground by way of an answer. "Stay down!" he ordered.

There was more laser fire and screaming. Guilt sliced through me when I realised I hadn't kept an eye on the jungle.

"Laser fire," I heard Mosuti whisper between shots. He'd landed facing Zhenna so I couldn't see their faces.

Another scream. Zhenna popped her head up, but quickly ducked back down, no doubt realising how foolish that move was.

I couldn't see much from my position, but movement caught my eye. Someone ran through the trees toward the shuttle. I didn't know who it was, but he didn't have long blonde hair. Pain sliced through my chest. What if Janssen was hit? What if he—

No. I couldn't go there. I couldn't lose another person I cared about. Not so soon after losing Gran.

I squeezed my eyes shut. I would not cry. I would not give in to my emotions right now. That would *not* help me. I needed to think. Who would be using laser weapons in the middle of a prehistoric jungle out on the edge of the Known Universe? Surely these primitives wouldn't have enemies who possessed advanced technology. That could only mean we were the target.

Who would want to attack us? We were just a group of scientists. It didn't make sense. Maybe it was another company that wanted to study these natives or take the planet's resources for themselves.

Surely they would go about it another way.

Or maybe they were a group of space pirates out for spoils. We had nothing of value besides the ship itself — a small shuttle used to ferry us from the Acronis to the surface. There was nothing on board worth the risks they were taking.

My attention was drawn to my hand, where a large beetle was making its way along my finger. I resisted the urge to flick it away. I needed to stay still.

My eyes darted around. The leaf litter teemed with life. A few more beetles and some ants crawled on me and there was something on Mosuti's arm. There were more crawling things on my legs and something on my shoulder. They didn't worry me too much; I'd been working in gardens since I was seven. I tried not to think about them crawling on me. As long as I kept still, I probably wouldn't get bitten. Maybe.

Another scream.

I tried to calm my breathing, but hearing more shots being fired all around us made it difficult.

All went quiet, but that wasn't necessarily a good thing. I waited for their next move.

The others lay with me on the ground, waiting, listening. Footsteps came closer and stopped. "These ones are good..."

I sucked in a breath. Slowly. Quietly. *Good for what?*

"Don't damage them," said another.

My blood ran cold thinking about what that could mean. My body tensed, waiting for a blow or the burn of a laser pistol. After all my efforts to avoid joining the armed forces back home, it seemed I was about to die at the hands of a gun anyway. How pathetically ironic.

Pain ripped through me and my body convulsed. The world faded to black.

Shakiran: Larissa's Story is available right now where all good books are sold

---

Keep reading for a chance to sign up for a free novelette, *THE ALIEN*

YOUR FREE BOOK IS WAITING

The novelette

THE ALIEN

is free for a limited time. You just need to tell me where to send it

When Lilliana crash-lands her spaceship on a Primitive planet, she'll have to rely on help from an attractive local to survive.

Use the QR Code to follow the link, then enter your name and email address to get your free book delivered to your inbox

Or type this link into your browser: https://www.subscribepage.com/thealien

ACKNOWLEDGEMENTS

Up until this book, I've always worked alone when writing. Sure, I've had the support of family and friends, but now I have a group of authors that understand what it's like and help me along my journey. I'd like to thank them personally. They are the 10K Readers + SPF – Sydney Meet Up group. I don't know where I'd be without you all.

And of course, I'd like to thank all of the members of the Sydney Shadows Club who have supported me. I am honoured to be a member of the club.

Lastly, to my family and friends, a big thank you.

Books by Susan McKenzie

THE JADORI SERIES (ONGOING SERIES):

Fire and Magic is being released in a serialized format (1 chapter per week) on reamstories.com right now!

———◆◆———

THE TAMISAN SERIES (COMPLETED SERIES):

Tamisan

Enigma

A Tamisan Novella – Shakiran: Larissa's Story

———◆◆———

THE LIGHTNING TOUCH SERIES (COMPLETED SERIES):

Touch of Lightning

Power of Lightning

---

*Just remember, a completed series means you can binge read the whole series now – no waiting for the next book to release.

ABOUT THE AUTHOR

Susan McKenzie is an Australian author who loves creating worlds of fantasy and science fiction with fascinating characters and slow-burn low-spice romance.

Her books are full of interesting and relatable characters who use their psychic abilities or magical powers to fight their way out of trouble.

She loves stories that hit you in the feels.

She's not a typical author coffee addict - but chocolate? Now that's a different story. When she's not writing, she loves to paint, draw, sing, and play the guitar.

———◆———

Get in touch with Sue.
Follow Sue on her Ream site for early access and bonus/deleted scenes:
https://reamstories.com/susanmckenzie
Follow Sue on her Amazon author page:
amazon.com/author/susancarter
Visit Sue's website:
http://susanmckenzieauthor.com

Follow Sue on Facebook:
https://www.facebook.com/SueMcKenzieAuthor